Stories of Wessex

Stories of Wessex

Thomas Hardy

LT

S

THORNDIKE
CHIVERS

This Large Print edition is published by Thorndike Press®,
Waterville, Maine USA and by BBC Audiobooks, Ltd, Bath,
England.

Originally published in 1888 and is now in Public Domain in
the United States and the United Kingdom.

U.S. Hardcover 0-7862-6942-1(Perennial Bestsellers)
U.K. Hardcover 1-4056-3137-6 (Chivers Large Print)

The text of this Large Print edition is unabridged. Other
aspects of the book may vary from the original edition.

Set in 16 pt. Plantin by Liana M. Walker.

Printed in the United States on permanent paper.

British Library Cataloguing-in-Publication Data available

Library of Congress Cataloging-in-Publication Data

Hardy, Thomas, 1840–1928.
    [Wessex tales]
    Stories of Wessex / Thomas Hardy.
        p. cm.
    ISBN 0-7862-6942-1 (lg. print : hc : alk. paper)
    1. England — Social life and customs — 19th century —
Fiction.   2. Wessex (England) — Fiction.   3. Large type
books.   I. Title.
PR4749.A1 2004
    823′.8—dc22   2004054752

Stories of Wessex

Contents

The Three Strangers

Among the few features of agricultural England which retain an appearance but little modified by the lapse of centuries may be reckoned the long, grassy and furzy downs, coombs, or ewe-leases, as they are called according to their kind, that fill a large area of certain counties in the south and south-west. If any mark of human occupation is met with hereon it usually takes the form of the solitary cottage of some shepherd.

Fifty years ago such a lonely cottage stood on such a down and may possibly be standing there now. In spite of its loneliness, however, the spot, by actual measurement, was not more than three miles from a county town. Yet that affected it little. Three miles of irregular upland, during the long inimical seasons, with their sleets, snows, rains, and mists, afford withdrawing space enough to isolate a Timon or Nebuchadnezzar; much less, in fair weather, to please that less repellent tribe, the poets, philosophers, artists, and others, who "conceive and meditate of pleasant things."

Some old earthen camp or barrow, some clump of trees, at least some starved fragment of ancient hedge, is usually taken advantage of in the erection of these forlorn dwellings. But in the present case such a kind of shelter had been disregarded. Higher Crowstairs, as the house was called, stood quite detached and undefended. The only reason for its precise situation seemed to be the crossing of two footpaths at right angles hard by, which may have crossed there and thus for a good five hundred years. Hence the house was exposed to the elements on all sides. But though the wind up here blew unmistakeably when it did blow, and the rain hit hard whenever it fell, the various weathers of the winter season were not quite so formidable on the down as they were imagined to be by dwellers on low ground. The raw rimes were not so pernicious as in the hollows, and the frosts were scarcely so severe. When the shepherd and his family who tenanted the house were pitied for their sufferings from the exposure, they said that upon the whole they were less inconvenienced by "wuzzes and flames" (hoarses and phlegms) than when they had lived by the stream of a snug neighbouring valley.

The night of the twenty eighth of March 182– was precisely one of the nights that were wont to call forth these expressions of commiseration. The level rain-storm smote walls, slopes, and hedges, like the cloth-yard shafts of Senlac and Crecy. Such sheep and out-door animals as had no shelter stood with their buttocks to the wind; while the tails of little birds trying to roost on some scraggy thorn were blown inside-out like umbrellas. The gable-end of the cottage was stained with wet, and the eaves-droppings flapped against the wall. Yet never was commiseration for the shepherd more misplaced. For that cheerful rustic was entertaining a large party in glorification of the christening of his second girl.

The guests had arrived before the rain began to fall, and they were all now assembled in the chief or living-room of the dwelling. A glance into the apartment at eight o'clock on this eventful evening would have resulted in the opinion that it was as cosy and comfortable a nook as could be wished for in boisterous weather. The calling of its inhabitant was proclaimed by a number of highly polished sheep-crooks without stems, that were hung ornamentally over the fireplace, the curl of each shining crook varying from the antiquated type engraved in the patriarchal pictures of old family bibles to the most approved fashion of the last local sheep-fair. The room was lighted by half a dozen candles, having wicks only a trifle smaller than the grease which enveloped them, in candlesticks that were never used but at high-days, holy-days, and family feasts. The lights were scattered about the room, two of them standing on the chimney-piece. This position of candles was in itself significant. Candles on the chimney-piece always meant a party.

On the hearth, in front of a back-brand to give substance, blazed a fire of thorns, that crackled "like the laughter of the fool."

Nineteen persons were gathered here. Of these, five women, wearing gowns of various bright hues, sat in chairs along the wall; girls shy and not shy filled the window bench; four men including Charley Jake the hedge-carpenter, Elijah

New, the parish-clerk and John Pitcher, a neighbouring dairyman, the shepherd's father-in-law, lolled in the settle; a young man and maid, who were blushing over tentative *pourparlers* on a life-companionship, sat beneath the corner-cupboard; and an elderly engaged man of fifty or upwards moved restlessly about from spots where his betrothed was not to the spot where she was. Enjoyment was pretty general, and so much the more prevailed in being unhampered by conventional restrictions. Absolute confidence in each other's good opinion begat perfect ease, while the finishing stroke of manner, amounting to a truly princely serenity, was lent to the majority by the absence of any expression or trait denoting that they wished to get on in the world, enlarge their minds, or do any eclipsing thing whatever — which nowadays so generally nips the bloom and *bonhomie* of all except the two extremes of the social scale.

Shepherd Fennel had married well, his wife being a dairyman's daughter from a vale at a distance, who brought fifty guineas in her pocket — and kept them there, till they should be required for administering to the needs of a coming family. This frugal woman had been somewhat exercised as to the character that should be given to the gathering. A sit-still party had its advantages; but an undisturbed position of ease in chairs and settles was apt to lead on the men to such an unconscionable deal of toping that they would sometimes fairly drink the house dry. A dancing-party was the alternative; but this, while avoiding the foregoing objection on the score of good drink, had a counterbalancing disadvantage in the matter of good victuals, the ravenous appetites engendered by the exercise causing immense havoc in the buttery. Shepherdess Fennel fell back upon the intermediate plan of mingling short dances with short periods of talk and singing, so as to hinder any ungovernable rage in either. But this scheme was entirely confined to her own gentle mind: the shepherd himself was in the mood to exhibit the most reckless phases of hospitality.

The fiddler was a boy of those parts, about twelve years of age, who had a wonderful dexterity in jigs and reels, though his fingers were so small and short as to necessitate a constant shifting for the high notes, from which he scrambled back to the first position with sounds not of unmixed purity of tone. At seven the shrill tweedle-dee of this youngster had begun, accompanied by a booming ground-bass from Elijah New, the parish-clerk, who had thoughtfully brought with him his favourite musical instrument, the serpent. Dancing was instantaneous, Mrs Fennel privately enjoining the players on no account to let the dance exceed the length of a quarter of an hour.

But Elijah and the boy, in the excitement of their position, quite forgot the injunction. Moreover Oliver Giles, a man of seventeen, one of the dancers, who was enamoured of his partner, a fair girl of thirty-three rolling years, had recklessly handed a new crown-piece to the musicians, as a bribe to keep going as long as they had muscle and wind. Mrs Fennel, seeing the steam begin to generate on the countenances of her guests, crossed over and touched the fiddler's elbow and put her hand on the serpent's mouth. But they took no notice, and fearing she might lose her character of genial hostess if she were to interfere too markedly she retired and sat down helpless. And so the dance whizzed on with cumulative fury, the performers moving in their planet-like courses, direct and retrograde, from apogee to perigee, till the hand of the well kicked clock at the bottom of the room had travelled over the circumference of an hour.

While these cheerful events were in course of enactment within Fennel's pastoral dwelling an incident having considerable bearing on the party had occurred in the gloomy night without. Mrs Fennel's concern about the growing fierceness of the dance corresponded in point of time with the ascent of a human figure to the solitary hill of Higher Crowstairs from the direction of the distant town. This personage strode on through the rain without a pause, following the little-worn path which, further on in its course skirted the shepherd's cottage.

It was nearly the time of full moon, and on this account, though the sky was lined with a uniform sheet of dripping cloud, ordinary objects out of doors were readily visible. The sad wan light revealed the lonely pedestrian to be a man of supple frame; his gait suggested that he had somewhat passed the period of perfect and instinctive agility, though not so far as to be otherwise than rapid of motion when occasion required. At a rough guess, he might have been about forty years of age. He appeared tall, but a recruiting-sergeant, or other person accustomed to the judging of men's heights by the eye, would have discerned that this was chiefly owing to his gauntness, and that he was not more than five feet eight or nine.

Notwithstanding the regularity of his tread there was caution in it, as in that of one who mentally feels his way; and despite the fact that it was not a black coat, nor a dark garment of any sort that he wore, there was something about him which suggested that he naturally belonged to the black coated tribes of men. His clothes were of fustian, and his boots hobnailed, yet in his progress he showed not the mud-accustomed bearing of hobnailed and fustianed peasantry.

By the time that he had arrived abreast of the shepherd's premises the rain came down, or rather came along, with yet more determined violence. The outskirts of the little settlement partially broke the force of wind and rain and this induced him to stand still. The most salient of the shepherd's domestic erections was an empty sty at the forward corner of his hedgeless garden, for in these latitudes the principle of masking the homelier features of your establishment by a conventional frontage was unknown. The traveller's eye was attracted to this small building by the pallid shine of the wet slates that covered it. He turned aside, and, finding it empty, stood under the pent-roof for shelter.

While he stood the boom of the serpent within the adjacent house, and the lesser strains of the fiddler, reached the spot as an accompaniment to the surging hiss of the flying rain on the sod, its louder beating on the cabbage-leaves of the garden, on the straw hackles of eight or ten bee-hives just discernible by the path, and its dripping from the eaves into a row of buckets and pans that had been placed under the walls of the cottage. For at Higher Crowstairs, as at all such elevated domiciles, the grand difficulty of house-keeping was an insufficiency of water: and a casual rainfall was utilized by turning out, as catchers, every utensil that the house contained. Some queer stories might be told of the contrivances for economy in suds and dish-waters that are absolutely necessitated in upland habitations during the droughts of summer. But at this season there were no such exigencies: a mere acceptance of what the skies bestowed was sufficient for an abundant store.

At last the notes of the serpent ceased, and the house was silent. This cessation of activity aroused the solitary pedestrian from the reverie into which he had lapsed, and emerging from the shed, with an apparently new intention, he walked up the path to the house-door. Arrived here his first act was to kneel down on a large stone beside the row of vessels, and to drink a copious draught from one of them. Having quenched his thirst he rose and lifted his hand to knock, but paused with his eye upon the panel. Since the dark surface of the wood revealed absolutely nothing it was evident that he must be mentally looking through the door, as if he wished to measure thereby all the possibilities that a house of this sort might include, and how they might bear upon the question of his entry. In his indecision he turned and surveyed the scene around. Not a soul was anywhere visible. The garden-path stretched downward from his feet, gleaming like the track of a snail; the roof of the little well (mostly dry), the well-cover, the top-rail of the garden-gate, were varnished with the same dull liquid glaze; while far away in the vale a faint whiteness of more than usual extent showed that the rivers were high in the meads. Beyond all this winked a few bleared lamp-lights through the beating drops, lights that denoted the situation of the county-town from which he had appeared to come. The absence of all notes of life in that direction seemed to clinch his intentions, and he knocked at the door.

Within, a desultory chat had taken the place of movement and musical sound. The hedge-carpenter was suggesting a song to the company, which nobody just then was inclined to undertake, so that the knock afforded a not unwelcome diversion.

"Walk in!" said the shepherd promptly.

The latch clicked upward, and out of the night our pedestrian appeared upon the door-mat. The shepherd arose, snuffed two of the nearest candles, and turned to look at him.

Their light disclosed that the stranger was dark in complexion, and not unprepossessing as to feature. His hat, which for a moment he did not remove, hung low over his eyes, without concealing that they were large, open, and determined, moving with a flash rather than a glance round the room. He seemed pleased with the survey, and baring his shaggy head said in a rich deep voice "The rain is so heavy, friends, that I ask leave to come in and rest awhile."

"To be sure, stranger," said the shepherd. "And faith, you've been lucky in choosing yer time; for we are having a bit of a fling for a glad cause — though to be sure a man could hardly wish that glad cause to happen more than once a year."

"Nor less," spoke up a woman. "For 'tis best to get yer family over and done with as soon as you can, so as to be all the earlier out of the fag o't."

"And what may be this glad cause?" asked the stranger.

"A birth and christening," said the shepherd.

The stranger hoped his host might not be made unhappy either by too many or too few of such episodes, and being invited by a gesture to a pull at the mug he readily acquiesced. His manner which, before entering, had been so dubious, was now altogether that of a careless and candid man.

"Late to be traipsing athwart this coomb — hey?" said the engaged man of fifty.

"Late it is, master, as you say. — I'll take a seat in the chimney-corner if you have nothing to urge against it, ma'am; for I am a little moist on the side that was next the rain."

Mrs Shepherd Fennel assented, and made room for the self-inviting comer who, having got completely inside the chimney-corner, stretched out his legs and his arms with the expansiveness of a person quite at home.

"Yes — I am rather cracked in the vamp," he said freely, seeing that the eyes of the shepherd's wife fell upon his boots, "and I am not well-fitted, either. I have had some rough times lately, and have been forced to pick up what I can get in the way of wearing, but I must find a suit better fit for working-days when I reach home."

"One of hereabouts?" she inquired.

"Not quite that — further up the country."

"I thought so. And so be I; and by your tongue you come from my neighbourhood."

"But you would hardly have heard of me" he said quickly. "My time would be long before yours ma'am, you see."

This testimony to the youthfulness of his hostess had the effect of stopping her cross-examination.

"There is only one thing more wanted to make me happy" continued the newcomer. "And that is a little baccy which I am sorry to say I am out of."

"I'll fill your pipe," said the shepherd.

"I must ask you to lend me a pipe likewise."

"A smoker, and no pipe about 'ee?"

"I have dropped it somewhere on the road."

The shepherd filled and handed him a new clay pipe, saying as he did so, "Hand me your baccy-box — I'll fill that too now I am about it."

The man went through the movement of searching his pockets.

"Lost that too?" said his entertainer with some surprise.

"I am afraid so," said the man with some confusion. "Give it to me in a screw of paper." Lighting his pipe at the candle with a suction that drew the whole flame into the bowl he re-settled himself in the corner and bent his looks upon the faint steam from his damp legs, as if he wished to say no more.

Meanwhile the general body of guests had been taking little notice of this visitor by reason of an absorbing discussion in which they were engaged with the band about a tune for the next dance. The matter being settled they were about to stand up, when an interruption came in the shape of another knock at the door.

At sound of the same the man in the chimney-corner took up the poker and began stirring the brands as if doing it thoroughly were the one aim of his existence; and a second time the shepherd said "Walk in!" In a moment another man stood upon the straw-woven door-mat. He too was a stranger.

This individual was one of a type radically different from the first. There was more of the commonplace in his manner, and a certain jovial cosmopolitanism sat upon his features. He was several years older than the first arrival, his hair being slightly frosted, his eyebrows bristly, and his whiskers cut back from his cheeks. His face was rather full and flabby, and yet it was not altogether a face without power. A few grog-blossoms marked the neighbourhood of his nose. He flung back his long drab great coat, revealing that beneath it he wore a suit of cinder-grey shade throughout, large heavy seals, of some metal or other that would take a polish, dangling from his fob as his only personal ornament. Shaking the water-drops from his low-crowned glazed hat he said "I must ask for a few minutes shelter, comrades, or I shall be wetted to my skin before I get to Casterbridge."

"Make yourself at home, master," said the shepherd, perhaps a trifle less heartily than on the first occasion. Not that Fennel had the least tinge of niggardliness in his composition; but the room was far from large, spare chairs were not numerous, and damp companions were not altogether desirable at close quarters for the women and girls in their bright coloured gowns.

However, the second comer, after taking off his great-coat, and hanging his hat on a nail in one of the ceiling-beams as if he had been specially invited to put it there, advanced and sat down at the table. This had been pushed so closely into the chimney-corner, to give all available room to the dancers, that its inner edge grazed the elbow of the man who had ensconced himself by the fire; and thus the two strangers were brought into close companionship. They nodded to each other by way of breaking the ice of unacquaintance, and the first stranger handed his neighbour the family mug — a huge vessel of brown ware, having its upper edge worn away like a threshold by the rub of whole generations of thirsty lips that had gone the way of all flesh, and bearing the following inscription burnt upon its rotund side in yellow letters,

"THERE iS NO FUN
"UNTiLL i CUM"

The other man, nothing loth, raised the mug

25

to his lips, and drank on and on and on — till a curious blueness overspread the countenance of the shepherd's wife, who had regarded with no little surprise the first stranger's free offer to the second of what did not belong to him to dispense.

"I knew it!" said the toper to the shepherd with much satisfaction. "When I walked up your garden before coming in, and saw the hives all of a row I said to myself 'where there's bees there's honey, and where there's honey there's mead.' But mead of such a truly comfortable sort as this I really didn't expect to meet in my older days." He took yet another pull at the mug, till it assumed an ominous elevation.

"Glad you enjoy it!" said the shepherd warmly.

"It is goodish mead," assented Mrs Fennel with an absence of enthusiasm which seemed to say that it was possible to buy praise for one's cellar at too heavy a price. "It is trouble enough to make — and really I hardly think we shall make any more. For honey sells well, and we ourselves can make shift with a drop o' small mead and metheglin for common use from the comb-washings."

"O but you'll never have the heart!" reproachfully cried the stranger in cinder-grey, after taking up the mug a third time and setting it down empty. "I love mead when 'tis old like this, as I love to go to church o' Sundays or to relieve the needy any day of the week."

"Ha, ha, ha!" said the man in the chimney-corner who, in spite of the taciturnity induced by the pipe of tobacco could not or would not refrain from this slight testimony to his comrade's humour.

Now the old mead of those days, brewed of the purest first-year or maiden honey, four pounds to the gallon — with its due complement of white of eggs, cinnamon, ginger, cloves, mace, rosemary, yeast, and processes of working, bottling, and cellaring — tasted remarkably strong; but it did not taste so strong as it actually was. Hence, presently, the stranger in cinder-grey at the table, moved by its creeping influence, unbuttoned his waistcoat, threw himself back in his chair, spread his legs, and made his presence felt in various ways.

"Well, well, as I say" he resumed, "I am going to Casterbridge, and to Casterbridge I must go. I should have been almost there by this time; but the rain drove me in to your dwelling, and I'm not sorry for it."

"You don't live in Casterbridge?" said the shepherd.

"Not as yet; though I shortly mean to move there."

"Going to set up in trade perhaps?"

"No, no," said the shepherd's wife. "It is easy to see that the gentleman is rich, and don't want to work at anything."

The cinder-grey stranger paused, as if to consider whether he would accept that definition of himself. He presently rejected it by answering "Rich is not quite the word for me, dame. I do work, and I must work. And even if I only get to Casterbridge by midnight I must begin work there at eight to-morrow morning. Yes, het or wet, blow or snow, famine or sword, my day's work to-morrow must be done."

"Poor man! Then in spite o' seeming you be worse off than we?" replied the shepherd's wife.

" 'Tis the nature of my trade, men and maidens. 'Tis the nature of my trade more than my poverty. . . . But really and truly I must up and off, or I shan't get a lodging in the town." However, the speaker did not move, and directly added, "There's time for one more draught of friendship before I go; and I'd perform it at once if the mug were not dry."

"Here's a mug o' small," said Mrs Fennel. "Small we call it, though to be sure 'tis only the first wash o' the combs."

"No" said the stranger disdainfully. "I won't spoil your first kindness by partaking o' your second."

"Certainly not" broke in Fennel. "We don't increase and multiply every day, and I'll fill the mug again." He went away to the dark place under the stairs where the barrel stood. The shepherdess followed him.

"Why should you do this!" she said reproachfully as soon as they were alone. "He's emptied it once, though it held enough for ten people; and now he's not contented wi' the small, but must needs call for more o' the strong! And a stranger unbeknown to any of us. For my part I don't like the look o' the man at all."

"But he's in the house, my honey; and 'tis a wet night, and a christening. Daze it, what's a cup of mead more or less? There'll be plenty more next bee-burning."

"Very well — this time, then," she answered, looking wistfully at the barrel. "But what is the man's calling, and where is he one of, that he should come in and join us like this?"

"I don't know. I'll ask him again."

The catastrophe of having the mug drained dry at one pull by the stranger in cinder-grey was effectually guarded against this time by Mrs Fennel. She poured out his allowance in a small cup, keeping the large one at a discreet distance from him. When he had tossed off his portion the shepherd renewed his inquiry about the stranger's occupation.

The latter did not immediately reply, and the man in the chimney-corner with sudden demonstrativeness said "Anybody may know my trade — I'm a wheelwright."

"A very good trade for these parts," said the shepherd.

"And anybody may know mine — if they've the sense to find it out," said the stranger in cinder-grey.

"You may generally tell what a man is by his claws," observed the hedge-carpenter, looking at his own hands. "My fingers be as full of thorns as an old pincushion is of pins."

The hands of the man in the chimney-corner instinctively sought the shade, and he gazed into the fire as he resumed his pipe. The man at the table took up the hedge-carpenter's remark and added smartly "True; but the oddity of my trade is that, instead of setting a mark upon me, it sets a mark upon my customers."

No observation being offered by anybody in elucidation of this enigma the shepherd's wife once more called for a song. The same obstacles presented themselves as at the former time: one had no voice, another had forgotten the first verse. The stranger at the table, whose soul had now risen to a good working temperature, relieved the difficulty by exclaiming that, to start the company, he would sing himself. Thrusting one thumb into the arm-hole of his waistcoat, he waved the other hand in the air, and, with an extemporising gaze at the shining sheep-crooks above the mantel-piece, began:

"O my trade it is the rarest one,
Simple shepherds all,
My trade is a sight to see;
For my customers I tie,
   and take them up on high,
And waft 'em to a far countree."

The room was silent when he had finished the verse — with one exception, that of the man in the chimney-corner, who, at the singer's word "Chorus," joined him in a deep bass voice of musical relish —

"And waft 'em to a far countree."

Oliver Giles, John Pitcher the dairyman, the

parish-clerk, the engaged man of fifty, the row of young women against the wall, seemed lost in thought not of the gayest kind. The shepherd looked meditatively on the ground. The shepherdess gazed keenly at the singer, and with some suspicion; she was doubting whether this stranger were merely singing an old song from recollection, or was composing one there and then for the occasion. All were as perplexed at the obscure revelation as the guests at Belshazzar's feast, except the man in the chimney-corner who quietly said, "Second verse, stranger," and smoked on.

The singer thoroughly moistened himself from his lips inwards, and went on with the next stanza as requested:

"My tools are but common ones,
Simple shepherds all,
My tools are no sight to see;
A little hempen string,
  and a post whereon to swing,
Are implements enough for me."

Shepherd Fennel glanced round. There was no longer any doubt that the stranger was answering his question rhythmically. The guests one and all started back with suppressed exclamations. The young woman engaged to the man of fifty fainted half-way and would have proceeded, but finding him wanting in alacrity for catching her she sat down trembling.

"Oh — he's the — !" whispered the people in the background, mentioning the name of an ominous public officer. "He's come to do it. 'Tis to be at Casterbridge gaol tomorrow — the man for sheep stealing — the poor clock-maker we heard of, who used to live away at Shottsford and had no work to do — Timothy Summers, whose family were a starving, and so he went out of Shottsford by the high-road, and took a sheep in open daylight, defying the farmer and the farmer's wife and the farmer's lad, and every man jack among 'em. He" (and they nodded towards the stranger of the deadly trade) "is come from up the country to do it because there's not enough to do in his own county-town, and he's got the place here now our own county man's dead; he's going to live in the same cottage under the prison wall."

The stranger in cinder-grey took no notice of this whispered string of observations, but again wetted his lips. Seeing that his friend in the chimney-corner was the only one who reciprocated his joviality in any way, he held out his cup towards that appreciative comrade, who also held out his own. They clicked together, the eyes of the rest of the room hanging upon the singer's actions. He parted his lips for the third verse; but at that moment another knock was audible upon the door. This time the knock was faint and hesitating.

The company seemed scared; the shepherd looked with consternation towards the entrance, and it was with some effort that he resisted his alarmed wife's deprecatory glance, and uttered for the third time the welcoming words "Walk in!"

The door was gently opened, and another man stood upon the mat. He, like those who had preceded him, was a stranger. This time it was a short small personage, of fair complexion, and dressed in a decent suit of dark clothes.

"Can you tell me the way to —," he began; when, gazing round the room to observe the nature of the company amongst whom he had fallen, his eyes lighted on the stranger in cinder-grey. It was just at the instant when the latter, who had thrown his mind into his song with such a will that he scarcely heeded the interruption, silenced all whispers and inquiries by bursting into his third verse:

"To-morrow is my working-day
Simple shepherds all,
To-morrow is a working-day for me;
For the farmer's sheep is slain,
    and the lad who did it ta'en,
And on his soul may God ha' merc-y!"

The stranger in the chimney-corner, waving cups with the singer so heartily that his mead splashed over on the hearth, repeated in his bass voice as before:

"And on his soul may God ha' merc-y!"

All this time the third stranger had been standing in the doorway. Finding now that he did not come forward or go on speaking the guests particularly regarded him. They noticed to their surprise that he stood before them the picture of abject terror — his knees trembling, his hand shaking so violently that the door-latch by which he supported himself rattled audibly; his white lips were parted, and his eyes fixed on the merry officer of justice in the middle of the room. A moment more and he had turned, closed the door, and fled.

"What a man can it be?" said the shepherd.

The rest, between the awfulness of their

late discovery and the odd conduct of this third visitor, looked as if they knew not what to think, and said nothing. Instinctively they withdrew further and further from the grim gentleman in their midst, whom some of them seemed to take for the Prince of Darkness himself, till they formed a remote circle, an empty space of floor being left between them and him:

". . . . circulus, cujus centrum diabolus."

The room was so silent — though there were more than twenty people in it — that nothing could be heard but the patter of the rain against the window-shutters, accompanied by the occasional hiss of a stray drop that fell down the chimney into the fire, and the steady puffing of the man in the corner, who had now resumed his pipe of long clay.

The stillness was unexpectedly broken. The distant sound of a gun reverberated through the air — apparently from the direction of the county-town.

"Be jiggered!" cried the stranger who had sung the song, jumping up.

"What does that mean?" asked several.

"A prisoner escaped from the gaol — that's what it means."

All listened. The sound was repeated,

36

and none of them spoke but the man in the chimney-corner who said quietly "I've often been told that in this county they fire a gun at such times; but I never heard it till now."

"I wonder if it is *my* man," murmured the personage in cinder-grey.

"Surely it is!" said the shepherd involuntarily. "And surely we've zeed him? That little man who looked in at the door by now, and quivered like a leaf when he zeed ye and heard your song!"

"His teeth chattered, and the breath went out of his body," said the dairyman.

"And his heart seemed to sink within him like a stone," said Oliver Giles.

"And he bolted as if he'd been shot at," said the hedge-carpenter.

"True — his teeth chattered; and his heart seemed to sink; and he bolted as if he'd been shot at," slowly summed up the man in the chimney-corner.

"I didn't notice it," remarked the hangman.

"We were all a wondering what made him run off in such a fright" faltered one of the women against the wall. "And now 'tis explained."

The firing of the alarm-gun went on at intervals, low and sullenly, and their suspicions became a certainty. The sinister gentleman in cinder-grey roused himself. "Is there a constable here?" he asked in thick tones. "If so, let him step forward."

The engaged man of fifty stepped quavering out from the wall, his betrothed beginning to sob on the back of the chair.

"You are a sworn constable?"

"I be sir."

"Then pursue the criminal at once, with assistance, and bring him back here. He can't have gone far."

"I will sir — I will — when I've got my staff. I'll go home and get it, and come sharp here, and start in a body."

"Staff! — never mind your staff — the man'll be gone!"

"But I can't do nothing without my staff — can I William, and John, and Charles Jake? No — for there's the king's royal crown a painted on en in yaller and gold, and the lion and the unicorn, so as when I raise en up and hit my prisoner 'tis made a lawful blow thereby. I wouldn't 'tempt to take up a man without my staff — no, not I. If I hadn't the law to gie me courage, why, instead o' my taking up him he might take up me!"

"Now, I'm a king's man myself, and can give you authority enough for this," said the formidable officer in grey. "Now then, all of ye — be ready. Have ye any lanterns?"

"Yes — have ye any lanterns — I demand it," said the constable.

"And the rest of you able-bodied —"

"Able-bodied men — yes — the rest of ye," said the constable.

"Have you some good stout staves and pitchforks —"

"Staves and pitchforks — in the name o' the law. And take 'em in yer hands and go in quest, and do as we in authority tell ye."

Thus aroused the men prepared to give chase. The evidence was, indeed, though circumstantial, so convincing, that but little argument was needed to show the shepherd's guests that after what they had seen it would look very much like connivance if they did not instantly pursue the unhappy third stranger, who could not as yet have gone more than a few hundred yards over such uneven country.

A shepherd is always well-provided with lanterns, and lighting these hastily, and with hurdle-staves in their hands, they poured out of the door — taking a direction along the crest of the hill, away from the town, the rain having fortunately a little abated.

Disturbed by the noise, or possibly by unpleasant dreams of her baptism, the child who had been christened began to cry heartbrokenly in the room overhead. These notes of grief came down through the chinks of the floor to the ears of the women below, who jumped up one by one, and seemed glad of the excuse to ascend and comfort the baby, for the incidents of the last half-hour greatly oppressed them. Thus in the space of two or three minutes the room on the ground floor was deserted quite.

But it was not for long. Hardly had the sound of footsteps died away when a man returned round the corner of the house from the direction the pursuers had taken. Peeping in at the door and seeing nobody there he entered leisurely. It was the stranger of the chimney-corner, who had gone out with the rest. The motive of his return was shown by his helping himself to a cut piece of skimmer-cake that lay on a ledge beside where he had sat, and which he had apparently forgotten to take with him. He also poured out half a cup more mead from the quantity that remained, ravenously eating and drinking these as he stood. He had not finished when another figure came in just as qui-

40

etly — his friend in cinder-grey.

"Oh — you here," said the latter smiling. "I thought you had gone to help in the capture." And this speaker also revealed the object of his return by looking solicitously round for the fascinating mug of old mead. "And I thought you had gone," said the other, continuing his skimmer-cake with some effort.

"Well, on second thoughts I felt there were enough without me" said the first confidentially. "And such a night as it is too. Besides 'tis the business o' the Government to take care of its criminals — not mine."

"True — so it is. And I felt as you did, that there were enough without me."

"I don't want to break my limbs running over the humps and hollows of this wild country."

"Nor I neither, between you and me."

"These shepherd-people are used to it — simple minded souls, you know, stirred up to anything in a moment. They'll have him ready for me before the morning, and no trouble to me at all."

"They'll have him; and we shall have saved ourselves all labour in the matter."

"True, true. Well, my way is to Casterbridge; and 'tis as much as my legs will do to take me that far. Going the same way?"

"No — I am sorry to say. I have to get home over there" (he nodded indefinitely to the right) "and I feel as you do, that it is quite enough for my legs to do before bedtime."

The other had by this time finished the mead in the mug, after which, shaking hands heartily at the door and wishing each other well, they went their several ways.

In the meantime the company of pursuers had reached the end of the hog's-back elevation which dominated this part of the down. They had decided on no particular plan of action; and, finding that the man of the baleful trade was no longer in their company, they seemed quite unable to form any such plan now. They descended in all directions down the hill, and straightway several of the party fell into the snare set by Nature for all misguided midnight ramblers over this part of the cretaceous formation. The "lanchets," or flint slopes, which belted the escarpment at intervals of a dozen yards, took the less cautious ones unawares, and losing their footing on the rubbly steep they slid sharply downwards, the lanterns rolling from their hands to the bottom and there lying on their sides till the horn was scorched through.

When they had again gathered themselves together the shepherd, as the man who knew the country best, took the lead and guided them round these treacherous inclines. The lanterns, which seemed rather to dazzle their eyes and warn the fugitive than to assist them in the exploration, were extinguished, due silence was observed; and in this more rational order they plunged into the vale. It was a grassy, briary, moist defile, affording some shelter to any person who had sought it; but the party perambulated it in vain, and ascended on the other side. Here they wandered apart, and after an interval closed together again to report progress. At the second time of closing in they found themselves near a lonely ash, the single tree on this part of the coomb, probably sown there by a passing bird some fifty years before. And here, standing a little to one side of the trunk, as motionless as the trunk itself, appeared the man they were in quest of, his outline being well-defined against the sky beyond. The band noiselessly drew up and faced him.

"Yer money or yer life!" said the constable sternly to the still figure.

"No, no," whispered John Pitcher. " 'Tisn't our side ought to say that. That's the doctrine of vagabonds like him, and we be on the side of the law."

"Well well," replied the constable impatiently; "I must say something, mustn't I? — and if you had all the weight o' this undertaking upon your mind, perhaps you'd say the wrong thing too. Prisoner at the bar, surrender, in the name of the fath— the crown I mane!"

The man under the tree seemed now to notice them for the first time, and giving them no opportunity whatever for exhibiting their courage he strolled slowly towards them. He was indeed the little man, the third stranger; but his trepidation had in a great measure gone.

"Well travellers," he said "did I hear ye speak to me?"

"You did — you've got to come and be our prisoner at once," said the constable. "We arrest ye on the charge of not biding in Casterbridge jail in a decent proper manner to be hung to-morrow morning. Neighbours, do your duty, and seize the culpet!"

On hearing the charge the man seemed enlightened, and saying not another word resigned himself with preternatural civility to the search-party, who, with their stakes in their hands, surrounded him on all sides and marched him back towards the shepherd's cottage.

It was eleven o'clock by the time they arrived. The light shining from the open door, a sound of men's voices within, proclaimed to them as they approached the house that some new events had arisen in their absence. On entering they discovered the shepherd's living-room to be invaded by two officers from Casterbridge gaol, and a well-known magistrate who lived at the nearest country-seat, intelligence of the escape having become generally circulated.

"Gentlemen," said the constable "I have brought back your man not without risk and danger; but every one must do his duty. He is inside this circle of ablebodied persons, who have lent me useful aid considering their ignorance of Crown work. Men, bring forward your prisoner." And the third stranger was led to the light.

"Who is this?" said one of the officials.

"The man" said the constable.

"Certainly not," said the turnkey; and the first corroborated his statement.

"But how can it be otherwise?" asked the

constable. "Or why was he so terrified at sight o' the singing instrument of the law who sat there?" Here he related the strange behaviour of the third stranger on entering the house during the hangman's song.

"Can't understand it," said the officer coolly. "All I know is that 'taint the condemned man. He's quite a different character from this one — a gauntish fellow, with dark hair and eyes, rather good-looking, and with a musical bass voice that if you heard it once you'd never mistake as long as you lived."

"Why — souls — 'twas the man in the chimney-corner!"

"Hey — what?" said the magistrate coming forward after inquiring particulars from the shepherd in the background. "Haven't you got the man after all?"

"Well sir," said the constable, "he's the man we were in search of, that's true; and yet he's not the man we were in search of. For the man we were in search of was not the man we wanted, sir, if you understand my everyday way; for 'twas the man in the chimney-corner."

"A pretty kettle of fish, altogether!" said the magistrate. "You had better start for the other man at once."

The prisoner now spoke for the first

time. The mention of the man in the chimney-corner seemed to have moved him as nothing else could do. "Sir," he said, stepping forward to the magistrate "take no more trouble about me. The time is come when I may as well speak. I have done nothing: my crime is that the condemned man is my brother. Early this afternoon I left home at Shottsford to tramp it all the way to Casterbridge gaol to bid him farewell. I was benighted, and called here to rest and ask the way. When I opened the door I saw before me the very man, my brother, that I thought to see in the condemned cell at Casterbridge. He was in this chimney-corner; and jammed close to him, so that he could not have got out if he had tried, was the executioner who'd come to take his life, singing a song about it, and not knowing that it was his victim who was close by, joining in, to save appearances. My brother threw a glance of agony at me, and I knew he meant 'Don't reveal what you see — my life depends on it.' I was so terror-struck that I could hardly stand, and not knowing what I did I turned and hurried away."

The narrator's manner and tone had the stamp of truth, and his story made a great impression on all around. "And do you know where your brother is at the present time?" asked the magistrate.

"I do not. I have never seen him since I closed this door."

"I can testify to that, for we've been between ye ever since," said the constable.

"Where does he think to fly to — what is his occupation?"

"He's a watch and clock-maker, sir."

" 'A said 'a was a wheelwright — a wicked rogue," said the constable.

"The wheels o' clocks and watches he meant, no doubt," said Shepherd Fennel. "I thought his hands were palish for's trade."

"Well, it appears to me that nothing can be gained by retaining this poor man in custody," said the magistrate. "Your business lies with the other unquestionably."

And so the little man was released offhand; but he looked nothing the less sad on that account, it being beyond the power of magistrate or constable to raze out the written troubles in his brain, for they concerned another whom he regarded with more solicitude than himself. When this was done, and the man had gone his way, the night was found to be so far advanced that it was deemed useless to renew the search before the next morning.

Next day, accordingly, the quest for the clever sheep stealer become general and keen — to all appearance at least. But the intended punishment was cruelly disproportioned to the transgression, and the sympathy of a great many country-folk in that district was strongly on the side of the fugitive. Moreover his marvellous coolness and daring in hob-and-nobbing with the hangman, under the unprecedented circumstances of the shepherd's party, won their admiration. So that it may be questioned if all those who ostensibly made themselves so busy in exploring woods and fields and lanes were quite so thorough when it came to the private examination of their own lofts and outhouses. Stories were afloat of a mysterious figure being occasionally seen in some old overgrown trackway or other, remote from turnpike-roads; but when a search was instituted in any of these suspected quarters nobody was found. Thus the days and weeks passed without tidings.

In brief, the bass-voiced man of the chimney-corner was never recaptured. Some said that he went across the sea, others that he did not, but buried himself in the depths of a populous city. At any rate the gentleman in cinder-grey never did his morning's work at Casterbridge, nor met anywhere at all for business purposes the genial comrade with whom he had passed an hour of relaxation in the lonely house on the slope of the coomb.

The grass has long been green on the graves of Shepherd Fennel and his frugal wife; the guests who made up the christening-party have mainly followed their entertainers to the tomb; the baby in whose honour they all had met is a matron in the sere and yellow leaf. But the arrival of the three strangers at the shepherd's that night, and the details connected therewith, is a story as well known as ever in the country about Higher Crowstairs.

March 1883.

A Tradition of
Eighteen Hundred and Four

The widely discussed possibility of an invasion of England through a Channel tunnel has more than once recalled old Solomon Selby's story to my mind.

The occasion on which I numbered myself among his audience was one evening when he was sitting in the yawning chimney-corner of the inn-kitchen, with some others who had gathered there, and I entered for shelter from the rain. Withdrawing the stem of his pipe from the dental notch in which it habitually rested, he leaned back in the recess behind him and smiled into the fire. The smile was neither mirthful nor sad, not precisely humorous nor altogether thoughtful. We who knew him recognized it in a moment: it was his narrative smile. Breaking off our few desultory remarks we drew up closer, and he thus began: —

"My father, as you mid know, was a shepherd all his life, and lived out by the Cove four miles yonder, where I was born and lived likewise, till I moved here shortly afore I was married. The cottage that first knew me stood on the top of the down, near the sea; there was no house within a mile and a half of it; it was built o' purpose for the farm-shepherd, and had no other use. They tell me that it is now pulled down, but that you can see where it stood by the mounds of earth and a few broken bricks that are still lying about. It was a bleak and dreary place in winter-time, but in summer it was well enough, though the garden never came to much, because we could not get up a good shelter for the vegetables and currant bushes; and where there is much wind they don't thrive.

"Of all the years of my growing up the ones that bide clearest in my mind were eighteen hundred and three, four, and five. This was for two reasons: I had just then grown to an age when a child's eyes and ears take in and note down everything about him, and there was more at that date to bear in mind than there ever has been since with me. It was, as I need hardly tell ye, the time after the first peace, when Bonaparte was scheming his descent upon England. He had crossed the great Alp mountains, fought in Egypt, drubbed the Turks, the Austrians, and the Proossians, and now thought he'd have a slap at us. On the other side of the Channel, scarce out of sight and hail of a man standing on our English shore, the French army of a hundred and sixty thousand men and fifteen thousand horses had been brought together from all parts, and were drilling every day. Bonaparte had been three years a-making his preparations; and to ferry these soldiers and cannon and horses across he had contrived a couple of thousand flat-bottomed boats. These boats were small things, but wonderfully built. A good few of 'em were so made as to have a little stable on board each for the two horses that were to haul the cannon carried at the stern. To get in order all these, and other things required, he had assembled there five or six thousand fellows that worked at trades — carpenters, blacksmiths, wheelwrights, saddlers, and what not. O 'twas a curious time!

"Every morning Neighbour Boney would muster his multitude of soldiers on the beach, draw 'em up in line, practise 'em in the manœuvre of embarking, horses and all, till they could do it without a single hitch. My father drove a flock of ewes up into Sussex that year, and as he went along the drover's track over the high downs thereabout he could see this drilling actually going on — the accoutrements of the rank and file glittering in the sun like silver. It was thought and always said by my uncle Job, sergeant of foot (who used to know all about these matters), that Bonaparte meant to cross with oars on a calm night. The grand query with us was, Where would my gentleman land? Many of the common people thought it would be at Dover; others, who knew how unlikely it was that any skilful general would make a business of landing just where he was expected, said he'd go either east into the River Thames, or west'ard to some convenient place, most likely one of the little hays inside the Isle of Portland, between the Beal and St. Alban's Head — and for choice the three-quarter-round Cove, screened from every mortal eye, that seemed made o' purpose, out by where we lived, and which I've climmed up with two tubs of brandy across my shoulders on scores o' dark nights in my younger days.

Some had heard that a part o' the French fleet would sail right round Scotland, and come up the Channel to a suitable haven. However, there was much doubt upon the matter; and no wonder, for after-years proved that Bonaparte himself could hardly make up his mind upon that great and very particular point, where to land. His uncertainty came about in this wise, that he could get no news as to where and how our troops lay in waiting, and that his knowledge of possible places where flat-bottomed boats might be quietly run ashore, and the men they brought marshalled in order, was dim to the last degree. Being flat-bottomed, they didn't require a harbour for unshipping their cargo of men, but a good shelving beach away from sight, and with a fair open road toward London. How the question posed that great Corsican tyrant (as we used to call him), what pains he took to settle it, and, above all, what a risk he ran on one particular night in trying to do so, were known only to one man here and there; and certainly to no maker of newspapers or printer of books, or my account o't would not have had so many heads shaken over it as it has by gentry who only believe what they see in printed lines.

"The flocks my father had charge of fed all about the downs near our house, over-looking the sea and shore each way for miles. In winter and early spring father was up a deal at nights, watching and tending the lambing. Often he'd go to bed early, and turn out at twelve or one; and on the other hand, he'd sometimes stay up till twelve or one, and then turn in to bed. As soon as I was old enough I used to help him, mostly in the way of keeping an eye upon the ewes while he was gone home to rest. This is what I was doing in a partic-ular month in either the year four or five — I can't certainly fix which, but it was long before I was took away from the sheep-keeping to be bound prentice to a trade. Every night at that time I was at the fold, about half a mile, or it may be a little more, from our cottage, and no living thing at all with me but the ewes and young lambs. Afeard? No; I was never afeard of being alone at these times; for I had been reared in such an out-step place that the lack o' human beings at night made me less fearful than the sight of 'em. Directly I saw a man's shape after dark in a lonely place I was frightened out of my senses.

"One day in that month we were sur-prised by a visit from my uncle Job, the sergeant in the Sixty-first foot, then in camp on the downs above King George's watering-place, several miles to the west yonder. Uncle Job dropped in about dusk, and went up with my father to the fold for an hour or two. Then he came home, had a drop to drink from the tub of sperrits that the smugglers kept us in for housing their liquor when they'd made a run, and for burning 'em off when there was danger. After that he stretched himself out on the settle to sleep. I went to bed: at one o'clock father came home, and waking me to go and take his place, according to custom, went to bed himself. On my way out of the house I passed Uncle Job on the settle. He opened his eyes, and upon my telling him where I was going he said it was a shame that such a youngster as I should go up there all alone; and when he had fastened up his stock and waist-belt he set off along with me, taking a drop from the sperrit-tub in a little flat bottle that stood in the corner-cupboard.

"By and by we drew up to the fold, saw that all was right, and then, to keep ourselves warm, curled up in a heap of straw that lay inside the thatched hurdles we had set up to break the stroke of the wind when there was any. To-night, however, there was none. It was one of those very still nights when, if you stand on the high hills anywhere within two or three miles of the sea, you can hear the rise and fall of the tide along the shore, coming and going every few moments like a sort of great snore of the sleeping world. Over the lower ground there was a bit of a mist, but on the hill where we lay the air was clear, and the moon, then in her last quarter, flung a fairly good light on the grass and scattered straw.

"While we lay there Uncle Job amused me by telling me strange stories of the wars he had served in and the wownds he had got. He had already fought the French in the Low Countries, and hoped to fight 'em again. His stories lasted so long that at last I was hardly sure that I was not a soldier myself, and had seen such service as he told of. The wonders of his tales quite bewildered my mind, till I fell asleep and dreamed of battle, smoke, and flying soldiers, all of a kind with the doings he had been bringing up to me.

"How long my nap lasted I am not prepared to say. But some faint sounds over and above the rustle of the ewes in the straw, the bleat of the lambs, and the tinkle of the sheep-bell brought me to my waking senses. Uncle Job was still beside me; but he too had fallen asleep. I looked out from the straw, and saw what it was that had aroused me. Two men, in boat-cloaks, cocked hats, and swords, stood by the hurdles about twenty yards off.

"I turned my ear thitherward to catch what they were saying, but though I heard every word o't, not one did I understand. They spoke in a tongue that was not ours — in French, as I afterward found. But if I could not gain the meaning of a word, I was shrewd boy enough to find out a deal of the talkers' business. By the light o' the moon I could see that one of 'em carried a roll of paper in his hand, while every moment he spoke quick to his comrade, and pointed right and left with the other hand to spots along the shore. There was no doubt that he was explaining to the second gentleman the shapes and features of the coast. What happened soon after made this still clearer to me.

"All this time I had not waked Uncle Job, but now I began to be afeared that they might light upon us, because uncle breathed so heavily through's nose. I put my mouth to his ear and whispered, 'Uncle Job.'

" 'What is it, my boy?' he said, just as if

he hadn't been asleep at all.

" 'Hush!' says I. 'Two French generals —'

" 'French?' says he.

" 'Yes,' says I. 'Come to see where to land their army!'

"I pointed 'em out; but I could say no more, for the pair were coming at that moment much nearer to where we lay. As soon as they got as near as eight or ten yards, the officer with a roll in his hand stooped down to a slanting hurdle, unfastened his roll upon it, and spread it out. Then suddenly he sprung a dark lantern open on the paper, and showed it to be a map.

" 'What be they looking at?' I whispered to Uncle Job.

" 'A chart of the Channel,' says the sergeant (knowing about such things).

"The other French officer now stooped likewise, and over the map they had a long consultation, as they pointed here and there on the paper, and then hither and thither at places along the shore beneath us. I noticed that the manner of one officer was very respectful toward the other, who seemed much his superior, the second in rank calling him by a sort of title that I did not know the sense of. The head one, on the other hand, was quite familiar with his friend, and more than once clapped him on the shoulder.

"Uncle Job had watched as well as I, but though the map had been in the lantern-light, their faces had always been in shade. But when they rose from stooping over the chart the light flashed upward, and fell smart upon one of 'em's features. No sooner had this happened than Uncle Job gasped, and sank down as if he'd been in a fit.

" 'What is it — what is it, Uncle Job?' said I.

" 'O good God!' says he, under the straw.

" 'What?' says I.

" 'Boney!' he groaned out.

" 'Who?' says I.

" 'Bonaparty,' he said. 'The Corsican ogre. O that I had got but my new-flinted firelock, that there man should die! But I haven't got my new-flinted firelock, and that there man must live. So lie low, as you value your life!'

"I did lie low, as you mid suppose. But I couldn't help peeping. And then I too, lad as I was, knew that it was the face of Bonaparte. Not know Boney? I should think I did know Boney. I should have known him by half the light o' that lantern. If I had seen a picture of his features once,

61

I had seen it a hundred times. "There was his bullet head, his short neck, his round yaller cheeks and chin, his gloomy face, and his great glowing eyes. He took off his hat to blow himself a bit, and there was the forelock in the middle of his forehead, as in all the draughts of him. In moving, his cloak fell a little open, and I could see for a moment his white-fronted jacket and one of his epaulets.

"But none of this lasted long. In a minute he and his general had rolled up the map, shut the lantern, and turned to go down toward the shore.

"Then Uncle Job came to himself a bit. 'Slipped across in the night-time to see how to put his men ashore,' he said. 'The like o' that man's coolness eyes will never again see! Nephew, I must act in this, and immediate, or England's lost!'

"When they were over the brow, we crope out, and went some little way to look after them. Half-way down they were joined by two others, and six or seven minutes brought them to the shore. Then, from behind a rock, a boat came out into the weak moonlight of the Cove, and they jumped in; it put off instantly, and vanished in a few minutes between the two rocks that stand at the mouth of the Cove as we all know. We climmed back to where we had been before, and I could see, a short way out, a larger vessel, though still not very large. The little boat drew up alongside, was made fast at the stern as I suppose, for the largest sailed away, and we saw no more.

"My uncle Job told his officers as soon as he got back to camp; but what they thought of it I never heard — neither did he. Boney's army never came, and a good job for me; for the Cove below my father's house was where he meant to land, as this secret visit showed. We coast-folk should have been cut down one and all, and I should not have sat here to tell this tale."

We who listened to old Selby that night have been familiar with his simple gravestone for these ten years past. Thanks to the incredulity of the age his tale has been seldom repeated. But if anything short of the direct testimony of his own eyes could persuade an auditor that Bonaparte had examined these shores for himself with a view to a practicable landing-place, it would have been Solomon Selby's manner of narrating the adventure which befell him on the down.

Christmas 1882.

The
Melancholy Hussar
of the
German Legion

I

Here stretch the downs, high and breezy and green, absolutely unchanged since those eventful days. A plough has never disturbed the turf, and the sod that was uppermost then is uppermost now. Here stood the camp; here are distinct traces of the banks thrown up for the horses of the cavalry, and spots where the midden-heaps lay are still to be observed. At night when I walk across the lonely place it is impossible to avoid hearing, amid the scourings of the wind over the grass-bents and thistles, the old trumpet and bugle calls, the rattle of the halters; to help seeing rows of spectral tents and the *impedimenta* of the soldiery; from within the canvases come guttural syllables of foreign tongues, and broken songs of the fatherland; for they were mainly regiments of the King's German legion that slept round the tent-poles hereabout at that time.

It was nearly ninety years ago. The British uniform of the period, with its immense epaulettes, queer cocked hat, breeches, gaiters, ponderous cartridge-box, buckled shoes, and what not, would look strange and barbarous now. Ideas have changed; invention has followed invention. Soldiers were monumental objects then. A divinity still hedged kings here and there; and war was considered a glorious thing.

Secluded old manor-houses and hamlets lie in the ravines and hollows among these hills, where a stranger had hardly ever been seen till the King chose to take the baths yearly at the sea-side watering-place a few miles to the south; as a consequence of which battalions descended in a cloud upon the open country around. Is it necessary to add that the echoes of many characteristic tales, dating from that picturesque time, still linger about here, in more or less fragmentary form to be caught by the attentive ear? Some of them

I have repeated; most of them I have forgotten; one I have never repeated, and assuredly can never forget.

Phyllis told me the story with her own lips. She was then an old lady of seventy-five, and her auditor a lad of fifteen. She enjoined silence as to her share in the incident till she should be "dead, buried, and forgotten." Her life was prolonged twelve years after the day of her narration, and she has now been dead nearly twenty. The oblivion which, in her modesty and humility, she courted for herself, has only partially fallen on her, with the unfortunate result of inflicting an injustice upon her memory; since such fragments of her story as got abroad at the time, and have been kept alive ever since, are precisely those which are most unfavourable to her character.

It all began with the arrival of the York Hussars, one of the foreign regiments above alluded to. Before that day scarcely a soul had been seen near her father's house for weeks. When a noise like the brushing skirt of a visitor was heard on the doorstep it proved to be a scudding leaf; when a carriage seemed to be nearing the door it was her father grinding his sickle on the stone in the garden for his favourite relaxation of trimming the box-tree borders to the plots. A sound like luggage thrown down from the coach was a gun far away at sea; and what looked like a tall man by the gate at dusk was a yew bush cut into a quaint and attenuated shape. There is no such solitude in country places now as there was in those old days.

Yet all the while King George and his court were at his favourite sea-side resort, not more than five miles off.

The daughter's seclusion was great, but beyond the seclusion of the girl lay the seclusion of the father. If her social condition was twilight his was darkness. Yet he enjoyed his darkness while her twilight oppressed her. Dr Grove had been a professional man whose taste for lonely meditation over metaphysical questions had diminished his practice till it no longer paid him to keep it going; after which he had relinquished it and hired at a nominal rent the small, dilapidated, half farm half manor-house of this obscure inland nook, to make a sufficiency of an income which in a town would have been inadequate for their maintenance. He stayed in his garden the greater part of the day, growing more and more irritable with the lapse of time, and the increasing perception that he had wasted his life in the pursuit of illusions. He saw his friends less and less frequently. Phyllis became so shy that if she met a stranger anywhere in her short rambles she felt ashamed at his gaze, walked awkwardly, and blushed to her shoulders.

Yet Phyllis was discovered even here by an admirer, and her hand most unexpectedly asked in marriage.

The king as aforesaid was at the neighbouring town, where he had taken up his abode at Gloucester Lodge; and his presence in the town naturally brought many county people thither. Among these idlers, many of whom professed to have connections and interests with the Court, was one Humphrey Gould, a bachelor; a personage neither young nor old; neither good-looking nor positively plain. Too steady going to be "a buck" (as fast and unmarried men were then called) he was an approximately fashionable man of a mild type. This bachelor of thirty found his way to the village on the down; beheld Phyllis, made her father's acquaintance in order to make hers; and by some means or other she sufficiently inflamed his heart to lead him in that direction almost daily: till he became engaged to marry her.

As he was of an old local family, some of

whose members were held in respect in the county, Phyllis, in bringing him to her feet, had accomplished what was considered a brilliant move for one in her constrained position. How she had done it was not quite known to Phyllis herself. In those days unequal marriages were regarded rather as a violation of the laws of nature than as a mere infringement of convention, the more modern view; and hence when Phyllis of the watering-place *bourgeoisie* was chosen by such a gentlemanly fellow it was as if she were going to be taken to Heaven; though perhaps the uninformed would have seen no great difference in the respective positions of the pair, the said Gould being as poor as a crow.

This pecuniary condition was his excuse — probably a true one — for postponing their union; and as the winter drew nearer, and the king departed for the season, Mr Humphrey Gould set out for Bath, promising to return to Phyllis in a few weeks. The winter arrived, the date of his promise passed; yet Gould postponed his coming, on the ground that he could not very easily leave his father in the city of their sojourn, the elder having no other relative near him. Phyllis, though lonely in the extreme, was content. The man who had asked her in marriage was a desirable husband for her in many ways; her father highly approved of his suit: but this neglect of her was awkward if not painful for Phyllis. Love him in the true sense of the word she assured me she never did; but she had a genuine regard for him; admired a certain methodical and dogged way in which he sometimes took his pleasure; valued his knowledge of what the Court was doing, had done, or was about to do; and she was not without a feeling of pride that he had chosen her when he might have exercised a more ambitious choice.

But he did not come; and the spring developed. His letters were regular though formal; and it is not to be wondered that the uncertainty of her position, linked with the fact that there was not much passion in her thoughts of Humphrey, bred an indescribable dreariness in the heart of Phyllis Grove. The spring was soon summer, and the summer brought the king; but still no Humphrey Gould. All this while the engagement by letter was maintained intact.

At this point of time a golden radiance flashed in upon the lives of people here, and charged all youthful thought with emotional interest. This radiance was the aforesaid York Hussars.

The present generation has probably but a very dim notion of the celebrated York Hussars of ninety years ago. They were one of the regiments of the King's German Legion and (though they somewhat degenerated later on) their brilliant uniform, their splendid horses, and above all, their foreign air, and mustachios (rare appendages then) drew crowds of admirers of both sexes wherever they went. These, with other regiments had come to encamp on the downs and pastures, because of the presence of the king in the neighbouring town.

The spot was high and airy, and the view extensive, commanding Portland — the Isle of Slingers — in front, and reaching to St. Aldhelm's Head eastward, and almost to the Start on the west.

Phyllis, though not precisely a girl of the village, was as interested as any of them in this military investment. Her father's home stood somewhat apart, and on the highest point of ground, to which the lane ascended, so that it was almost level with the top of the church tower in the lower part of the parish. Immediately from the outside of the garden wall the grass spread away to a great distance, and it was crossed by a path which came close to the wall. Ever since her childhood it had been Phyllis's pleasure to clamber up this fence, and sit on the top, a feat not so difficult as it may seem, the walls in this district being built of rubble, without mortar so that there were plenty of crevices for small toes.

She was sitting up here one day, listlessly surveying the pasture without, when her attention was arrested by a solitary figure walking along the path. It was one of the renowned German Hussars, and he moved onward with his eyes on the ground, and with the manner of one who wished to escape company. His head would probably have been bent like his eyes but for his stiff neck-gear. On nearer view she perceived that his face was marked with deep sadness. Without observing her he advanced by the footpath till it brought him almost immediately under the wall.

Phyllis was much surprised to see a fine tall soldier in such a mood as this. Her theory of the military, and of the York Hussars in particular (derived entirely from hearsay, for she had never talked to a soldier in her life) was that their hearts were as gay as their accoutrements.

At this moment the Hussar lifted his eyes and noticed her on her perch, the white muslin neckerchief which covered her shoulders and neck where left bare by her low gown, and her white raiment in general, showing conspicuously in the bright sunlight of this summer day. He blushed a little at the suddenness of the encounter, and without halting a moment from his pace passed on.

All that day the foreigner's face haunted Phyllis; its aspect was so striking, so handsome, and his eyes were so blue, and sad, and abstracted. It was perhaps only natural that on some following day at the same hour she should look over that wall again, and wait till he had passed a second time. On this occasion he was reading a letter, and at the sight of her his manner was that of one who had half expected or hoped to discover her. He almost stopped, smiled, and made a courteous salute. The end of the meeting was that they exchanged a few words. She asked him what he was reading, and he readily informed her that he was reperusing letters from his mother in Germany; he did not get them often, he said, and was forced to read the old ones a great many times. This was all that passed at the present interview; but others of the same kind followed.

Phyllis used to say that his English,

though not good, was quite intelligible to her, so that their acquaintance was never hindered by difficulties of speech. Whenever the subject became too delicate, subtle, or tender, for such words of English as were at his command, the eyes no doubt helped out the tongue, and — though this was later on — the lips helped out the eyes. In short this acquaintance, unguardedly made, and rash enough on her part, developed, and ripened. Like Desdemona, she pitied him, and learnt his history.

His name was Matthäus Tina, and Saarbruck his native town, where his mother was still living. His age was twenty-two, and he had already risen to the grade of corporal, though he had not long been in the army. Phyllis used to assert that no such refined or well-educated young man could have been found in the ranks of the purely English regiments, some of these foreign soldiers having rather the graceful manner and presence of our native officers than of our rank and file.

She by degrees learnt from her foreign friend a circumstance about himself and his comrades which Phyllis would least have expected of the York Hussars. So far from being as gay as its uniform the regi-

ment was pervaded by a dreadful melancholy, a chronic home-sickness, which
depressed many of the men to such an extent that they could hardly attend to their
drill. The worst sufferers were the younger
soldiers who had not been over here long.
They hated England and English life; they
took no interest whatever in King George
and his island kingdom, and they only
wished to be out of it and never to see it
any more. Their bodies were here, but
their hearts and minds were always far
away in their dear fatherland, of which —
brave men and stoical as they were in
many ways — they would speak with tears
in their eyes. One of the worst of the sufferers from this home-woe, as he called it
in his own tongue, was Matthäus Tina,
whose dreamy musing nature felt the
gloom of exile still more intensely from the
fact that he had left a lonely mother at
home with nobody to cheer her.

Though Phyllis, touched by all this, and
interested in his history, did not disdain her
soldier's acquaintance, she declined (according to her own account at least) to
permit the young man to over-step the line
of mere friendship for a long while — as
long, indeed, as she considered herself likely
to become the possession of another; though

it is probable that she had lost her heart to Matthäus before she was herself aware. The stone wall of necessity made anything like intimacy difficult; and he had never ventured to come, or to ask to come, inside the garden, so that all their conversation had been overtly conducted across this boundary.

III

But news reached the village from a friend of Phyllis's father, concerning Mr Humphrey Gould, her remarkably cool and patient betrothed. This gentleman had been heard to say in Bath that he considered his overtures to Miss Phyllis Grove to have reached only the stage of a half-understanding; and in view of his enforced absence on his father's account, who was too great an invalid now to attend to his affairs, he thought it best that there should be no definite promise as yet on either side. He was not sure, indeed, that he might not cast his eyes elsewhere.

This account — though only a piece of hearsay and as such entitled to no absolute credit — tallied so well with the infrequency of his letters, and their lack of warmth, that Phyllis did not doubt its truth for one moment; and from that hour she felt herself free to bestow her heart as she should choose. Not so her father; he declared the whole story to be a fabrication. He had known Mr Gould's family from his boyhood: and if there was one proverb which expressed the matrimonial aspect of that family well it was "Love me little love me long." Humphrey was an honourable man who would not think of treating his engagement so lightly. "Do you wait in patience," he said. "All will be right enough in time."

From these words Phyllis at first imagined that her father was in correspondence with Mr Gould; and her heart sank within her; for in spite of her original intentions she had been relieved to hear that her engagement had come to nothing. But she presently learnt that her father had heard no more of Humphrey Gould than she herself had done: while he would not write and address her affianced directly on the subject lest it should be deemed an imputation on that bachelor's honour.

"You want an excuse for encouraging one or other of those foreign fellows to flatter you with his unmeaning attentions," her father exclaimed, his mood having of late been a very unkind one towards her. "I

78

see more than I say. Don't you ever set foot outside that garden-fence without my permission. If you want to see the camp I'll take you myself some Sunday afternoon."

Phyllis had not the smallest intention of disobeying him in her actions, but she assumed herself to be independent with respect to her feelings. She no longer checked her fancy for the Hussar, though she was far from regarding him as her lover in the serious sense in which an Englishman might have been regarded as such. The young foreign soldier was almost an ideal being to her, with none of the appurtenances of an ordinary house-dweller; one who had descended she knew not whence, and would disappear she knew not whither; the subject of a fascinating dream, no more.

They met continually now — mostly at dusk — during the brief interval between the going down of the sun and the minute at which the last trumpet-call summoned him to his tent. Perhaps her manner had become less restrained latterly: at any rate that of the Hussar was so; he had grown more tender every day, and at parting after these hurried interviews she reached down her hand from the top of the wall that he might press it. One evening he held it such a while that she exclaimed, "The wall is white, and somebody in the field may see your shape against it."

He lingered so long that night that it was with the greatest difficulty that he could run across the intervening stretch of ground and enter the camp in time. On the next occasion of his awaiting her she did not appear in her usual place at the usual hour. His disappointment was unspeakably keen: he remained staring blankly at the spot, like a man in a trance. The trumpets and tattoo sounded, and still he did not go.

She had been delayed purely by an accident. When she arrived she was anxious because of the lateness of the hour, having heard as well as he the sounds denoting the closing of the camp. She implored him to leave immediately.

"No," he said, gloomily. "I shall not go in yet — the moment you come — I have thought of your coming all day."

"But you may be disgraced at being after time?"

"I don't mind that. I should have disappeared from the world some time ago if it had not been for two persons — my beloved, here; and my mother in Saarbruck. I hate the army. I care more for a minute of

80

your company than for all the promotion in the world."

Thus he stayed and talked to her, and told her interesting details of his native place, and incidents of his childhood, till she was in a simmer of distress at his recklessness in remaining. It was only because she insisted on bidding him good night and leaving the wall that he returned to his quarters.

The next time that she saw him he was without the stripes that had adorned his sleeve. He had been broken to the level of private for his lateness that night: and as Phyllis considered herself to be the cause of his disgrace her sorrow was great. But the position was now reversed: it was his turn to cheer her.

"Don't grieve meine Liebliche!" he said. "I have got a remedy for whatever comes. First, even supposing I regain my stripes, would your father allow you to marry a non-commissioned officer in the York Hussars?"

She flushed. This practical step had not been in her mind in relation to such an unrealistic person as he was; and a moment's reflection was enough for it. "My father would not — certainly would not," she answered unflinchingly. "It cannot be thought of! My dear friend, please do forget me: I fear I am ruining you and your prospects!"

"Not at all!" said he. "You are giving this country of yours just sufficient interest to me to make me care to keep alive in it. If my dear land were here also, and my old parent, with you, I could be happy as I am, and would do my best as a soldier. But it is not so. And now listen. This is my plan. That you go with me to my own country, and be my wife there, and live there with my mother and me. I am not a Hanoverian, as you know, though I entered the army as such, my country is by the Saar, and is at peace with France, and if I were once in it I should be free."

"But how get there?" she asked. Phyllis had been rather amazed than shocked at his proposition. Her position in her father's house was growing irksome and painful in the extreme; his parental affection seemed to be quite dried up. She was not a native of the village, like all the joyous girls around her; and in some way Matthäus Tina had infected her with his own passionate longing for his country and mother and home.

"But how?" she repeated, finding that he did not answer. "Will you buy your discharge?"

"Ah, no," he said. "That's impossible in these times. No. I came here against my will: why should I not escape? Now is the time, as we shall soon be striking camp, and I might see you no more. This is my scheme. I will ask you to meet me on the highway two miles off on some calm night next week that may be appointed. There will be nothing unbecoming in it, or to cause you shame; you will not fly alone with me, for I will bring with me my devoted young friend Christoph, an Alsatian, who has lately joined the regiment, and who has agreed to assist in this enterprise. We shall have come from yonder harbour, where we shall have examined the boats, and found one suited to our purpose. Christoph has already a chart of the channel, and we will then go to the harbour, and at midnight cut the boat from her moorings, and row away round the point out of sight; and by the next morning we are on the coast of France, near Cherbourg. The rest is easy, for I have saved money for the land journey, and can get a change of clothes. I will write to my mother; who will meet us on the way."

He added details in reply to her inquiries which left no doubt in Phyllis's mind of the feasibility of the undertaking. But its magnitude almost appalled her; and it is questionable if she would ever have gone further in the wild adventure if, on entering the house that night, her father had not accosted her in the most significant terms.

"How about the York Hussars?" he said.

"They are still at the Camp; but they are soon going away, I believe."

"It is useless for you to attempt to cloak your actions in that way. You have been meeting one of those fellows: you have been seen walking with him — foreign barbarians not much better than the French themselves. I have made up my mind — don't speak a word till I have done please! — I have made up my mind that you shall stay here no longer while they are on the spot. You shall go to your Aunt's."

It was useless for her to protest that she had never taken a walk with any soldier or man under the sun except himself. Her protestations were feeble too, for though he was not literally correct in his assertion he was virtually only half in error.

The house of her father's sister was a prison to Phyllis. She had quite recently undergone experience of its gloom; and when her father went on to direct her to pack what would be necessary for her to take her heart died within her. In after years she never attempted to excuse her conduct during this week of agitation; but the result of her self-communing was that she decided to join in the scheme of her lover and his friend, and fly to the country which he had coloured with such lovely hues in her imagination. She always said that the one feature in his proposal which overcame her hesitation was the obvious purity and straightforwardness of his intentions. He showed himself to be so virtuous and kind: he treated her with a respect to which she had never before been accustomed; and she was braced to the obvious risks of the voyage by her confidence in him.

IV

It was on a soft, dark evening of the following week that they engaged in the adventure. Tina was to meet her at a point in the highway at which the lane to the village branched off. Christoph was to go ahead of them to the harbour where the boat lay, row it round the Nothe — or Look-out as it was called in those days — and pick them up on the other side of the promontory, which they were to reach by crossing the harbour bridge on foot, and climbing over the Look-out hill.

As soon as her father had ascended to his room she left the house, and, bundle in hand, proceeded at a trot along the lane. At such an hour not a soul was afoot anywhere in the village, and she reached the junction of the lane with the highway unobserved. Here she took up her position in the obscurity formed by the angle of a fence, whence she could discern every one who approached along the turnpike road, without being herself seen.

She had not remained thus waiting for her lover longer than a minute — though from the tension of her nerves the lapse of even that short time was trying — when, instead of the expected footsteps the stagecoach could be heard descending the hill. She knew that Tina would not show himself till the road was clear, and waited impatiently for the coach to pass. Nearing the corner where she was it slackened speed, and, instead of going by as usual, drew up within a few yards of her. A passenger alighted, and she heard his voice. It was Humphrey Gould's.

He had brought a friend with him, and luggage. The luggage was deposited on the grass, and the coach went on its route to the royal watering-place.

"I wonder where that young man is with the horse and trap?" said her former admirer to his companion. "I hope we shan't have to wait here long. I told him half-past nine o'clock precisely."

"Have you got her present safe?"

"Phyllis's? O yes. It is in this trunk. I hope it will please her."

"Of course it will. What woman would not be pleased with such a handsome peace-offering."

"Well — she deserves it. I've treated her rather badly. But she has been in my mind these last two days much more than I should care to confess to everybody. Ah well; I'll say no more about that. It cannot be that she is so bad as they make out. I am quite sure that a girl of her good wit would know better than to get entangled with any of those Hanoverian soldiers. I won't believe it of her, and there's an end on't."

More words in the same strain were casually dropped as the two men waited; words which revealed to her, as by a sudden illumination, the enormity of her conduct. The conversation was at length cut off by the arrival of the man with the vehicle. The luggage was placed in it, and they mounted, and were driven on in the direction from which she had just come.

Phyllis was so conscience-stricken that she was at first inclined to follow them: but a moment's reflection led her to feel that it would only be bare justice to Matthäus to wait till he arrived, and explain candidly that she had changed her mind — difficult as the struggle would be when she stood face to face with him. She bitterly reproached herself for having believed reports which represented Humphrey Gould as false to his engagement, when, from what she now heard from his own lips she gathered that he had been living full of trust in her; but she knew well enough who had won her love. Without him her life seemed a dreary prospect; yet the more she looked at his proposal the more she feared to accept it — so wild as it was, so vague, so venturesome. She had promised Humphrey Gould, and it was only his assumed faithlessness which had led her to treat that promise as nought. His solicitude in bringing her these gifts touched her; her promise must be kept, and esteem must take the place of love. She would preserve her self-respect. She would stay at home, and marry him, and suffer.

Phyllis had thus braced herself to an exceptional fortitude when, a few minutes later, the outline of Matthäus Tina appeared behind a field-gate; over which he lightly leapt as she stepped forward. There was no evading it: he pressed her to his breast.

"It is the first and last time!" she wildly thought as she stood encircled by his arms.

How Phyllis got through the terrible ordeal of that night she could never clearly recollect. She always attributed her success in carrying out her resolve to her lover's honour, for as soon as she declared to him in feeble words that she had changed her mind, and felt that she could not, dared not, fly with him, he forbore to urge her, grieved as he was at her decision. Unscrupulous pressure on his part, seeing how romantically she had become attached to him, would no doubt have turned the balance in his favour. But he did nothing to tempt her unduly or unfairly.

On her side, fearing for his safety, she begged him to remain. This, he declared, could not be. "I cannot break faith with my friend," said he. Had he stood alone he would have abandoned his plan. But Christoph, with the boat and compass and chart, was waiting on the shore; the tide would soon turn; his mother had been warned of his coming; go he must.

Many precious minutes were lost while he tarried, unable to tear himself away. Phyllis held to her resolve, though it cost her many a bitter pang. At last they parted, and he went down the hill. Before his footsteps had quite died away she felt a desire to behold at least his outline once more, and running noiselessly after him regained view of his diminishing figure. For one moment she was sufficiently excited to be on the point of rushing forward and linking her fate with his. But she could not. The courage which at the critical instant failed Cleopatra of Egypt could scarcely be expected of Phyllis Grove.

A dark shape similar to his own joined him in the highway: it was Christoph his friend. She could see no more; they had hastened on in the direction of the town and harbour, four miles ahead. With a feeling akin to despair she turned and slowly pursued her way homeward. Tattoo sounded in the camp; but there was no camp for her now. It was as dead as the camp of the Assyrians after the passage of the destroying angel.

She noiselessly entered the house, seeing

nobody; and went to bed. Grief, which kept her awake at first, ultimately wrapt her in a heavy sleep. The next morning her father met her at the foot of the stairs.

"Mr. Gould is come!" he said triumphantly.

Humphrey was staying at the inn, and had already called to inquire for her. He had brought her a present of a very handsome looking-glass in a frame of *repoussé* silver-work, which her father held in his hand. He had promised to call again in the course of an hour, to ask Phyllis to walk with him.

Pretty mirrors were rarer in country-houses at that day than they are now, and the one before her won Phyllis's admiration. She looked into it, saw how heavy her eyes were, and endeavoured to brighten them. She was in that wretched state of mind which leads a woman to move mechanically onward in what she conceives to be her allotted path. Mr Humphrey had, in his undemonstrative way, been adhering all along to the old understanding: it was for her to do the same; and to say not a word of her own lapse. She put on her bonnet and tippet, and when he arrived at the hour named she was at the door awaiting him.

V

Phyllis thanked him for his beautiful gift; but the talking was soon entirely on Humphrey's side as they walked along. He told her of the latest movements of the world of fashion — a subject which she willingly discussed to the exclusion of anything more personal — and his measured language helped to still her disquieted heart and brain. Had not her own sadness been what it was she must have observed his embarrassment. At last he abruptly changed the subject.

"I am glad you are pleased with my little present," he said. "The truth is that I brought it to propitiate 'ee, and to get you to help me out of a mighty difficulty."

It was inconceivable to Phyllis that this independent bachelor — whom she admired in some respects — could have a difficulty.

"Phyllis — I'll tell you my secret at once; for I have a monstrous secret to confide before I can ask your counsel. The case is, then, that I am married: yes, I have privately married a dear young *belle*, and if you knew her, and I hope you will, you would say everything in her praise. But she is not quite the one that my father would have chose for me — you know the pa-

92

ternal idea as well as I — and I have kept it secret. There will be a terrible noise, no doubt; but I think that with your help I may get over it. If you would only do me this good turn — when I have told my father I mean — say that you never could have married me, you know, or something of that sort — 'pon my life it will help to smooth the way vastly. I am so anxious to win him round to my point of view, and not to cause any estrangement."

What Phyllis replied she scarcely knew, or how she counselled him as to his unexpected situation. Yet the relief that his announcement brought her was perceptible. To have confided her trouble in return was what her aching heart longed to do; and had Humphrey been a woman she would instantly have poured out her tale. But to him she feared to confess; and there was a real reason for silence till a sufficient time had elapsed to allow her lover and his comrade to get out of harm's way.

As soon as she reached home again she sought a solitary place, and spent the time in half regretting that she had not gone away, and in dreaming over the meetings with Matthäus Tina from their beginning to their end. In his own country, amongst his own countrywomen, he would possibly soon forget her, even to her very name.

Her listlessness was such that she did not go out of the house for several days. There came a morning which broke in fog and mist, behind which the down could be discerned in greenish gray; and the outlines of the tents, and the rows of horses at the ropes. The smoke from the canteen fires drooped heavily.

The spot at the bottom of the garden where she had been accustomed to climb the wall to meet Matthäus was the only inch of English ground in which she took any interest; and in spite of the disagreeable haze prevailing she walked out there till she reached the well-known corner. Every blade of grass was weighted with little liquid globes, and slugs and snails had crept out upon the plots. She could hear the usual faint noises from the camp, and in the other direction the trot of farmers on the road to the town, for it was market-day. She observed that her frequent visits to this corner had quite trodden down the grass in the angle of the wall and left marks of garden-soil on the stepping-stones by which she had mounted to look over the top: seldom having gone there till dusk she had not considered that her traces might be visible by day. Perhaps it was these which had revealed her trysts to her father.

While she paused in melancholy regard she fancied that the customary sounds from the tents were changing their character. Indifferent as Phyllis was to camp doings now, she mounted by the steps to the old place. What she beheld at first awed and perplexed her: then she stood rigid, her fingers hooked to the wall, her eyes starting out of her head, and her face as if hardened to stone.

On the open green stretching before her all the regiments in the camp were drawn up in line, in the mid-front of which two empty coffins lay on the ground. The unwonted sounds which she had noticed came from an advancing procession; it consisted of the band of the York Hussars playing a dead march; next two soldiers of that regiment in a mourning coach, guarded on each side, and accompanied by two priests. Behind came a crowd of rustics who had been attracted by the event. The melancholy procession marched along the front of the line, returned to the centre, and halted beside the coffins, where the two condemned men were blind-folded, and each placed kneeling on his coffin; a few minutes pause was now given, while they prayed.

A firing-party of twenty-four men stood ready with levelled carbines. The commanding officer, who had his sword drawn, waved it through some cuts of the sword-exercise till he reached the downward stroke, whereat the firing party discharged their volley. The two victims fell, one upon his face across his coffin, the other backwards.

As the volley resounded there arose a shriek from the wall of Dr Grove's garden, and some one fell down inside; but nobody among the spectators without noticed it at the time.

The two executed hussars were Matthäus Tina and his friend Christoph. The soldiers on guard placed the bodies in the coffins almost instantly; but the Colonel of the regiment — an Englishman — rode up and exclaimed in a stern voice: "Turn them out — as an example to the men!"

The coffins were lifted endwise, and the dead Germans flung out upon their faces on the grass. Then all the regiments wheeled in sections, and marched past the spot in slow time. When the survey was over the corpses were again coffined, and borne away.

Meanwhile Dr Grove, attracted by the noise of the volley, had rushed out into his garden, where he saw his wretched daughter lying motionless against the wall. She was taken indoors, but it was long before she recovered consciousness; and for weeks they despaired of her reason.

It transpired that the luckless deserters from the York Hussars had cut the boat from her moorings in the adjacent harbour, according to their plan, and, with two other comrades who were smarting under ill-treatment from their Colonel, had sailed in safety across the Channel. But mistaking their bearings they steered into Jersey, thinking that island the French coast. Here they were perceived to be deserters, and delivered up to the authorities. Matthäus and Christoph interceded for the other two at the court-martial, saying that it was entirely by the formers' representations that these were induced to go. Their sentence was accordingly commuted to flogging, the death punishment being reserved for their leaders.

The visitor to the well-known old Georgian watering-place, who may care to ramble to the neighbouring village under the hills, and examine the register of burials, will there find two entries in these words: — *"Matth. Tina (Corpl.) in His Majesty's Regmt. of York Hussars and Shot for Desertion was Buried June 30th 1801, aged 22 Years. Born in the town of Sarrbruk Germany.*

"Christopher Bless belonging to His Majesty's Regmt. of York Hussars who was Shot for Desertion was Buried June 30th 1801, aged 22 Years. Born at Lothaargen Alsassia."

Their graves were dug at the back of the little church, near the wall. There is no memorial to mark the spot, but Phyllis pointed it out to me. While she lived she used to keep their mounds neat; but now they are over-grown with nettles, and sunk nearly flat. The older villagers, however, who know of the episode from their parents, still recollect the place where the soldiers lie. Phyllis lies near.

October 1889.

The Withered Arm

I.   A Lorn Milkmaid

It was an eighty-cow dairy, and the troop of milkers, regular and supernumerary, were all at work; for, though the time of year was as yet but early April, the feed lay entirely in water-meadows and the cows were "in full pail." The hour was about six in the evening, and three-fourths of the large, red, rectangular animals having been finished off, there was opportunity for a little conversation.

"He do bring home his bride to-morrow, I hear. They've come as far as Anglebury to-day."

The voice seemed to proceed from the belly of the cow called Cherry, but the speaker was a milking-woman, whose face was buried in the flank of that motionless beast.

"Hav' anybody seen her?" said another.

There was a negative response from the

first. "Though they say she's a rosy-cheeked, tisty-tosty little body enough," she added; and as the milkmaid spoke she turned her face so that she could glance past her cow's tail to the other side of the barton, where a thin fading woman of thirty milked somewhat apart from the rest.

"Years younger than he, they say," continued the second, with also a glance of reflectiveness in the same direction. "How old do you call him, then?"

"Thirty or so."

"More like forty," broke in an old milkman near, in a long white pinafore or "wropper," and with the brim of his hat tied down, so that he looked like a woman. " 'A was born before our Great Weir was builded, and I hadn't man's wages when I laved water there."

The discussion waxed so warm that the purr of the milk-streams became jerky, till a voice from another cow's belly cried with authority, "Now, then, what the Turk do it matter to us about Farmer Lodge's age, or Farmer Lodge's new mis'ess! I shall have to pay him nine pound a-year for the rent of every one of these milchers, whatever his age or hers. Get on with your work, or 'twill be dark afore we have done.

The evening is pinking in a'ready." This speaker was the dairyman himself, by whom the milkmaids and men were employed.

Nothing more was said publicly about Farmer Lodge's wedding; but the first woman murmured under her cow to her next neighbour, " 'Tis hard for *she*," signifying the thin worn milkmaid aforesaid.

"Oh no," said the second. "He ha'n't spoke to Rhoda Brook for years."

When the milking was done they washed their pails and hung them on a many-forked stand made as usual of the peeled limb of an oak-tree, set upright in the earth, and resembling a colossal antlered horn. The majority then dispersed in various directions homeward. The thin woman who had not spoken was joined by a boy of twelve or thereabout, and the twain went away up the field also.

Their course lay apart from that of the others, to a lonely spot high above the water-meads, and not far from the border of Egdon Heath, whose dark countenance was visible in the distance as they drew nigh to their home.

"They've just been saying down in barton that your father brings his young wife home from Anglebury to-morrow," the woman observed. "I shall want to send you for a few things to market, and you'll be pretty sure to meet 'em."

"Yes, mother," said the boy. "Is father married, then?"

"Yes. . . . You can give her a look, and tell me what she's like, if you do see her."

"Yes, mother."

"If she's dark or fair, and if she's tall — as tall as I. And if she seems like a woman who has ever worked for a living, or one that has been always well off, and has never done anything, and shows marks of the lady on her, as I expect she do."

"Yes."

They crept up the hill in the twilight, and entered the cottage. It was built of mud-walls, the surface of which had been washed by many rains into channels and depressions that left none of the original flat face visible; while here and there in the thatch above a rafter showed like a bone protruding through the skin.

She was kneeling down in the chimney-corner, before two pieces of turf laid together with the heather inwards, blowing at the red-hot ashes with her breath till the turves flamed. The radiance lit her pale cheek, and made her dark eyes, that had once been handsome, seem handsome anew. "Yes," she resumed, "see if she is dark or fair, and if you can, notice if her hands be white; if not, see if they look as though she had ever done housework, or are milker's hands like mine."

The boy again promised, inattentively this time, his mother not observing that he was cutting a notch with his pocket-knife in the beech-backed chair.

II.   The Young Wife

The road from Anglebury to Holmstoke is in general level; but there is one place where a sharp ascent breaks its monotony. Farmers homeward-bound from the former market-town, who trot all the rest of the way, walk their horses up this short incline.

The next evening, while the sun was yet bright, a handsome new gig, with a lemon-coloured body and red wheels, was spinning westward along the level highway at the heels of a powerful mare. The driver was a yeoman in the prime of life, cleanly shaven like an actor, his face being toned to that bluish-vermilion hue which so often graces a thriving farmer's features when returning home after successful dealings in the town. Beside him sat a woman, many years his junior — almost, indeed, a girl. Her face too was fresh in colour, but it was of a totally different quality — soft and evanescent, like the light under a heap of rose-petals.

Few people travelled this way, for it was not a main road; and the long white riband of gravel that stretched before them was empty, save of one small scarce-moving speck, which presently resolved itself into the figure of a boy, who was creeping on at a snail's pace, and continually looking behind him — the heavy bundle he carried being some excuse for, if not the reason of, his dilatoriness. When the bouncing gig-party slowed at the bottom of the incline above mentioned, the pedestrian was only a few yards in front. Supporting the large bundle by putting one hand on his hip, he turned and looked straight at the farmer's wife as though he would read her through and through, pacing along abreast of the horse.

The low sun was full in her face, rendering every feature, shade, and contour distinct, from the curve of her little nostril to the colour of her eyes. The farmer, though he seemed annoyed at the boy's persistent presence, did not order him to get out of the way; and thus the lad preceded them, his hard gaze never leaving her, till they reached the top of the ascent, when the farmer trotted on with relief in his lineaments — having taken no outward notice of the boy whatever.

"How that poor lad stared at me!" said the young wife.

"Yes, dear; I saw that he did."

"He is one of the village, I suppose?"

"One of the neighbourhood. I think he lives with his mother a mile or two off."

"He knows who we are, no doubt?"

"Oh yes. You must expect to be stared at just at first, my pretty Gertrude."

"I do, — though I think the poor boy may have looked at us in the hope we might relieve him of his heavy load, rather than from curiosity."

"Oh no," said her husband, off-handedly. "These country lads will carry a hundred-weight once they get it on their backs; besides, his pack had more size than weight in it. Now, then, another mile and I shall be able to show you our house in the distance — if it is not too dark before we get there." The wheels spun round, and particles flew from their periphery as before, till a white house of ample dimensions revealed itself, with farm-buildings and ricks at the back.

Meanwhile the boy had quickened his pace, and turning up a by-lane some mile and half short of the white farmstead, ascended towards the leaner pastures, and so on to the cottage of his mother.

She had reached home after her day's milking at the outlying dairy, and was washing cabbage at the doorway in the declining light. "Hold up the net a moment," she said, without preface, as the boy came up.

He flung down his bundle, held the edge of the cabbage-net, and as she filled its meshes with the dripping leaves she went on, "Well, did you see her?"

"Yes; quite plain."

"Is she ladylike?"

"Yes; and more. A lady complete."

"Is she young?"

"Well, she's growed up, and her ways be quite a woman's."

"Of course. What colour is her hair and face?"

"Her hair is lightish, and her face as comely as a live doll's."

"Her eyes, then, are not dark like mine?"

"No — of a bluish turn, and her mouth is very nice and red; and when she smiles, her teeth show white."

"Is she tall?" said the woman sharply.

"I couldn't see. She was sitting down."

"Then do you go to Holmstoke church to-morrow morning: she's sure to be there. Go early and notice her walking in, and come home and tell me if she's taller than I."

"Very well, mother. But why don't you go and see for yourself?"

"*I* go to see her! I wouldn't look up at her if she were to pass my window this instant. She was with Mr Lodge, of course. What did he say or do?"

"Just the same as usual."

"Took no notice of you?"

"None."

Next day the mother put a clean shirt on the boy, and started him off for Holmstoke church. He reached the ancient little pile when the door was just being opened, and he was the first to enter. Taking his seat by the font, he watched all the parishioners file in. The well-to-do Farmer Lodge came nearly last; and his young wife, who accompanied him, walked up the aisle with the shyness natural to a modest woman who had appeared thus for the first time. As all other eyes were fixed upon her, the youth's stare was not noticed now.

When he reached home his mother said "Well?" before he had entered the room.

"She is not tall. She is rather short," he replied.

"Ah!" said his mother, with satisfaction.

"But she's very pretty — very. In fact, she's lovely." The youthful freshness of the yeoman's wife had evidently made an impression even on the somewhat hard nature of the boy.

"That's all I want to hear," said his mother quickly. "Now, spread the table-cloth. The hare you wired is very tender; but mind that nobody catches you. — You've never told me what sort of hands she had."

"I have never seen 'em. She never took off her gloves."

"What did she wear this morning?"

"A white bonnet and a silver-coloured gownd. It whewed and whistled so loud when it rubbed against the pews that the lady coloured up more than ever for very shame at the noise, and pulled it in to keep it from touching; but when she pushed into her seat, it whewed more than ever. Mr Lodge, he seemed pleased, and his waist-coat stuck out, and his great golden seals hung like a lord's; but she seemed to wish her noisy gownd anywhere but on her."

"Not she! However, that will do now."

These descriptions of the newly married

couple were continued from time to time by the boy at his mother's request, after any chance encounter he had had with them. But Rhoda Brook, though she might easily have seen young Mrs Lodge for herself by walking a couple of miles, would never attempt an excursion towards the quarter where the farmhouse lay. Neither did she, at the daily milking in the dairyman's yard on Lodge's outlying second farm, ever speak on the subject of the recent marriage. The dairyman, who rented the cows of Lodge, and knew perfectly the tall milkmaid's history, with manly kindliness always kept the gossip in the cowbarton from annoying Rhoda. But the atmosphere thereabout was full of the subject during the first days of Mrs Lodge's arrival; and from her boy's description and the casual words of the other milkers, Rhoda Brook could raise a mental image of the unconscious Mrs Lodge that was realistic as a photograph.

III.   A Vision

One night, two or three weeks after the bridal return, when the boy was gone to bed, Rhoda sat a long time over the turf ashes that she had raked out in front of her to extinguish them. She contemplated so intently the new wife, as presented to her in her mind's eye over the embers, that she forgot the lapse of time. At last, wearied with her day's work, she too retired.

But the figure which had occupied her so much during this and the previous days was not to be banished at night. For the first time Gertrude Lodge visited the supplanted woman in her dreams. Rhoda Brook dreamed — since her assertion that she really saw, before falling asleep, was not to be believed — that the young wife, in the pale silk dress and white bonnet, but with features shockingly distorted, and wrinkled as by age, was sitting upon her chest as she lay. The pressure of Mrs Lodge's person grew heavier; the blue eyes peered cruelly into her face; and then the figure thrust forward its left hand mockingly, so as to make the wedding-ring it wore glitter in Rhoda's eyes. Maddened mentally, and nearly suffocated by pressure, the sleeper struggled; the incubus, still regarding her, withdrew to the foot of the bed, only, however, to come forward by degrees, resume her seat, and flash her left hand as before.

Gasping for breath, Rhoda, in a last desperate effort, swung out her right hand, seized the confronting spectre by its obtrusive left arm, and whirled it backward to the floor, starting up herself as she did so with a low cry.

"Oh, merciful heaven!" she cried, sitting on the edge of the bed in a cold sweat, "that was not a dream — she was here!"

She could feel her antagonist's arm within her grasp even now — the very flesh and bone of it, as it seemed. She looked on the floor whither she had whirled the spectre, but there was nothing to be seen.

Rhoda Brook slept no more that night, and when she went milking at the next dawn they noticed how pale and haggard she looked. The milk that she drew quivered into the pail; her hand had not calmed even yet, and still retained the feel of the arm. She came home to breakfast as wearily as if it had been supper-time.

"What was that noise in your chimmer, mother, last night?" said her son. "You fell off the bed, surely?"

"Did you hear anything fall? At what time?"

"Just when the clock struck two."

She could not explain, and when the meal was done went silently about her household work, the boy assisting her, for he hated going afield on the farms, and she indulged his reluctance. Between eleven and twelve the garden-gate clicked, and she lifted her eyes to the window. At the bottom of the garden, within the gate, stood the woman of her vision. Rhoda seemed transfixed.

"Ah, she said she would come!" exclaimed the boy, also observing her.

"Said so — when? How does she know us?"

"I have seen and spoken to her. I talked to her yesterday."

"I told you," said the mother, flushing indignantly, "never to speak to anybody in that house, or go near the place."

"I did not speak to her till she spoke to me. And I did not go near the place. I met her in the road."

"What did you tell her?"

"Nothing. She said, 'Are you the poor boy who had to bring the heavy load from market?' And she looked at my boots, and said they would not keep my feet dry if it came on wet, because they were so cracked. I told her I lived with my mother, and we had enough to do to keep ourselves, and that's how it was; and she said then, 'I'll come and bring you some better boots, and see your mother.' She gives

away things to other folks in the meads besides us."

Mrs Lodge was by this time close to the
door — not in her silk, as Rhoda had
dreamt of in the bed-chamber, but in a
morning hat, and gown of common light
material, which became her better than
silk. On her arm she carried a basket.

The impression remaining from the
night's experience was still strong. Brook
had almost expected to see the wrinkles,
the scorn, and the cruelty on her visitor's
face. She would have escaped an interview,
had escape been possible. There was, however, no back-door to the cottage, and in
an instant the boy had lifted the latch to
Mrs Lodge's gentle knock.

"I see I have come to the right house,"
said she, glancing at the lad, and smiling.
"But I was not sure till you opened the
door."

The figure and action were those of the
phantom; but her voice was so indescrib-
ably sweet, her glance so winning, her
smile so tender, so unlike that of Rhoda's
midnight visitant, that the latter could
hardly believe the evidence of her senses.
She was truly glad that she had not hidden
away in sheer aversion, as she had been inclined to do. In her basket Mrs Lodge

brought the pair of boots that she had promised to the boy, and other useful articles.

At these proofs of a kindly feeling towards her and hers, Rhoda's heart reproached her bitterly. This innocent young thing should have her blessing and not her curse. When she left them a light seemed gone from the dwelling. Two days later she came again to know if the boots fitted; and less than a fortnight after that paid Rhoda another call. On this occasion the boy was absent.

"I walk a good deal," said Mrs Lodge, "and your house is the nearest outside our own parish. I hope you are well. You don't look quite well."

Rhoda said she was well enough; and indeed, though the paler of the two, there was more of the strength that endures in her well-defined features and large frame, than in the soft-cheeked young woman before her. The conversation became quite confidential as regarded their powers and weaknesses; and when Mrs Lodge was leaving, Rhoda said, "I hope you will find this air agree with you, ma'am, and not suffer from the damp of the water meads."

The younger one replied that there was not much doubt of it, her general health being usually good. "Though, now you remind me," she added, "I have one little ailment which puzzles me. It is nothing serious, but I cannot make it out."

She uncovered her left hand and arm; and their outline confronted Rhoda's gaze as the exact original of the limb she had beheld and seized in her dream. Upon the pink round surface of the arm were faint marks of an unhealthy colour, as if produced by a rough grasp. Rhoda's eyes became riveted on the discolorations; she fancied that she discerned in them the shape of her own four fingers.

"How did it happen?" she said mechanically.

"I cannot tell," replied Mrs Lodge, shaking her head. "One night when I was sound asleep, dreaming I was away in some strange place, a pain suddenly shot into my arm there, and was so keen as to awaken me. I must have struck it in the daytime, I suppose, though I don't remember doing so." She added, laughing, "I tell my dear husband that it looks just as if he had flown into a rage and struck me there. Oh, I daresay it will soon disappear."

"Ha, ha! Yes. . . . On what night did it come?"

Mrs Lodge considered, and said it would

be a fortnight ago on the morrow. "When I awoke, I could not remember where I was," she added, "till the clock striking two reminded me."

She had named the night and the hour of Rhoda's spectral encounter, and Brook felt like a guilty thing. The artless disclosure startled her; she did not reason on the freaks of coincidence; and all the scenery of that ghastly night returned with double vividness to her mind.

"Oh, can it be," she said to herself, when her visitor had departed, "that I exercise a malignant power over people against my own will?" She knew that she had been slyly called a witch since her fall; but never having understood why that particular stigma had been attached to her, it had passed disregarded. Could this be the explanation, and had such things as this ever happened before?

IV. A Suggestion

The summer drew on, and Rhoda Brook almost dreaded to meet Mrs Lodge again, notwithstanding that her feeling for the young wife amounted wellnigh to affection. Something in her own individuality seemed to

convict Rhoda of crime. Yet a fatality sometimes would direct the steps of the latter to
the outskirts of Holmstoke whenever she left
her house for any other purpose than her
daily work; and hence it happened that their
next encounter was out of doors. Rhoda
could not avoid the subject which had so
mystified her, and after the first few words
she stammered, "I hope your — arm is well
again, ma'am?" She had perceived with consternation that Gertrude Lodge carried her
left arm stiffly.

"No; it is not quite well. Indeed it is no
better at all; it is rather worse. It pains me
dreadfully sometimes."

"Perhaps you had better go to a doctor,
ma'am."

She replied that she had already seen a
doctor. Her husband had insisted upon her
going to one. But the surgeon had not
seemed to understand the afflicted limb at
all; he had told her to bathe it in hot water,
and she had bathed it, but the treatment
had done no good.

"Will you let me see it?" said the
milkwoman.

Mrs Lodge pushed up her sleeve and
disclosed the place, which was a few inches
above the wrist. As soon as Rhoda Brook
saw it, she could hardly preserve her com-

posure. There was nothing of the nature of a wound, but the arm at that point had a shrivelled look, and the outline of the four fingers appeared more distinct than at the former time. Moreover, she fancied that they were imprinted in precisely the relative position of her clutch upon the arm in the trance; the first finger towards Gertrude's wrist, and the fourth towards her elbow.

What the impress resembled seemed to have struck Gertrude herself since their last meeting. "It looks almost like finger-marks," she said; adding with a faint laugh, "my husband says it is as if some witch, or the devil himself, had taken hold of me there, and blasted the flesh."

Rhoda shivered. "That's fancy," she said hurriedly. "I wouldn't mind it, if I were you."

"I shouldn't so much mind it," said the younger, with hesitation, "if — if I hadn't a notion that it makes my husband — dislike me — no, love me less. Men think so much of personal appearance."

"Some do — he for one."

"Yes; and he was very proud of mine, at first."

"Keep your arm covered from his sight."

"Ah — he knows the disfigurement is

there!" She tried to hide the tears that filled her eyes.

"Well, ma'am, I earnestly hope it will go away soon."

And so the milkwoman's mind was chained anew to the subject by a horrid sort of spell as she returned home. The sense of having been guilty of an act of malignity increased, affect as she might to ridicule her superstition. In her secret heart Rhoda did not altogether object to a slight diminution of her successor's beauty, by whatever means it had come about; but she did not wish to inflict upon her physical pain. For though this pretty young woman had rendered impossible any reparation which Lodge might have made Rhoda for his past conduct, everything like resentment at the unconscious usurpation had quite passed away from the elder's mind.

If the sweet and kindly Gertrude Lodge only knew of the dream-scene in that bedchamber, what would she think? Not to inform her of it seemed treachery in the presence of her friendliness; but tell she could not of her own accord — neither could she devise a remedy.

She mused upon the matter the greater part of the night; and the next day, after the morning milking, set out to obtain another glimpse of Gertrude Lodge if she could, being held to her by a gruesome fascination. By watching the house from a distance the milkmaid was presently able to discern the farmer's wife in a ride she was taking alone — probably to join her husband in some distant field. Mrs Lodge perceived her, and cantered in her direction.

"Good morning, Rhoda!" Gertrude said, when she had come up. "I was going to call."

Rhoda noticed that Mrs Lodge held the reins with some difficulty.

"I hope — the bad arm," said Rhoda.

"They tell me there is possibly one way by which I might be able to find out the cause, and so perhaps the cure, of it," replied the other anxiously. "It is by going to some clever man over in Egdon Heath. They did not know if he was still alive — and I cannot remember his name at this moment; but they said that you knew more of his movements than anybody else hereabout, and could tell me if he were still to be consulted. Dear me — what was his name? But you know."

"Not Conjuror Trendle?" said her thin companion, turning pale.

"Trendle — yes. Is he alive?"

"I believe so," said Rhoda, with reluctance.

"Why do you call him conjuror?"

"Well — they say — they used to say he was a — he had powers other folks have not."

"Oh, how could my people be so superstitious as to recommend a man of that sort! I thought they meant some medical man. I shall think no more of him."

Rhoda looked relieved, and Mrs Lodge rode on. The milkwoman had inwardly seen, from the moment she heard of her having been mentioned as a reference for this man, that there must exist a sarcastic feeling among the work-folk that a sorceress would know the whereabouts of the exorcist. They suspected her, then. A short time ago this would have given no concern to a woman of her common-sense. But she had a haunting reason to be superstitious now; and she had been seized with sudden dread that this Conjuror Trendle might name her as the malignant influence which was blasting the fair person of Gertrude, and so lead her friend to hate her for ever, and to treat her as some fiend in human shape.

But all was not over. Two days after, a shadow intruded into the window-pattern thrown on Rhoda Brook's floor by the afternoon sun. The woman opened the door at once, almost breathlessly.

"Are you alone?" said Gertrude. She seemed to be no less harassed and anxious than Brook herself.

"Yes," said Rhoda.

"The place on my arm seems worse, and troubles me!" the young farmer's wife went on. "It is so mysterious! I do hope it will not be an incurable wound. I have again been thinking of what they said about Conjuror Trendle. I don't really believe in such men, but I should not mind just visiting him, from curiosity — though on no account must my husband know. Is it far to where he lives?"

"Yes — five miles," said Rhoda, backwardly. "In the heart of Egdon."

"Well, I should have to walk. Could not you go with me to show me the way — say to-morrow afternoon?"

"Oh, not I — that is," the milkwoman murmured, with a start of dismay. Again the dread seized her that something to do with her fierce act in the dream might be revealed, and her character in the eyes of the most useful friend she had ever had be ruined irretrievably.

Mrs Lodge urged, and Rhoda finally assented, though with much misgiving. Sad as the journey would be to her, she could not conscientiously stand in the way of a possible remedy for her patron's strange affliction. It was agreed that, to escape suspicion of their mystic intent, they should meet at the edge of the heath, at the corner of a plantation which was visible from the spot where they now stood.

V.   Conjuror Trendle

By the next afternoon, Rhoda would have done anything to escape this inquiry. But she had promised to go. Moreover, there was a horrid fascination at times in becoming instrumental in throwing such possible light on her own character as would reveal her to be something greater in the occult world than she had ever herself suspected.

She started just before the time of day mentioned between them, and half an hour's brisk walking brought her to the southeastern extension of the Egdon tract of country, where the fir plantation was. A slight figure, cloaked and veiled, was already there. Rhoda recognised, almost with a shudder, that Mrs Lodge bore her left arm in a sling.

They hardly spoke to each other, and

immediately set out on their climb into the interior of this solemn country, which stood high above the rich alluvial soil they had left half an hour before. It was a long walk; thick clouds made the atmosphere dark, though it was as yet only early afternoon; and the wind howled dismally over the slopes of the heath — not improbably the same heath which had witnessed the agony of the Wessex King Ina, presented to after-ages as Lear. Gertrude Lodge talked most, Rhoda replying with monosyllabic preoccupation. She had a strange dislike to walking on the side of her companion where hung the afflicted arm, moving round to the other when inadvertently near it. Much heather had been brushed by their feet when they descended upon a cart-track, beside which stood the house of the man they sought.

He did not profess his remedial practices openly, or care anything about their continuance, his direct interests being those of a dealer in furze, turf, "sharp sand," and other local products. Indeed, he affected not to believe largely in his own powers, and when warts that had been shown him for cure miraculously disappeared — which it must be owned they infallibly did — he would say lightly, "Oh, I only drink a glass of grog upon 'em at your expense — perhaps it's all chance," and immediately turn the subject.

He was at home when they arrived, having in fact seen them descending into his valley. He was a grey-bearded man, with a reddish face, and he looked singularly at Rhoda the first moment he beheld her. Mrs Lodge told him her errand; and then with words of self-disparagement he examined her arm.

"Medicine can't cure it," he said, promptly. " 'Tis the work of an enemy."

Rhoda shrank into herself, and drew back.

"An enemy? What enemy?" asked Mrs. Lodge.

He shook his head. "That's best known to yourself," he said. "If you like I can show the person to you, though I shall not myself know who it is. I can do no more; and don't wish to do that."

She pressed him; on which he told Rhoda to wait outside where she stood, and took Mrs Lodge into the room. It opened immediately from the door; and, as the latter remained ajar, Rhoda Brook could see the proceedings without taking part in them. He brought a tumbler from the dresser, nearly filled it with water, and fetching an egg, prepared it in some private way; after which he broke it on the edge of the glass, so that the white went in and the yolk remained. As it was getting gloomy, he took the glass and its contents to the window, and told Gertrude to watch the mixture closely. They leant over the table together, and the milkwoman could see the opaline hue of the egg fluid changing form as it sank in the water, but she was not near enough to define the shape that it assumed.

"Do you catch the likeness of any face or figure as you look?" demanded the conjuror of the young woman.

She murmured a reply, in tones so low as to be inaudible to Rhoda, and continued to gaze intently into the glass. Rhoda turned, and walked a few steps away.

When Mrs Lodge came out, and her face was met by the light, it appeared exceedingly pale — as pale as Rhoda's — against the sad dun shades of the upland's garniture. Trendle shut the door behind her, and they at once started homeward together. But Rhoda perceived that her companion had quite changed.

"Did he charge much?" she asked, tentatively.

"Oh no — nothing. He would not take a

farthing," said Gertrude.

"And what did you see?" inquired Rhoda.

"Nothing I — care to speak of." The constraint in her manner was remarkable; her face was so rigid as to wear an oldened aspect, faintly suggestive of the face in Rhoda's bed-chamber.

"Was it you who first proposed coming here?" Mrs Lodge suddenly inquired, after a long pause. "How very odd, if you did."

"No. But I am not sorry we have come, all things considered," she replied. For the first time a sense of triumph possessed her, and she did not altogether deplore that the young thing at her side should learn that their lives had been antagonised by other influences than their own.

The subject was no more alluded to during the long and dreary walk home. But in some way or other a story was whispered about the many-dairied lowland that winter that Mrs Lodge's gradual loss of the use of her left arm was owing to her being "over-looked" by Rhoda Brook. The latter kept her own counsel about the incubus, but her face grew sadder and thinner; and in the spring she and her boy disappeared from the neighbourhood of Holmstoke.

VI.   A Second Attempt

Half-a-dozen years passed away, and Mr and Mrs Lodge's married experience sank into prosiness, and worse. The farmer was usually gloomy and silent: the woman whom he had wooed for her grace and beauty was contorted and disfigured in the left limb; moreover, she had brought him no child, which rendered it likely that he would be the last of a family who had occupied that valley for some two hundred years. He thought of Rhoda Brook and her son; and feared this might be a judgment from heaven upon him.

The once blithe-hearted and enlightened Gertrude was changing into an irritable, superstitious woman, whose whole time was given to experimenting upon her ailment with every quack remedy she came across. She was honestly attached to her husband, and was ever secretly hoping against hope to win back his heart again by regaining some at least of her personal beauty. Hence it arose that her closet was lined with bottles, packets, and ointment-pots of every description — nay, bunches of mystic herbs, charms, and books of necromancy, which in her schoolgirl time she would have ridiculed as folly.

"Damned if you won't poison yourself

with these apothecary messes and witch mixtures some time or other," said her husband, when his eye chanced to fall upon the multitudinous array.

She did not reply, but turned her sad soft glance upon him in such heart-swollen reproach that he looked sorry for his words, and added, "I only meant it for your good, you know, Gertrude."

"I'll clear out the whole lot, and destroy them," said she, huskily, "and try such remedies no more!"

"You want somebody to cheer you," he observed. "I once thought of adopting a boy; but he is too old now. And he is gone away I don't know where."

She guessed to whom he alluded; for Rhoda Brook's story had in the course of years become known to her; though not a word had ever passed between her husband and herself on the subject. Neither had she ever spoken to him of her visit to Conjuror Trendle, and of what was revealed to her, or she thought was revealed to her, by that solitary heath-man.

She was now five-and-twenty; but she seemed older. "Six years of marriage, and only a few months of love," she sometimes whispered to herself. And then she thought of the apparent cause, and said, with a tragic glance at her withering limb, "If I could only again be as I was when he first saw me!"

She obediently destroyed her nostrums and charms; but there remained a hankering wish to try something else — some other sort of cure altogether. She had never revisited Trendle since she had been conducted to the house of the solitary by Rhoda against her will; but it now suddenly occurred to Gertrude that she would, in a last desperate effort at deliverance from this seeming curse, again seek out the man, if he yet lived. He was entitled to a certain credence, for the indistinct form he had raised in the glass had undoubtedly resembled the only woman in the world who — as she now knew, though not then — could have a reason for bearing her ill-will. The visit should be paid.

This time she went alone, though she nearly got lost on the heath, and roamed a considerable distance out of her way. Trendle's house was reached at last, however: he was not indoors, and instead of waiting at the cottage she went to where his bent figure was pointed out to her at work a long way off. Trendle remembered her, and laying down the handful of furze-roots which he was gathering and throwing into a heap, he offered to accompany her in her homeward direction, as the distance was considerable and the days were short. So they walked together, his head bowed nearly to the earth, and his form of a colour with it.

"You can send away warts and other excrescences, I know," she said; "why can't you send away this?" And the arm was uncovered.

"You think too much of my powers!" said Trendle; "and I am old and weak now, too. No, no; it is too much for me to attempt in my own person. What have ye tried?"

She named to him some of the hundred medicaments and counter-spells which she had adopted from time to time. He shook his head.

"Some were good enough," he said, approvingly; "but not many of them for such as this. This is of the nature of a blight, not of the nature of a wound; and if you ever do throw it off, it will be all at once."

"If I only could!"

"There is only one chance of doing it known to me. It has never failed in kindred afflictions, — that I can declare. But it is hard to carry out, and especially for a woman."

"Tell me!" said she.

"You must touch with the limb the neck of a man who's been hanged."

She started a little at the image he had raised.

"Before he's cold — just after he's cut down," continued the conjuror, impassively.

"How can that do good?"

"It will turn the blood and change the constitution. But, as I say, to do it is hard. You must go to the jail when there's a hanging, and wait for him when he's brought off the gallows. Lots have done it, though perhaps not such pretty women as you. I used to send dozens for skin complaints. But that was in former times. The last I sent was in '13 — near twelve years ago."

He had no more to tell her; and, when he had put her into a straight track homeward, turned and left her, refusing all money as at first.

VII.   A Ride

The communication sank deep into Gertrude's mind. Her nature was rather a timid one; and probably of all remedies that the white wizard could have suggested there was not one which would have filled her with so much aversion as this, not to speak of the immense obstacles in the way of its adoption.

Casterbridge, the county-town, was a dozen or fifteen miles off; and though in those days, when men were executed for horse-stealing, arson, and burglary, an assize seldom passed without a hanging, it was not likely that she could get access to the body of the criminal unaided. And the fear of her husband's anger made her reluctant to breathe a word of Trendle's suggestion to him or to anybody about him.

She did nothing for months, and patiently bore her disfigurement as before. But her woman's nature, craving for renewed love, through the medium of renewed beauty (she was but twenty-five), was ever stimulating her to try what, at any rate, could hardly do her any harm. "What came by a spell will go by a spell surely," she would say. Whenever her imagination pictured the act she shrank in terror from the possibility of it: then the words of the conjuror, "It will turn your blood," were seen to be capable of a scientific no less than a ghastly interpretation; the mastering desire returned, and urged her on again.

There was at this time but one county paper, and that her husband only occasionally borrowed. But old-fashioned days had old-fashioned means, and news was extensively conveyed by word of mouth from market to market or from fair to fair; so that, whenever such an event as an execution was about to take place, few within a radius of twenty miles were ignorant of the coming sight; and, so far as Holmstoke was concerned, some enthusiasts had been known to walk all the way to Casterbridge and back in one day, solely to witness the spectacle. The next assizes were in March; and when Gertrude Lodge heard that they had been held, she inquired stealthily at the inn as to the result, as soon as she could find opportunity.

She was, however, too late. The time at which the sentences were to be carried out had arrived, and to make the journey and obtain admission at such short notice required at least her husband's assistance. She dared not tell him, for she had found by delicate experiment that these smouldering village beliefs made him furious if mentioned, partly because he half entertained them himself. It was therefore necessary to wait for another opportunity.

Her determination received a fillip from

learning that two epileptic children had attended from this very village of Holmstoke many years before with beneficial results, though the experiment had been strongly condemned by the neighbouring clergy. April, May, June passed; and it is no overstatement to say that by the end of the last-named month Gertrude wellnigh longed for the death of a fellow-creature. Instead of her formal prayers each night, her unconscious prayer was, "O Lord, hang some guilty or innocent person soon!"

This time she made earlier inquiries, and was altogether more systematic in her proceedings. Moreover, the season was summer, between the haymaking and the harvest, and in the leisure thus afforded him her husband had been holiday-taking away from home.

The assizes were in July, and she went to the inn as before. There was to be one execution — only one, for arson.

Her greatest problem was not how to get to Casterbridge, but what means she should adopt for obtaining admission to the jail. Though access for such purposes had formerly never been denied, the custom had fallen into desuetude; and in contemplating her possible difficulties, she was again almost driven to fall back upon her husband. But, on sounding him about the assizes, he was so uncommunicative, so more than usually cold, that she did not proceed, and decided that whatever she did she would do alone.

Fortune, obdurate hitherto, showed her unexpected favour. On the Thursday before the Saturday fixed for the execution, Lodge remarked to her that he was going away from home for another day or two on business at a fair, and that he was sorry he could not take her with him.

She exhibited on this occasion so much readiness to stay at home that he looked at her in surprise. Time had been when she would have shown deep disappointment at the loss of such a jaunt. However, he lapsed into his usual taciturnity, and on the day named left Holmstoke.

It was now her turn. She at first had thought of driving, but on reflection held that driving would not do, since it would necessitate her keeping to the turnpike-road, and so increase by tenfold the risk of her ghastly errand being found out. She decided to ride, and avoid the beaten track, notwithstanding that in her husband's stables there was no animal just at present which by any stretch of imagination could be considered a lady's mount, in spite of his promise before marriage to always keep a mare for her. He had, however, many cart-horses, fine ones of their kind; and among the rest was a serviceable creature, an equine Amazon, with a back as broad as a sofa, on which Gertrude had occasionally taken an airing when unwell. This horse she chose.

On Friday afternoon one of the men brought it round. She was dressed, and before going down looked at her shrivelled arm. "Ah!" she said to it, "if it had not been for you this terrible ordeal would have been saved me!"

When strapping up the bundle in which she carried a few articles of clothing, she took occasion to say to the servant, "I take these in case I should not get back to-night from the person I am going to visit. Don't be alarmed if I am not in by ten, and close up the house as usual. I shall be at home to-morrow for certain." She meant then to tell her husband privately: the deed accomplished was not like the deed projected. He would almost certainly forgive her.

And then the pretty palpitating Gertrude Lodge went from her husband's homestead; but though her goal was Casterbridge she did not take the direct route thither through Stickleford. Her cunning course at first was in precisely the opposite direction. As soon as she was out of sight, however, she tuned to the left, by a road which led into Egdon, and on entering the heath wheeled round, and set out in the true course, due westerly. A more private way down the county could not be imagined; and as to direction, she had merely to keep her horse's head to a point a little to the right of the sun. She knew that she would light upon a furze-cutter or cottager of some sort from time to time, from whom she might correct her bearing.

Though the date was comparatively recent, Egdon was much less fragmentary in character than now. The attempts — successful and otherwise — at cultivation on the lower slopes, which intrude and break up the original heath into small detached heaths, had not been carried far: Enclosure Acts had not taken effect, and the banks and fences which now exclude the cattle of those villagers who formerly enjoyed rights of commonage thereon, and the carts of those who had turbary privileges which kept them in firing all the year round, were not erected. Gertrude therefore rode along with no other obstacles than the prickly furze-bushes, the mats of heather, the white watercourses, and the natural steeps and declivities of the ground.

Her horse was sure, if heavy-footed and slow, and though a draught animal, was easy-paced; had it been otherwise, she was not a woman who could have ventured to ride over such a bit of country with a half-dead arm. It was therefore nearly eight o'clock when she drew rein to breathe her bearer on the last outlying high point of heath-land towards Casterbridge, previous to leaving Egdon for the cultivated valleys.

She halted before a pool called Rushy-pond, flanked by the ends of two hedges; a railing ran through the centre of the pond, dividing it in half. Over the railing she saw the low green country; over the green trees the roofs of the town; over the roofs a white flat façade, denoting the entrance to the county jail. On the roof of this front specks were moving about; they seemed to be workmen erecting something. Her flesh crept. She descended slowly, and was soon amid corn-fields and pastures. In another half-hour, when it was almost dusk, Gertrude reached the White Hart, the first inn of the town on that side.

Little surprise was excited by her arrival: farmers' wives rode on horseback then more than they do now; though for that matter, Mrs Lodge was not imagined to be a wife at all; the innkeeper supposed her some harum-scarum young woman who had come to attend "hang-fair" next day. Neither her husband nor herself ever dealt in Casterbridge market, so that she was unknown. While dismounting she beheld a crowd of boys standing at the door of a harness-maker's shop just above the inn, looking inside it with deep interest.

"What is going on there?" she asked of the ostler.

"Making the rope for to-morrow."

She throbbed responsively, and contracted her arm.

" 'Tis sold by the inch afterwards," the man continued. "I could get you a bit, miss, for nothing, if you'd like?"

She hastily repudiated any such wish, all the more from a curious creeping feeling that the condemned wretch's destiny was becoming interwoven with her own; and having engaged a room for the night, sat down to think.

Up to this time she had formed but the vaguest notions about her means of obtaining access to the prison. The words of the cunning-man returned to her mind. He had implied that she should use her beauty, impaired though it was, as a passkey. In her inexperience she knew little about jail functionaries; she had heard of a high sheriff and an under-sheriff, but dimly only. She knew, however, that there must be a hangman, and to the hangman she determined to apply.

VIII. A Water-side Hermit

At this date, and for several years after, there was a hangman to almost every jail. Gertrude found, on inquiry, that the Casterbridge official dwelt in a lonely cottage by a deep slow river flowing under the cliff on which the prison buildings were situate — the stream being the self-same one, though she did not know it, which watered the Stickleford and Holmstoke meads lower down in its course.

Having changed her dress, and before she had eaten or drunk — for she could not take her ease till she had ascertained some particulars — Gertrude pursued her way by a path along the water-side to the cottage indicated. Passing thus the outskirts of the jail, she discerned on the level roof over the gateway three rectangular lines against the sky, where the specks had been moving in her distant view; she recognised what the erection was, and passed quickly on. Another hundred yards brought her to the executioner's house, which a boy pointed out. It stood close to the same stream, and was hard by a weir, the waters of which emitted a steady roar.

While she stood hesitating the door opened, and an old man came forth shading a candle with one hand. Locking the door on the outside, he turned to a flight of wooden steps fixed against the end of the cottage, and began to ascend them, this being evidently the staircase to his bedroom. Gertrude hastened forward, but by the time she reached the foot of the ladder he was at the top. She called to him loudly enough to be heard above the roar of the weir; he looked down and said, "What d'ye want here?"

"To speak to you a minute."

The candle-light, such as it was, fell upon her imploring, pale, up-turned face, and Davies (as the hangman was called) backed down the ladder. "I was just going to bed," he said; " 'Early to bed and early to rise,' but I don't mind stopping a minute for such a one as you. Come into house." He reopened the door, and pre-ceded her to the room within.

The implements of his daily work, which

was that of a jobbing gardener, stood in a corner, and seeing probably that she looked rural, he said, "If you want me to undertake country work I can't come, for I never leave Casterbridge for gentle nor simple — not I. My real calling is officer of justice," he added formally.

"Yes, yes! That's it! To-morrow!"

"Ah! I thought so. Well, what's the matter about that? 'Tis no use to come here about the knot — folks do come continually, but I tell 'em one knot is as merciful as another if ye keep it under the ear. Is the unfortunate man a relation; or, I should say, perhaps" (looking at her dress) "a person who's been in your employ?"

"No. What time is the execution?"

"The same as usual — twelve o'clock, or as soon after as the London mail-coach gets in. We always wait for that, in case of a reprieve."

"Oh — a reprieve — I hope not!" she said involuntarily.

"Well, — he, he! — as a matter of business, so do I! But still, if ever a young fellow deserved to be let off, this one does; only just turned eighteen, and only present by chance when the rick was fired. Howsomever, there's not much risk of it, as they are obliged to make an example of

143

him, there having been so much destruction of property that way lately."

"I mean," she explained, "that I want to touch him for a charm, a cure of an affliction, by the advice of a man who has proved the virtue of the remedy."

"Oh yes, miss! Now I understand. I've had such people come in past years. But it didn't strike me that you looked of a sort to require blood-turning. What's the complaint? The wrong kind for this, I'll be bound."

"My arm." She reluctantly showed the withered skin.

"Ah! 'tis all a-scram!" said the hangman, examining it.

"Yes," said she.

"Well," he continued with interest, "that *is* the class o' subject, I'm bound to admit. I like the look of the wownd; it is truly as suitable for the cure as any I ever saw. 'Twas a knowing man that sent 'ee, whoever he was."

"You can contrive for me all that's necessary?" she said, breathlessly.

"You should really have gone to the governor of the jail, and your doctor with 'ee, and given your name and address — that's how it used to be done, if I recollect. Still, perhaps, I can manage it for a trifling fee."

"Oh, thank you! I would rather do it this way, as I should like it kept private."

"Lover not to know, eh?"

"No — husband."

"Aha! Very well. I'll get 'ee a touch of the corpse."

"Where is it now?" she said, shuddering.

"It? — *he*, you mean; he's living yet. Just inside that little small winder up there in the glum." He signified the jail on the cliff above.

She thought of her husband and her friends. "Yes, of course," she said; "and how am I to proceed?"

He took her to the door. "Now, do you be waiting at the little wicket in the wall, that you'll find up there in the lane, not later than one o'clock. I will open it from the inside, as I shan't come home to dinner till he's cut down. Good night. Be punctual; and if you don't want anybody to know 'ee, wear a veil. Ah — once I had such a daughter as you!"

She went away, and climbed the path above, to assure herself that she would be able to find the wicket next day. Its outline was soon visible to her — a narrow opening in the outer wall of the prison precincts. The steep was so great that, having reached the wicket, she stopped a moment to breathe; and looking back upon the water-side cot, saw the hangman again ascending his outdoor staircase. He entered the loft or chamber to which it led, and in a few minutes extinguished his light.

The town clock struck ten, and she returned to the White Hart as she had come.

IX. A Rencounter

It was one o'clock on Saturday. Gertrude Lodge, having been admitted to the jail as above described, was sitting in a waiting-room within the second gate, which stood under a classic archway of ashlar, then comparatively modern, and bearing the inscription, "COVNTY GAOL: 1793." This had been the façade she saw from the heath the day before. Near at hand was a passage to the roof on which the gallows stood.

The town was thronged, and the market suspended; but Gertrude had seen scarcely a soul. Having kept her room till the hour of the appointment, she had proceeded to the spot by a way which avoided the open space below the cliff where the spectators had gathered; but she could, even now, hear the multitudinous babble of their voices, out of which rose at intervals the hoarse croak of a single voice, uttering the words, "Last dying speech and confession!" There had been no reprieve, and the execution was over; but the crowd still waited to see the body taken down.

Soon the persistent woman heard a trampling overhead, then a hand beckoned to her, and, following directions, she went out and crossed the inner paved court beyond the gatehouse, her knees trembling so that she could scarcely walk. One of her arms was out of its sleeve, and only covered by her shawl.

On the spot at which she had now arrived were two trestles, and before she could think of their purpose she heard heavy feet descending stairs somewhere at her back. Turn her head she would not, or could not, and, rigid in this position, she was conscious of a rough coffin passing her shoulder, borne by four men. It was open, and in it lay the body of a young man, wearing the smockfrock of a rustic, and fustian breeches. The corpse had been thrown into the coffin so hastily that the skirt of the smockfrock was hanging over. The burden was temporarily deposited on the trestles.

By this time the young woman's state was such that a grey mist seemed to float before her eyes, on account of which, and the veil she wore, she could scarcely discern anything: it was as though she had nearly died, but was held up by a sort of galvanism.

"Now," said a voice close at hand, and she was just conscious that the word had been addressed to her.

By a last strenuous effort she advanced, at the same time hearing persons approaching behind her. She bared her poor curst arm; and Davies, uncovering the face of the corpse, took Gertrude's hand, and held it so that her arm lay across the dead man's neck, upon a line the colour of an unripe blackberry, which surrounded it.

Gertrude shrieked: "the turn o' the blood," predicted by the conjuror, had taken place. But at that moment a second shriek rent the air of the enclosure: it was not Gertrude's, and its effect upon her was to make her start round.

Immediately behind her stood Rhoda Brook, her face drawn, and her eyes red with weeping. Behind Rhoda stood Gertrude's own husband; his countenance lined, his eyes dim, but without a tear.

"D—n you! what are you doing here?" he said, hoarsely.

"Hussy — to come between us and our

child now!" cried Rhoda. "This is the meaning of what Satan showed me in the vision! You are like her at last!" And clutching the bare arm of the younger woman, she pulled her unresistingly back against the wall. Immediately Brook had loosened her hold the fragile young Gertrude slid down against the feet of her husband. When he lifted her up she was unconscious.

The mere sight of the twain had been enough to suggest to her that the dead young man was Rhoda's son. At that time the relatives of an executed convict had the privilege of claiming the body for burial, if they chose to do so; and it was for this purpose that Lodge was awaiting the inquest with Rhoda. He had been summoned by her as soon as the young man was taken in the crime, and at different times since; and he had attended in court during the trial. This was the "holiday" he had been indulging in of late. The two wretched parents had wished to avoid exposure; and hence had come themselves for the body, a waggon and sheet for its conveyance and covering being in waiting outside.

Gertrude's case was so serious that it was deemed advisable to call to her the surgeon who was at hand. She was taken out of the jail into the town; but she never reached home alive. Her delicate vitality, sapped perhaps by the paralysed arm, collapsed under the double shock that followed the severe strain, physical and mental, to which she had subjected herself during the previous twenty-four hours. Her blood had been "turned" indeed — too far. Her death took place in the town three days after.

Her husband was never seen in Casterbridge again; once only in the old market-place at Anglebury, which he had so much frequented, and very seldom in public anywhere. Burdened at first with moodiness and remorse, he eventually changed for the better, and appeared as a chastened and thoughtful man. Soon after attending the funeral of his poor young wife, he took steps towards giving up the farms in Holmstoke and the adjoining parish, and, having sold every head of his stock, he went away to Port-Bredy, at the other end of the county, living there in solitary lodgings till his death two years later of a painless decline. It was then found that he had bequeathed the whole of his not inconsiderable property to a reformatory for boys, subject to the payment of a small annuity to Rhoda Brook, if she could be found to claim it.

For some time she could not be found; but eventually she reappeared in her old parish, — absolutely refusing, however, to have anything to do with the provision made for her. Her monotonous milking at the dairy was resumed, and followed for many long years, till her form became bent, and her once abundant dark hair white and worn away at the forehead — perhaps by long pressure against the cows. Here, sometimes, those who knew her experiences would stand and observe her, and wonder what sombre thoughts were beating inside that impassive, wrinkled brow, to the rhythm of the alternating milkstreams.

Blackwood's Magazine, January 1888.

Fellow-Townsmen

I

The shepherd on the east hill could shout
out lambing intelligence to the shepherd on
the west hill, over the intervening town
chimneys, without great inconvenience to
his voice, so nearly did the steep pastures en-
croach upon the burghers' back yards. And
at night it was possible to stand in the very
midst of the town, and hear from their native
paddocks on the lower slopes of greensward
the mild lowing of the farmers' heifers, and
the profound, warm blowings of breath in
which those creatures indulge. But the com-
munity which had jammed itself in the valley
thus flanked formed a veritable town, with a
real mayor and corporation, and a staple
manufacture.

During a certain damp evening five-and-
thirty years ago, before the twilight was far
advanced, a pedestrian of professional ap-

pearance, carrying a small bag in his hand
and an elevated umbrella, was descending
one of these hills by the turnpike road
when he was overtaken by a phaeton.

"Hullo, Downe — is that you?" said the
driver of the vehicle, a young man of pale
and refined appearance. "Jump up here
with me, and ride down to your door."

The other turned a plump, cheery, rather
self-indulgent face over his shoulder towards the hailer.

"Oh! good-evening, Mr. Barnet —
thanks," he said, and mounted beside his
acquaintance.

They were fellow-burgesses of the town
which lay beneath them, but though old
and very good friends, they were differ-
ently circumstanced. Barnet was a richer
man than the struggling young lawyer
Downe, a fact which was to some extent
perceptible in Downe's manner towards
his companion, though nothing of it ever
showed in Barnet's manner towards the solicitor. Barnet's position in the town was
none of his own making; his father had
been a very successful flax-merchant in the
same place, where the trade was still carried on as briskly as the small capacities of
its quarters would allow. Having acquired
a fair fortune, old Mr. Barnet had retired

from business, bringing up his son as a gentleman-burgher, and, it must be added, as a well-educated, liberal-minded young man.

"How is Mrs. Barnet?" asked Downe.

"Mrs. Barnet was very well when I left home," the other answered constrainedly, exchanging his meditative regard of the horse for one of self-consciousness.

Mr. Downe seemed to regret his inquiry, and immediately took up another thread of conversation. He congratulated his friend on his election as a councilman; he thought he had not seen him since that event took place; Mrs. Downe had meant to call and congratulate Mrs. Barnet, but he feared that she had failed to do so as yet.

Barnet seemed hampered in his replies. "We should have been glad to see you. I — my wife would welcome Mrs. Downe at any time, as you know. . . . Yes, I am a member of the corporation — rather an in-experienced member, some of them say. It is quite true; and I should have declined the honour as premature — having other things on my hands just now, too — if it had not been pressed upon me so very heartily."

"There is one thing you have on your

hands which I can never quite see the necessity for," said Downe, with good-humoured freedom. "What the deuce do you want to build that new mansion for, when you have already got such an excellent house as the one you live in?"

Barnet's face acquired a warmer shade of colour; but as the question had been idly asked by the solicitor while regarding the surrounding flocks and fields, he answered after a moment with no apparent embarrassment —

"Well, we wanted to get out of the town, you know; the house I am living in is rather old and inconvenient."

Mr. Downe declared that he had chosen a pretty site for the new building. They would be able to see for miles and miles from the windows. Was he going to give it a name? He supposed so.

Barnet thought not. There was no other house near that was likely to be mistaken for it. And he did not care for a name.

"But I think it has a name!" Downe observed: "I went past — when was it? — this morning; and I saw something, — 'Château Ringdale,' I think it was, stuck up on a board!"

"It was an idea she — we had for a short time," said Barnet hastily. "But we have decided finally to do without a name — at any rate such a name as that. It must have been a week ago that you saw it. It was taken down last Saturday. . . . Upon that matter I am firm!" he added grimly.

Downe murmured in an unconvinced tone that he thought he had seen it yesterday.

Talking thus they drove into the town. The street was unusually still for the hour of seven in the evening; an increasing drizzle from the sea had prevailed since the afternoon, and now formed a gauze across the yellow lamps, and trickled with a gentle rattle down the heavy roofs of stone tile, that bent the house-ridges hollow-backed with its weight, and in some instances caused the walls to bulge outwards in the upper story. Their route took them past the little town-hall, the Black-Bull Hotel, and onward to the junction of a small street on the right, consisting of a row of those two-and-two windowed brick residences of no particular age, which are exactly alike wherever found, except in the people they contain.

"Wait — I'll drive you up to your door," said Barnet, when Downe prepared to alight at the corner. He thereupon turned into the narrow street, when the faces of three little girls could be discerned close to the panes of a lighted window a few yards ahead, surmounted by that of a young matron, the gaze of all four being directed eagerly up the empty street. "You are a fortunate fellow, Downe," Barnet continued, as mother and children disappeared from the window to run to the door. "You must be happy if any man is. I would give a hundred such houses as my new one to have a home like yours."

"Well — yes, we get along pretty comfortably," replied Downe complacently.

"That house, Downe, is none of my ordering," Barnet broke out, revealing a bitterness hitherto suppressed, and checking the horse a moment to finish his speech before delivering up his passenger. "The house I have already is good enough for me, as you supposed. It is my own freehold; it was built by my grandfather, and is stout enough for a castle. My father was born there, lived there, and died there. I was born there, and have always lived there; yet I must needs build a new one."

"Why do you?" said Downe.

"Why do I? To preserve peace in the household. I do anything for that; but I don't succeed. I was firm in resisting 'Château Ringdale,' however; not that I

158

would not have put up with the absurdity of the name, but it was too much to have your house christened after Lord Ringdale, because your wife once had a fancy for him. If you only knew everything, you would think all attempt at reconciliation hopeless. In your happy home you have had no such experiences; and God forbid that you ever should. See, here they are all ready to receive you!"

"Of course! And so will your wife be waiting to receive you," said Downe. "Take my word for it she will! And with a dinner prepared for you far better than mine."

"I hope so," Barnet replied dubiously.

He moved on to Downe's door, which the solicitor's family had already opened. Downe descended, but being encumbered with his bag and umbrella, his foot slipped, and he fell upon his knees in the gutter.

"Oh, my dear Charles!" said his wife, running down the steps; and, quite ignoring the presence of Barnet, she seized hold of her husband, pulled him to his feet, and kissed him, exclaiming, "I hope you are not hurt, darling!" The children crowded round, chiming in piteously, "Poor papa!"

"He's all right," said Barnet, perceiving that Downe was only a little muddy, and

159

looking more at the wife than at the husband. Almost at any other time — certainly during his fastidious bachelor years — he would have thought her a too demonstrative woman; but those recent circumstances of his own life to which he had just alluded made Mrs. Downe's solicitude so affecting that his eye grew damp as he witnessed it. Bidding the lawyer and his family good-night he left them, and drove slowly into the main street towards his own house.

The heart of Barnet was sufficiently impressionable to be influenced by Downe's parting prophecy that he might not be so unwelcome home as he imagined: the dreary night might, at least on this one occasion, make Downe's forecast true. Hence it was in a suspense that he could hardly have believed possible that he halted at his door. On entering his wife was nowhere to be seen, and he inquired for her. The servant informed him that her mistress had the dressmaker with her, and would be engaged for some time.

"Dressmaker at this time of day!"

"She dined early, sir, and hopes you will excuse her joining you this evening."

"But she knew I was coming to-night?"

"Oh yes, sir."

"Go up and tell her I am come."

The servant did so; but the mistress of the house merely transmitted her former words.

Barnet said nothing more, and presently sat down to his lonely meal, which was eaten abstractedly, the domestic scene he had lately witnessed still impressing him by its contrast with the situation here. His mind fell back into past years upon a certain pleasing and gentle being whose face would loom out of their shades at such times as these. Barnet turned in his chair, and looked with unfocused eyes in a direction southward from where he sat, as if he saw not the room but a long way beyond. "I wonder if she lives there still!" he said.

II

He rose with a sudden rebelliousness, put on his hat and coat, and went out of the house, pursuing his way along the glistening pavement while eight o'clock was striking from St. Mary's tower, and the apprentices and shopmen were slamming up the shutters from end to end of the town. In two minutes only those shops which could boast of no attendant save the master or the mistress remained with open eyes. These were ever somewhat less prompt to exclude customers than the others: for their owners' ears the closing hour had scarcely the cheerfulness that it possessed for the hired servants of the rest. Yet the night being dreary the delay was not for long, and their windows, too, blinked together one by one.

During this time Barnet had proceeded with decided step in a direction at right angles to the broad main thoroughfare of the town, by a long street leading due southward. Here, though his family had no more to do with the flax manufacture, his own name occasionally greeted him on gates and warehouses, being used allusively by small rising tradesmen as a recommendation, in such words as "Smith, from Barnet and Co." — "Robinson, late manager at Barnet's." The sight led him to reflect upon his father's busy life, and he questioned if it had not been far happier than his own.

The houses along the road became fewer, and presently open ground appeared between them on either side, the tract on the right hand rising to a higher level till it merged in a knoll. On the summit a row of builders' scaffold-poles probed the indistinct sky like spears, and at their bases could be discerned the lower courses of a building lately begun. Barnet slackened his pace and stood for a few moments without leaving the centre of the road, apparently not much interested in the sight, till suddenly his eye was caught by a post in the fore part of the ground, bearing a white board at the top. He went to the rails, vaulted over, and walked in far enough to discern painted upon the board "Château Ringdale."

A dismal irony seemed to lie in the words, and its effect was to irritate him. Downe, then, had spoken truly. He stuck his umbrella into the sod and seized the post with both hands, as if intending to loosen and throw it down. Then, like one bewildered by an opposition which would exist none the less though its manifestations were removed, he allowed his arms to sink to his side.

"Let it be," he said to himself. "I have declared there shall be peace — if possible."

Taking up his umbrella, he quietly left the enclosure, and went on his way, still keeping his back to the town. He had advanced with more decision since passing the new building, and soon a hoarse murmur rose upon the gloom; it was the sound of the sea. The road led to the harbour, at a distance of a mile from the town, from which the trade of the district was fed. After seeing the obnoxious name-board Barnet had forgotten to open his umbrella, and the rain tapped smartly on his hat, and occasionally stroked his face as he went on.

Though the lamps were still continued at the roadside they stood at wider intervals than before, and the pavement had given place to rough gravel. Every time he came to a lamp an increasing shine made itself visible upon his shoulders, till at last they quite glistened with wet. The murmur from the shore grew stronger, but it was still some distance off when he paused before one of the smallest of the detached houses by the wayside, standing in its own garden, the latter being divided from the road by a row of wooden palings. Scrutinising the spot to ensure that he was not mistaken, he opened the gate and gently knocked at the cottage door.

When he had patiently waited minutes enough to lead any man in ordinary cases to knock again, the door was heard to open; though it was impossible to see by whose hand, there being no light in the passage. Barnet said at random, "Does

Miss Savile live here?"

A youthful voice assured him that she did live there, and by a sudden after-thought asked him to come in. It would soon get a light, it said; but, the night being wet, mother had not thought it worth while to trim the passage lamp.

"Don't trouble yourself to get a light for me," said Barnet hastily; "it is not necessary at all. Which is Miss Savile's sitting-room?"

The young person, whose white pinafore could just be discerned, signified a door in the side of the passage, and Barnet went forward at the same moment, so that no light should fall upon his face. On entering the room he closed the door behind him, pausing till he heard the retreating foot-steps of the child.

He found himself in an apartment which was simply and neatly, though not poorly furnished; everything, from the miniature chiffonnier, to the shining little daguerreo-type which formed the central ornament of the mantelpiece, being in scrupulous order. The picture was enclosed by a frame of embroidered cardboard — evidently the work of feminine hands — and it was the portrait of a thin-faced, elderly lieutenant in the navy. From behind the lamp on the table a female form now rose into view, that of a young girl, and a resemblance between her and the portrait was early discoverable. She had been so absorbed in some occupation on the other side of the lamp as to have barely found time to realise her visitor's presence.

They both remained standing for a few seconds without speaking. The face that confronted Barnet had a beautiful outline; the Raffaelesque oval of its contour was remarkable for an English countenance, and that countenance housed in a remote country-road to an unheard-of harbour. But her features did not do justice to this splendid beginning: Nature had recollected that she was not in Italy; and the young lady's lineaments, though not so inconsistent as to make her plain, would have been accepted rather as pleasing than as correct. The preoccupied expression which, like images on the retina, remained with her for a moment after the state that caused it had ceased, now changed into a reserved, half-proud, and slightly indignant look, in which the blood diffused itself quickly across her cheek, and additional brightness broke the shade of her rather heavy eyes.

"I know I have no business here," he said, answering the look. "But I had a great wish to see you, and enquire how you were. You can give your hand to me, seeing how often I have held it in past days?"

"I would rather forget than remember all that, Mr. Barnet," she answered, as she coldly complied with the request. "When I think of the circumstances of our last meeting, I can hardly consider it kind of you to allude to such a thing as our past — or, indeed, to come here at all."

"There was no harm in it surely? I don't trouble you often, Lucy."

"I have not had the honour of a visit from you for a very long time, certainly, and I did not expect it now," she said, with the same stiffness in her air. "I hope Mrs. Barnet is very well?"

"Yes, yes!" he impatiently returned. "At least I suppose so — though I only speak from inference!"

"But she is your wife, sir," said the young girl tremulously.

The unwonted tones of a man's voice in that feminine chamber had startled a canary that was roosting in its cage by the window; the bird awoke hastily, and fluttered against the bars. She went and stilled it by laying her face against the cage and murmuring a coaxing sound. It might partly have been done to still herself.

"I didn't come to talk of Mrs. Barnet," he pursued; "I came to talk of you, of yourself alone; to enquire how you are getting on since your great loss." And he turned towards the portrait of her father.

"I am getting on fairly well, thank you."

The force of her utterance was scarcely borne out by her look; but Barnet courteously reproached himself for not having guessed a thing so natural; and to dissipate all embarrassment, added, as he bent over the table, "What were you doing when I came? — painting flowers, and by candle-light."

"Oh no," she said, "not painting them — only sketching the outlines. I do that at night to save time — I have to get three dozen done by the end of the month."

Barnet looked as if he regretted it deeply. "You will wear your poor eyes out," he said, with more sentiment than he had hitherto shown. "You ought not to do it. There was a time when I should have said you must not. Well — I almost wish I had never seen light with my own eyes when I think of that!"

"Is this a time or place for recalling such matters?" she asked, with dignity. "You used to have a gentlemanly respect for me, and for yourself. Don't speak any more as you have spoken, and don't come again. I cannot think that this visit is serious, or was closely considered by you."

"Considered: well, I came to see you as an old and good friend — not to mince matters, to visit a woman I loved. Don't be angry! I could not help doing it, so many things brought you into my mind. . . . This evening I fell in with an acquaintance, and when I saw how happy he was with his wife and family welcoming him home, though with only one-tenth of my income and chances, and thought what might have been in my case, it fairly broke down my discretion, and off I came here. Now I am here I feel that I am wrong to some extent. But the feeling that I should like to see you, and talk of those we used to know in common, was very strong."

"Before that can be the case a little more time must pass," said Miss Savile quietly; "a time long enough for me to regard with some calmness what at present I remember far too impatiently — though it may be you almost forget it. Indeed you must have forgotten it long before you acted as you did." Her voice grew stronger and more vivacious as she added: "But I am doing my best to forget it too, and I know I shall succeed from the progress I have made already."

She had remained standing till now, when she turned and sat down, facing half away from him.

Barnet watched her moodily. "Yes, it is only what I deserve," he said. "Ambition pricked me on — no, it was not ambition, it was wrongheadedness. Had I but reflected. . . ." He broke out vehemently: "But always remember this, Lucy: if you had written to me only one little line after that misunderstanding, I declare I should have come back to you. That ruined me!" He slowly walked as far as the little room would allow him to go, and remained with his eyes on the skirting.

"But, Mr. Barnet, how could I write to you? There was no opening for my doing so."

"Then there ought to have been," said Barnet, turning. "That was my fault!"

"Well, I don't know anything about that; but as there had been nothing said by me which required any explanation by letter, I did not send one. Everything was so indefinite, and feeling your position to be so much wealthier than mine, I fancied I might have mistaken your meaning. And when I heard of the other lady — a woman of whose family even you might be proud — I thought how foolish I had been, and said nothing."

"Then I suppose it was destiny — accident — I don't know what, that separated us, dear Lucy. Anyhow you were the woman I ought to have made my wife — and I let you slip, like the foolish man that I was!"

"Oh, Mr. Barnet," she said, almost in tears, "don't revive the subject to me; I am the wrong one to console you — think, sir — you should not be here — it would be so bad for me if it were known!"

"It would — it would, indeed," he said hastily. "I am not right in doing this, and I won't do it again."

"It is a very common folly of human nature, you know, to think the course you did *not* adopt must have been the best," she continued, with gentle solicitude, as she followed him to the door of the room. "And you don't know that I should have accepted you, even if you had asked me to be your wife." At this his eye met hers, and she dropped her gaze. She knew that her voice belied her. There was a silence till she looked up to add, in a voice of soothing playfulness, "My family was so much poorer than yours, even before I lost my dear father, that — perhaps your companions would have made it unpleasant for us on account of my deficiencies."

"Your disposition would soon have won them round," said Barnet.

She archly expostulated: "Now, never mind my disposition; try to make it up with your wife! Those are my commands to you. And now you are to leave me at once."

"I will. I must make the best of it all, I suppose," he replied, more cheerfully than he had as yet spoken. "But I shall never again meet with such a dear girl as you!" And he suddenly opened the door, and left her alone. When his glance again fell on the lamps that were sparsely ranged along the dreary level road, his eyes were in a state which showed straw-like motes of light radiating from each flame into the surrounding air.

On the other side of the way Barnet observed a man under an umbrella, walking parallel with himself. Presently this man left the footway, and gradually converged on Barnet's course. The latter then saw that it was Charlson, a surgeon of the town, who owed him money. Charlson was a man not without ability; yet he did not prosper. Sundry circumstances stood in his way as a medical practitioner; he was needy; he was not a coddle; he gossiped with men instead of with women; he had married a stranger instead of one of the town young ladies; and he was given to conversational buffoonery. Moreover, his look was quite erroneous. Those only proper features in the family doctor, the quiet eye, and the thin straight passionless lips which never curl in public either for laughter or for scorn, were not his; he had a full curved mouth, and a bold black eye that made timid people nervous. His companions were what in old times would have been called boon companions — an expression which, though of irreproachable root, suggests fraternisation carried to the point of unscrupulousness. All this was against him in the little town of his adoption.

Charlson had been in difficulties, and to oblige him Barnet had put his name to a bill; and, as he had expected, was called upon to meet it when it fell due. It had been only a matter of fifty pounds, which Barnet could well afford to lose, and he bore no ill-will to the thriftless surgeon on account of it. But Charlson had a little too much brazen indifferentism in his composition to be altogether a desirable acquaintance.

"I hope to be able to make that little bill-business right with you in the course of three weeks, Mr. Barnet," said Charlson, with hail-fellow friendliness.

Barnet replied good-naturedly that there was no hurry.

This particular three weeks had moved on in advance of Charlson's present with the precision of a shadow for some considerable time.

"I've had a dream," Charlson continued. Barnet knew from his tone that the surgeon was going to begin his characteristic nonsense, and did not encourage him. "I've had a dream," repeated Charlson, who required no encouragement. "I dreamed that a gentleman, who has been very kind to me, married a haughty lady in haste, before he had quite forgotten a nice little girl he knew before, and that one wet evening, like the present, as I was walking up the harbour-road, I saw him come out of that dear little girl's present abode."

Barnet glanced towards the speaker. The rays from a neighbouring lamp struck through the drizzle under Charlson's umbrella, so as just to illumine his face against the shade behind, and show that his eye was turned up under the outer corner of its lid, whence it leered with impish jocoseness as he thrust his tongue into his cheek.

"Come," said Barnet, gravely, "we'll have no more of that."

"No, no — of course not," Charlson hastily answered, seeing that his humour had carried him too far, as it had done many times before. He was profuse in his apologies, but Barnet did not reply. Of one thing he was certain — that scandal was a plant of quick root, and that he was bound to obey Lucy's injunction for Lucy's own sake.

III

He did so, to the letter; and though, as the crocus followed the snowdrop and the daffodil the crocus in Lucy's garden, the harbour-road was a not unpleasant place to walk in, Barnet's feet never trod its stones, much less approached her door. He avoided a saunter that way as he would have avoided a dangerous dram, and took his airings a long distance northward, among severely square and brown ploughed fields, where no other townsman came. Sometimes he went round by the lower lanes of the borough, where the rope walks stretched in which his family formerly had share, and looked at the rope-makers walking backwards, overhung by apple-trees and bushes, and intruded on by cows and calves, as if trade had established itself there at considerable inconvenience to nature.

One morning, when the sun was so warm as to raise a steam from the southeastern slopes of those flanking hills that looked so lovely above the old roofs, but made every low-chimneyed house in the town as smoky as Tophet, Barnet glanced from the windows of the town-council room for lack of interest in what was proceeding within. Several members of the corporation were present, but there was not much business doing, and in a few minutes Downe came leisurely across to him, saying that he seldom saw Barnet now.

Barnet owned that he was not often present.

Downe looked at the crimson curtain which hung down beside the panes, reflecting its hot hues into their faces, and then out of the window. At that moment there passed along the street a tall commanding lady, in whom the solicitor recognised Barnet's wife. Barnet had done the same thing, and turned away.

"It will be all right some day," said Downe, with cheering sympathy.

"You have heard, then, of her last outbreak?"

Downe depressed his cheerfulness to its very reverse in a moment. "No, I have not heard of anything serious," he said, with as long a face as one naturally round could be turned into at short notice. "I only hear vague reports of such things."

"You may think it will be all right," said Barnet, drily. "But I have a different opinion. . . . No, Downe, we must look the thing in the face. Not poppy nor mandragora — however, how are your wife and children?"

Downe said that they were all well, thanks; they were out that morning somewhere; he was just looking to see if they were walking that way. Ah, there they were, just coming down the street, and Downe pointed to the figures of two children with a nursemaid, and a lady walking behind them.

"You will come out and speak to her?" he asked.

"Not this morning. The fact is I don't care to speak to anybody just now."

"You are too sensitive, Mr. Barnet. At school I remember you used to get as red as a rose if anybody uttered a word that hurt your feelings."

177

Barnet mused. "Yes," he admitted, "there is a grain of truth in that. It is because of that I often try to make peace at home. Life would be tolerable then at any rate, even if not particularly bright."

"I have thought more than once of proposing a little plan to you," said Downe with some hesitation. "I don't know whether it will meet your views, but take it or leave it, as you choose. In fact, it was my wife who suggested it; that she would be very glad to call on Mrs. Barnet and get into her confidence. She seems to think that Mrs. Barnet is rather alone in the town, and without advisers. Her impression is that your wife will listen to reason. Emily has a wonderful way of winning the hearts of people of her own sex."

"And of the other sex too, I think. She is a charming woman, and you were a lucky fellow to find her."

"Well, perhaps I was," simpered Downe, trying to wear an aspect of being the last man in the world to feel pride. "However, she will be likely to find out what ruffles Mrs. Barnet. Perhaps it is some misunderstanding, you know — something that she is too proud to ask you to explain, or some little thing in your conduct that irritates her because she does not fully comprehend you. The truth is, Emily would have been more ready to make advances if she had been quite sure of her fitness for Mrs. Barnet's society, who has of course been accustomed to London people of good position, which made Emily fearful of intruding."

Barnet expressed his warmest thanks for the well-intentioned proposition. There was reason in Mrs. Downe's fear — that he owned. "But do let her call," he said. "There is no woman in England I would so soon trust on such an errand. I am afraid there will not be any brilliant result; still I shall take it as the kindest and nicest thing if she will try it, and not be frightened at a repulse."

When Barnet and Downe had parted, the former went to the Town Savings-Bank, of which he was a trustee, and endeavoured to forget his troubles in the contemplation of low sums of money, and figures in a network of red and blue lines. He sat and watched the working-people making their deposits, to which at intervals he signed his name. Before he left in the afternoon Downe put his head inside the door.

"Emily has seen Mrs. Barnet," he said, in a low voice. "She has got Mrs. Barnet's promise to take her for a drive down to the shore to-morrow, if it is fine. Good afternoon!"

Barnet shook Downe by the hand without speaking, and Downe went away.

IV

The next day was as fine as the arrangement could possibly require. As the sun passed the meridian and declined westward, the tall shadows from the scaffold-poles of Barnet's rising residence streaked the ground as far as to the middle of the highway. Barnet himself was there inspecting the progress of the works for the first time during several weeks. A building in an old-fashioned town five-and-thirty years ago did not, as in the modern fashion, rise from the sod like a booth at a fair. The foundations and lower courses were put in and allowed to settle for many weeks before the superstructure was built up, and a whole summer of drying was hardly sufficient to do justice to the important issues involved. Barnet stood within a window-niche which had as yet received no frame, and thence looked down a slope into the road. The wheels of a chaise were heard, and then his handsome Xantippe, in the company of Mrs. Downe, drove past on their way to the shore. They were driving slowly; there was a pleasing light in Mrs. Downe's face, which seemed faintly to reflect itself upon the countenance of her companion — that *politesse du cœur* which was so natural to her having possibly begun already to work results. But whatever the situation, Barnet resolved not to interfere, or do anything to hazard the promise of the day. He might well afford to trust the issue to another when he could never direct it but to ill himself. His wife's clenched rein-hand in its lemon-coloured glove, her stiff erect figure, clad in velvet and lace, and her boldly outlined face, passed on, exhibiting their owner as one fixed for ever above the level of her companion — socially by her early breeding, and materially by her higher cushion.

Barnet decided to allow them a proper time to themselves, and then stroll down to the shore and drive them home. After lingering on at the house for another hour he started with this intention. A few hundred yards below "Château Ringdale" stood the cottage in which the late lieutenant's daughter had her lodging. Barnet had not been so far that way for a long time, and as he approached the forbidden ground a curious warmth passed into him, which led him to perceive that, unless he were careful, he might have to fight the battle with himself about Lucy over again. A tenth of his present excuse would, however, have justified him in travelling by that road to-day.

He came opposite the dwelling, and turned his eyes for a momentary glance into the little garden that stretched from the palings to the door. Lucy was in the enclosure; she was walking and stooping to gather some flowers, possibly for the purpose of painting them, for she moved about quickly, as if anxious to save time. She did not see him; he might have passed unnoticed; but a sensation which was not in strict unison with his previous sentiments that day led him to pause in his walk and watch her. She went nimbly round and round the beds of anemones, tulips, jonquils, polyanthuses, and other old-fashioned flowers, looking a very charming figure in her half-mourning bonnet, and with an incomplete nosegay in her left hand. Raising herself to pull down a lilac blossom she observed him.

"Mr. Barnet!" she said, innocently smiling. "Why, I have been thinking of you many times since Mrs. Barnet went by in the pony carriage, and now here you are!"

"Yes, Lucy," he said.

Then she seemed to recall particulars of their last meeting, and he believed that she flushed, though it might have been only the fancy of his own super-sensitiveness.

"I am going to the harbour," he added.

"Are you?" Lucy remarked, simply. "A great many people begin to go there now the summer is drawing on."

Her face had come more into his view as she spoke, and he noticed how much thinner and paler it was than when he had seen it last. "Lucy, how weary you look! tell me, can I help you?" he was going to cry out. — "If I do," he thought, "it will be the ruin of us both!" He merely said that the afternoon was fine, and went on his way.

As he went a sudden blast of air came over the hill as if in contradiction to his words, and spoilt the previous quiet of the scene. The wind had already shifted violently, and now smelt of the sea.

The harbour-road soon began to justify its name. A gap appeared in the rampart of hills which shut out the sea, and on the left of the opening rose a vertical cliff, coloured a burning orange by the sunlight, the companion cliff on the right being livid in shade. Between these cliffs, like the

Libyan bay which sheltered the ship-wrecked Trojans, was a little haven, seemingly a beginning made by Nature herself of a perfect harbour, which appealed to the passer-by as only requiring a little human industry to finish it and make it famous, the ground on each side as far back as the daisied slopes that bounded the interior valley being a mere layer of blown sand. But the Port-Bredy burgesses a mile inland had, in the course of ten centuries, responded many times to that mute appeal, with the result that the tides had invariably choked up their works with sand and shingle as soon as completed. There were but few houses here: a rough pier, a few boats, some stores, an inn, a residence or two, a ketch unloading in the harbour, were the chief features of the settlement. On the open ground by the shore stood his wife's pony-carriage, empty, the boy in attendance holding the horse.

When Barnet drew near, he saw an indigo-coloured spot moving swiftly along beneath the radiant base of the eastern cliff, which proved to be a man in a jersey, running with all his might. He held up his hand to Barnet, as it seemed, and they approached each other. The man was local, but a stranger to him.

"What is it, my man?" said Barnet.

"A terrible calamity!" the boatman hastily explained. Two ladies had been capsized in a boat — they were Mrs. Downe and Mrs. Barnet of the old town; they had driven down there that afternoon — they had alighted, and it was so fine, that, after walking about a little while, they had been tempted to go out for a short sail round the cliff. Just as they were putting into the shore, the wind shifted with a sudden gust, the boat listed over, and it was thought they were both drowned. How it could have happened was beyond his mind to fathom, for John Green knew how to sail a boat as well as any man there.

"Which is the way to the place?" said Barnet.

It was just round the cliff.

"Run to the carriage and tell the boy to bring it to the place as soon as you can. Then go to the Harbour Inn and tell them to ride to town for a doctor. Have they been got out of the water?"

"One lady has."

"Which?"

"Mrs. Barnet. Mrs. Downe, it is feared, has fleeted out to sea."

Barnet ran on to that part of the shore

which the cliff had hitherto obscured from his view, and there discerned, a long way ahead, a group of fishermen standing. As soon as he came up one or two recognised him, and, not liking to meet his eye, turned aside with misgiving. He went amidst them and saw a small sailing-boat lying draggled at the water's edge; and, on the sloping shingle beside it, a soaked and sandy woman's form in the velvet dress and yellow gloves of his wife.

V

All had been done that could be done. Mrs. Barnet was in her own house under medical hands, but the result was still uncertain. Barnet had acted as if devotion to his wife were the dominant passion of his existence. There had been much to decide — whether to attempt restoration of the apparently lifeless body as it lay on the shore — whether to carry her to the Harbour Inn — whether to drive with her at once to his own house. The first course, with no skilled help or appliances near at hand, had seemed hopeless. The second course would have occupied nearly as much time as a drive to the town, owing to the intervening ridges of shingle, and the necessity of crossing the harbour by boat to get to the house, added to which much time must have elapsed before a doctor could have arrived down there. By bringing her home in the carriage some precious moments had slipped by; but she had been laid in her own bed in seven minutes, a doctor called to her side, and every possible restorative brought to bear upon her.

At what a tearing pace he had driven up that road, through the yellow evening sunlight, the shadows flapping irksomely into his eyes as each wayside object rushed past between him and the west! Tired workmen with their baskets at their backs had turned on their homeward journey to wonder at his speed. Half-way between the shore and Port-Bredy town he had met Charlson, who had been the first surgeon to hear of the accident. He was accompanied by his assistant in a gig. Barnet had sent on the latter to the coast in case that Downe's poor wife should by that time have been reclaimed from the waves, and had brought Charlson back with him to the house.

Barnet's presence was not needed here, and he felt it to be his next duty to set off at once and find Downe, that no other than himself might break the news to him.

He was quite sure that no chance had been lost for Mrs. Downe by his leaving the shore. By the time that Mrs. Barnet had been laid in the carriage, a much larger group had assembled to lend assistance in finding her friend, rendering his own help superfluous. But the duty of breaking the news was made doubly painful by the circumstance that the catastrophe which had befallen Mrs. Downe was solely the result of her own and her husband's loving-kindness towards himself.

He found Downe in his office. When the solicitor comprehended the intelligence he turned pale, stood up, and remained for a moment perfectly still, as if bereft of his faculties; then his shoulders heaved, he pulled out his handkerchief and began to cry like a child. His sobs might have been heard in the next room. He seemed to have no idea of going to the shore, or of doing anything; but when Barnet took him gently by the hand, and proposed to start at once he quietly acquiesced, neither uttering any further word nor making any effort to repress his tears.

Barnet accompanied him to the shore, where, finding that no trace had as yet been seen of Mrs. Downe, and that his stay would be of no avail, he left Downe with his friends and the young doctor, and once more hastened back to his own house.

At the door he met Charlson. "Well!" Barnet said.

"I have just come down," said the doctor; "we have done everything; but without result. I sympathise with you in your bereavement."

Barnet did not much appreciate Charlson's sympathy, which sounded to his ears as something of a mockery from the lips of a man who knew what Charlson knew about his domestic relations. Indeed there seemed an odd spark in Charlson's full black eye as he said the words; but that might have been imaginary.

"And, Mr. Barnet," Charlson resumed, "that little matter between us — I hope to settle it finally in three weeks at least."

"Never mind that now," said Barnet abruptly. He directed the surgeon to go to the harbour in case his services might even now be necessary there; and himself entered the house.

The servants were coming from his wife's chamber, looking helplessly at each other and at him. He passed them by and entered the room, where he stood regarding the shape on the bed for a few minutes, after which he walked into his own dressing-room adjoining, and there paced up and down. In a minute or two he noticed what a strange and total silence had come over the upper part of the house; his own movements, muffled as they were by the carpet, seemed noisy; and his thoughts to disturb the air like articulate utterances. His eye glanced through the window. Far down the road to the harbour a roof detained his gaze: out of it rose a red chimney, and out of the red chimney a curl of smoke, as from a fire newly kindled. He had often seen such a sight before. In that house lived Lucy Savile; and the smoke was from the fire which was regularly lighted at this time to make her tea.

After that he went back to the bedroom, and stood there some time regarding his wife's silent form. She was a woman some years older than himself, but had not by any means over-passed the maturity of good looks and vigour. Her passionate features, well-defined, firm, and statuesque in life, were doubly so now: her mouth and brow, beneath her purplish black hair, showed only too clearly that the turbulency of character which had made a bear-garden of his house had been no tempo-rary phase of her existence. While he reflected, he suddenly said to himself, I wonder if all has been done?

The thought was led up to by his having fancied that his wife's features lacked in its completeness the expression which he had been accustomed to associate with the faces of those whose spirits have fled for ever. The effacement of life was not so marked but that, entering uninformed, he might have supposed her sleeping. Her complexion was that seen in the numerous faded portraits by Sir Joshua Reynolds; it was pallid in comparison with life; but there was visible on a close inspection the remnant of what had once been a flush; the keeping between the cheeks and the hollows of the face being thus preserved, although positive colour was gone. Long orange rays of evening sun stole in through chinks in the blind, striking on the large mirror, and being thence reflected upon the crimson hangings and woodwork of the heavy bedstead, so that the general tone of light was remarkably warm; and it was probable that something might be due to this circumstance. Still the fact impressed him as strange. Charlson had been gone more than a quarter of an hour: could it be possible that he had left too soon, and that his attempts to restore her had operated so

191

sluggishly as only now to have made themselves felt? Barnet laid his hand upon her chest, and fancied that ever and anon a faint flutter of palpitation, gentle as that of a butterfly's wing, disturbed the stillness there — ceasing for a time, then struggling to go on, then breaking down in weakness and ceasing again.

Barnet's mother had been an active practitioner of the healing art among her poorer neighbours, and her inspirations had all been derived from an octavo volume of Domestic Medicine, which at this moment was lying, as it had lain for many years, on a shelf in Barnet's dressing-room. He hastily fetched it, and there read under the head "Drowning": —

"Exertions for the recovery of any person who has not been immersed for a longer period than half-an-hour should be continued for at least four hours, as there have been many cases in which returning life has made itself visible even after a longer interval.

"Should, however, a weak action of any of the organs show itself when the case seems almost hopeless, our efforts must be redoubled; the feeble spark in this case requires to be solicited; it will certainly disappear under a relaxation of labour."

Barnet looked at his watch; it was now barely two hours and a half from the time when he had first heard of the accident. He threw aside the book and turned quickly to reach a stimulant which had previously been used. Pulling up the blind for more light, his eye glanced out of the window. There he saw that red chimney still smoking cheerily, and that roof, and through the roof that somebody. His mechanical movements stopped, his hand remained on the blind-cord, and he seemed to become breathless, as if he had suddenly found himself treading a high rope.

While he stood a sparrow lighted on the window-sill, saw him, and flew away. Next a man and a dog walked over one of the green hills which bulged above the roofs of the town. But Barnet took no notice.

We may wonder what were the exact images that passed through his mind during those minutes of gazing upon Lucy Savile's house, the sparrow, the man and the dog, and Lucy Savile's house again. There are honest men who will not admit to their thoughts, even as idle hypotheses, views of the future that assume as done a deed which they would recoil from doing; and there are other honest men for whom morality ends at the surface of their own heads, who will deliberate what the first will not so much as suppose. Barnet had a wife whose presence distracted his home; she now lay as in death; by merely doing nothing — by letting the intelligence which had gone forth to the world lie undisturbed — he would effect such a deliverance for himself as he had never hoped for, and open up an opportunity of which till now he had never dreamed. Whether the conjuncture had arisen through any unscrupulous, ill-considered impulse of Charlson to help out of a strait the friend who was so kind as never to press him for what was due could not be told; there was nothing to prove it; and it was a question which could never be asked. The triangular situation — himself — his wife — Lucy Savile — was the one clear thing.

From Barnet's actions we may infer that he *supposed* such and such a result, for a moment, but did not deliberate. He withdrew his hazel eyes from the scene without, calmly turned, rang the bell for assistance, and vigorously exerted himself to learn if life still lingered in that motionless frame. In a short time another surgeon was in attendance; and then Barnet's surmise proved to be true. The slow life timidly heaved again; but much care and patience were needed to catch and retain it, and a considerable period elapsed before it could be said with certainty that Mrs. Barnet lived. When this was the case, and there was no further room for doubt, Barnet left the chamber. The blue evening smoke from Lucy's chimney had died down to an imperceptible stream, and as he walked about downstairs he murmured to himself, "My wife was dead, and she is alive again."

It was not so with Downe. After three hours' immersion his wife's body had been recovered, life, of course, being quite extinct. Barnet, on descending, went straight to his friend's house, and there learned the result. Downe was helpless in his wild grief, occasionally even hysterical. Barnet said little, but finding that some guiding hand was necessary in the sorrow-stricken household, took upon him to supervise and manage till Downe should be in a state of mind to do so for himself.

VI

One September evening, four months later, when Mrs. Barnet was in perfect health, and Mrs. Downe but a weakening memory, an errand-boy paused to rest himself in front of

Mr. Barnet's old house, depositing his basket on one of the windowsills. The street was not yet lighted, but there were lights in the house, and at intervals a flitting shadow fell upon the blind at his elbow. Words also were audible from the same apartment, and they seemed to be those of persons in violent altercation. But the boy could not gather their purport, and he went on his way.

Ten minutes afterwards the door of Barnet's house opened, and a tall closely-veiled lady in a travelling-dress came out and descended the freestone steps. The servant stood in the doorway watching her as she went with a measured tread down the street. When she had been out of sight for some minutes Barnet appeared at the door from within.

"Did your mistress leave word where she was going?" he asked.

"No, sir."

"Is the carriage ordered to meet her anywhere?"

"No, sir."

"Did she take a latch-key?"

"No, sir."

Barnet went in again, sat down in his chair, and leaned back. Then in solitude and silence he brooded over the bitter emotions that filled his heart. It was for

196

this that he had gratuitously restored her to life, and made his union with another impossible! The evening drew on, and nobody came to disturb him. At bedtime he told the servants to retire, that he would sit up for Mrs. Barnet himself; and when they were gone he leaned his head upon his hand and mused for hours.

The clock struck one, two; still his wife came not, and, with impatience added to depression, he went from room to room till another weary hour had passed. This was not altogether a new experience for Barnet; but she had never before so prolonged her absence. At last he sat down again and fell asleep.

He awoke at six o'clock to find that she had not returned. In searching about the rooms he discovered that she had taken a case of jewels which had been hers before her marriage. At eight a note was brought him; it was from his wife, in which she stated that she had gone by the coach to the house of a distant relative near London, and expressed a wish that certain boxes, articles of clothing and so on, might be sent to her forthwith. The note was brought to him by a waiter at the Black-Bull Hotel, and had been written by Mrs. Barnet immediately before she took her place in the stage.

By the evening this order was carried out, and Barnet, with a sense of relief, walked out into the town. A fair had been held during the day, and the large clear moon which rose over the most prominent hill flung its light upon the booths and standings that still remained in the street, mixing its rays curiously with those from the flaring naphtha lamps. The town was full of country-people who had come in to enjoy themselves, and on this account Barnet strolled through the streets unobserved. With a certain recklessness he made for the harbour-road, and presently found himself by the shore, where he walked on till he came to the spot near which his friend the kindly Mrs. Downe had lost her life, and his own wife's life had been preserved. A tremulous pathway of bright moonshine now stretched over the water which had engulfed them, and not a living soul was near.

Here he ruminated on their characters, and next on the young girl in whom he now took a more sensitive interest than at the time when he had been free to marry her. Nothing, so far as he was aware, had ever appeared in his own conduct to show that such an interest existed. He had made it a point of the utmost strictness to hinder that feeling from influencing in the faintest degree his attitude towards his wife; and this was made all the more easy for him by the small demand Mrs. Barnet made upon his attentions, for which she ever evinced the greatest contempt; thus unwittingly giving him the satisfaction of knowing that their severance owed nothing to jealousy, or, indeed, to any personal behaviour of his at all. Her concern was not with him or his feelings, as she frequently told him; but that she had, in a moment of weakness, thrown herself away upon a common burgher when she might have aimed at, and possibly brought down, a peer of the realm. Her frequent depreciation of Barnet in these terms had at times been so intense that he was sorely tempted to retaliate on her egotism by owning that he loved at the same low level on which he lived; but prudence had prevailed, for which he was now thankful.

Something seemed to sound upon the shingle behind him over and above the raking of the wave. He looked round, and a slight girlish shape appeared quite close to him. He could not see her face because it was in the direction of the moon.

"Mr Barnet?" the rambler said, in timid surprise. The voice was the voice of Lucy Savile.

"Yes," said Barnet. "How can I repay you for this pleasure?"

"I only came because the night was so clear. I am now on my way home."

"I am glad we have met. I want to know if you will let me do something for you, to give me an occupation, as an idle man? I am sure I ought to help you, for I know you are almost without friends."

She hesitated. "Why should you tell me that?" she said.

"In the hope that you will be frank with me."

"I am not altogether without friends here. But I am going to make a little change in my life — to go out as a teacher of free-hand drawing and practical perspective, of course I mean on a comparatively humble scale, because I have not been specially educated for that profession. But I am sure I shall like it much."

"You have an opening?"

"I have not exactly got it, but I have advertised for one."

"Lucy, you must let me help you!"

"Not at all."

"You need not think it would compromise you, or that I am indifferent to delicacy. I bear in mind how we stand. It is very unlikely that you will succeed as

200

teacher of the class you mention, so let me do something of a different kind for you. Say what you would like, and it shall be done."

"No; if I can't be a drawing-mistress or governess, or something of that sort, I shall go to India and join my brother."

"I wish I could go abroad, anywhere, everywhere with you, Lucy, and leave this place and its associations for ever!"

She played with the end of her bonnet-string, and hastily turned aside. "Don't ever touch upon that kind of topic again," she said, with a quick severity not free from anger. "It simply makes it impossible for me to see you, much less receive any guidance from you. No, thank you, Mr. Barnet; you can do nothing for me at present; and as I suppose my uncertainty will end in my leaving for India, I fear you never will. If ever I think you *can* do anything, I will take the trouble to ask you. Till then, good-bye."

The tone of her latter words was equivocal, and while he remained in doubt whether a gentle irony was or was not inwrought with their sound, she swept lightly round and left him alone. He saw her form get smaller and smaller along the damp belt of sea-sand between ebb and flood;

and when she had vanished round the cliff into the harbour-road, he himself followed in the same direction.

That her hopes from an advertisement should be the single thread which held Lucy Savile in England was too much for Barnet. On reaching the town he went straight to the residence of Downe, now a widower with four children. The young motherless brood had been sent to bed about a quarter-of-an-hour earlier, and when Barnet entered he found Downe sitting alone. It was the same room as that from which the family had been looking out for Downe at the beginning of the year, when Downe had slipped into the gutter and his wife had been so enviably tender towards him. The old neatness had gone from the house; articles lay in places which could show no reason for their presence, as if momentarily deposited there some months ago, and forgotten ever since; there were no flowers; things were jumbled together on the furniture which should have been in cupboards; and the place in general had that stagnant, unrenovated air which usually pervades the maimed home of the widower.

Downe soon renewed his customary full-worded lament over his wife, and even when he had worked himself up to tears, went on volubly, as if a listener were a luxury to be enjoyed whenever he could be caught.

"She was a treasure beyond compare, Mr. Barnet! I shall never see such another. Nobody now to nurse me — nobody to console me in those daily troubles, you know, Barnet, which make consolation so necessary to a nature like mine. It would be unbecoming to repine, for her spirit's home was elsewhere — the tender light in her eyes always showed it; but it is a long dreary time that I have before me, and nobody else can ever fill the void left in my heart by her loss — nobody — nobody!" And Downe wiped his eyes again.

"She was a good woman in the highest sense," gravely answered Barnet, who, though Downe's words drew genuine compassion from his heart, could not help feeling that a tender reticence would have been a finer tribute to Mrs. Downe's really sterling virtues than such a second-class lament as this.

"I have something to show you," Downe resumed, producing from a drawer a sheet of paper on which was an elaborate design for a canopied tomb. "This has been sent me by the architect, but it is not exactly what I want."

"You have got Jones to do it, I see, the man who is carrying out my house," said Barnet, as he glanced at the signature to the drawing.

"Yes, but it is not quite what I want. I want something more striking — more like a tomb I have seen in St. Paul's Cathedral. Nothing less will do justice to my feelings, and how far short of them that will fall!"

Barnet privately thought the design a sufficiently imposing one as it stood, even extravagantly ornate; but, feeling that he had no right to criticise, he said gently, "Downe, should you not live more in your children's lives at the present time, and soften the sharpness of regret for your own past by thinking of their future?"

"Yes, yes; but what can I do more?" asked Downe, wrinkling his forehead hopelessly.

It was with anxious slowness that Barnet produced his reply — the secret object of his visit to-night. "Did you not say one day that you ought by rights to get a governess for the children?"

Downe admitted that he had said so, but that he could not see his way to it. "The kind of woman I should like to have," he said, "would be rather beyond my means. No; I think I shall send them to school in the town when they are old enough to go out alone."

"Now I know of something better than that. The late Lieutenant Savile's daughter, Lucy, wants to do something for herself in the way of teaching. She would be inexpensive, and would answer your purpose as well as anybody for six or twelve months. She would probably come daily if you were to ask her, and so your housekeeping arrangements would not be much affected."

"I thought she had gone away," said the solicitor, musing. "Where does she live?"

Barnet told him, and added that, if Downe should think of her as suitable, he would do well to call as soon as possible, or she might be on the wing. "If you do see her," he said, "it would be advisable not to mention my name. She is rather stiff in her ideas of me, and it might prejudice her against a course if she knew that I recommended it."

Downe promised to give the subject his consideration, and nothing more was said about it just then. But when Barnet rose to go, which was not till nearly bed-time, he reminded Downe of the suggestion, and went up the street to his own solitary home with a sense of satisfaction at his promising diplomacy in a charitable cause.

VII

The walls of his new house were carried up nearly to their full height. By a curious though not infrequent reaction, Barnet's feelings about that unnecessary structure had undergone a change; he took considerable interest in its progress as a long-neglected thing, his wife before her departure having grown quite weary of it as a hobby. Moreover, it was an excellent distraction for a man in the unhappy position of having to live in a provincial town with nothing to do. He was probably the first of his line who had ever passed a day without toil, and perhaps something like an inherited instinct disqualifies such men for a life of pleasant inaction, such as lies in the power of those whose leisure is not a personal accident, but a vast historical accretion which has become part of their natures.

Thus Barnet got into a way of spending many of his leisure hours on the site of the new building, and he might have been seen on most days at this time trying the temper of the mortar by punching the joints with his stick, looking at the grain of a floor-board, and meditating where it grew, or picturing under what circumstances the last fire would be kindled in the at present sootless chimney. One day when thus occupied he saw three children pass by in the company of a fair young woman, whose sudden appearance caused him to flush perceptibly.

"Ah, she is there," he thought. "That's a blessed thing."

Casting an interested glance over the rising building and the busy workmen, Lucy Savile and the little Downes passed by; and after that time it became a regular though almost unconscious custom of Barnet to stand in the half-completed house and look from the ungarnished windows at the governess as she tripped towards the sea-shore with her young charges, which she was in the habit of doing on most fine afternoons. It was on one of these occasions, when he had been loitering on the first-floor landing, near the hole left for the staircase, not yet erected, that there appeared above the edge of the floor a little hat, followed by a little head.

Barnet withdrew through a doorway, and the child came to the top of the ladder, stepping on to the floor and crying to her sisters and Miss Savile to follow. Another head rose above the floor, and another, and then Lucy herself came into view. The troop ran hither and thither through the empty, shaving-strewn rooms, and Barnet came forward.

Lucy uttered a small exclamation: she was very sorry that she had intruded; she had not the least idea that Mr. Barnet was there: the children had come up, and she had followed.

Barnet replied that he was only too glad to see them there. "And now, let me show you the rooms," he said.

She passively assented, and he took her round. There was not much to show in such a bare skeleton of a house, but he made the most of it, and explained the different ornamental fittings that were soon to be fixed here and there. Lucy made but few remarks in reply, though she seemed pleased with her visit, and stole away down the ladder, followed by her companions.

After this the new residence became yet more of a hobby for Barnet. Downe's children did not forget their first visit, and when the windows were glazed, and the handsome staircase spread its broad low steps into the hall, they came again, prancing in unwearied succession through every room from ground-floor to attics, while Lucy stood waiting for them at the door. Barnet, who rarely missed a day in coming to inspect progress, stepped out from the drawing-room.

"I could not keep them out," she said, with an apologetic blush. "I tried to do so very much; but they are rather wilful, and we are directed to walk this way for the sea air."

"Do let them make the house their regular playground, and you yours," said Barnet. "There is no better place for children to romp and take their exercise in than an empty house, particularly in muddy or damp weather, such as we shall get a good deal of now; and this place will not be furnished for a long long time — perhaps never. I am not at all decided about it."

"Oh, but it must!" replied Lucy, looking round at the hall. "The rooms are excellent, twice as high as ours; and the views from the windows are so lovely."

"I dare say, I dare say," he said, absently.

"Will all the furniture be new?" she asked.

"All the furniture be new — that's a thing I have not thought of. In fact I only come here and look on. My father's house would have been large enough for me, but another person had a voice in the matter, and it was settled that we should build. However, the place grows upon me, its recent associations are cheerful, and I am getting to like it fast."

A certain uneasiness in Lucy's manner showed that the conversation was taking too personal a turn for her. "Still as modern tastes develope, people require more room to gratify them in," she said, withdrawing to call the children; and serenely bidding him good afternoon she went on her way.

Barnet's life at this period was singularly lonely, and yet he was happier than he could have expected. His wife's estrangement and absence, which promised to be permanent, left him free as a boy in his movements, and the solitary walks that he took gave him ample opportunity for chastened reflection on what might have been his lot if he had only shown wisdom enough to claim Lucy Savile when there was no bar between their lives, and she was to be had for the asking. He would occasionally call at the house of his friend Downe; but there was scarcely enough in common between their two natures to make them more than friends of that excellent sort whose personal knowledge of each other's history and character is always in excess of intimacy, whereby they are not so likely to be severed by a clash of sentiment as in cases where intimacy springs up in excess of knowledge. Lucy was never visible at these times, being either engaged in the school-room, or in taking an airing out of doors; but, knowing that she was now comfortable, and had given up the, to him, depressing idea of going off to the other side of the globe, he was quite content.

The new house had so far progressed that the gardeners were beginning to grass down the front. During an afternoon which he was passing in marking the curve for the carriage-drive, he beheld her coming in boldly towards him from the road. Hitherto Barnet had only caught her on the premises by stealth; and this advance seemed to show that at last her reserve had broken down.

A smile gained strength upon her face as she approached, and it was quite radiant when she came up, and said, without a trace of embarrassment, "I find I owe you a hundred thanks — and it comes to me quite as a surprise! It was through your kindness that I was engaged by Mr.

Downe. Believe me, Mr. Barnet, I did not know it until yesterday, or I should have thanked you long and long ago!"

"I had offended you — just a trifle — at the time, I think?" said Barnet smiling, "and it was best that you should not know."

"Yes, yes," she returned hastily. "Don't allude to that; it is past and over, and we will let it be. The house is finished almost, is it not? How beautiful it will look when the evergreens are grown! Do you call the style Palladian, Mr. Barnet?"

"I — really don't quite know what it is. Yes, it must be Palladian, certainly. But I'll ask Jones, the architect; for, to tell the truth, I had not thought much about the style: I had nothing to do with choosing it, I am sorry to say."

She would not let him harp on this gloomy refrain, and talked on bright matters till she said, producing a small roll of paper which he had noticed in her hand all the while, "Mr. Downe wished me to bring you this revised drawing of the late Mrs. Downe's tomb, which the architect has just sent him. He would like you to look it over."

The children came up with their hoops, and she went off with them down the harbour-road as usual. Barnet had been glad to get those words of thanks; he had been thinking for many months that he would like her to know of his share in finding her a home, such as it was; and what he could not do for himself, Downe had now kindly done for him. He returned to his desolate house with a lighter tread; though in reason he hardly knew why his tread should be light.

On examining the drawing, Barnet found that, instead of the vast altar-tomb and canopy Downe had determined on at their last meeting, it was to be a more modest memorial even than had been suggested by the architect; a coped tomb of good solid construction, with no useless elaboration at all. Barnet was truly glad to see that Downe had come to reason of his own accord; and he returned the drawing with a note of approval.

He followed up the house-work as before, and as he walked up and down the rooms, occasionally gazing from the windows over the bulging green hills and the quiet harbour that lay between them, he murmured words and fragments of words, which, if listened to, would have revealed all the secrets of his existence. Whatever his reason in going there, Lucy did not call

213

again: the walk to the shore seemed to be abandoned: he must have thought it as well for both that it should be so, for he did not go anywhere out of his accustomed ways to endeavour to discover her.

VIII

The winter and the spring had passed, and the house was complete. It was a fine morning in the early part of June, and Barnet, though not in the habit of rising early, had taken a long walk before breakfast; returning by way of the new building. A sufficiently exciting cause of his restlessness to-day might have been the intelligence which had reached him the night before, that Lucy Savile was going to India after all, and notwithstanding the representations of her friends that such a journey was unadvisable in many ways for an unpractised girl, unless some more definite advantage lay at the end of it than she could show to be the case. Barnet's walk up the slope to the building betrayed that he was in a dissatisfied mood. He hardly saw that the dewy time of day lent an unusual freshness to the bushes and trees which had so recently put on their summer habit of heavy leafage, and made his newly-laid lawn look as well-established as an old manorial meadow. The house had been so adroitly placed between six tall elms which were growing on the site beforehand, that they seemed like real ancestral trees; and the rooks, young and old, cawed melodiously to their visitor.

The door was not locked, and he entered. No workmen appeared to be present, and he walked from sunny window to sunny window of the empty rooms, with a sense of seclusion which might have been very pleasant but for the antecedent knowledge that his almost paternal care of Lucy Savile was to be thrown away by her wilfulness. Footsteps echoed through an adjoining room; and, bending his eyes in that direction, he perceived Mr. Jones, the architect. He had come to look over the building before giving the contractor his final certificate. They walked over the house together. Everything was finished except the papering: there were the latest improvements of the period in bell-hanging, ventilating, smoke jacks, firegrates, and French windows. The business was soon ended, and Jones, having directed Barnet's attention to a book of wallpaper patterns which lay on a bench for his choice, was leaving to keep another engagement, when Barnet said, "Is the tomb finished yet for Mrs. Downe?"

"Well — yes: it is at last," said the architect, coming back and speaking as if he were in a mood to make a confidence. "I have had no end of trouble in the matter, and, to tell the truth, I am heartily glad it is over."

Barnet expressed his surprise. "I thought poor Downe had given up those extravagant notions of his? then he has gone back to the altar and canopy after all? Well, he is to be excused, poor fellow!"

"Oh, no — he has not at all gone back to them — quite the reverse," Jones hastened to say. "He has so reduced design after design, that the whole thing has been nothing but waste labour for me; till in the end it has become a common headstone, which a mason put up in half a day."

"A common headstone?" said Barnet.

"Yes. I held out for some time for the addition of a foot-stone at least. But he said, 'Oh, no — he couldn't afford it.'"

"Ah, well — his family is growing up, poor fellow, and his expenses are getting serious."

"Yes, exactly," said Jones, as if the subject were none of his. And again directing Barnet's attention to the wall-papers, the bustling architect left him to keep some other engagement.

"A common headstone," murmured Barnet, left again to himself. He mused a minute or two, and next began looking over and selecting from the patterns; but had not long been engaged in the work when he heard another footstep on the gravel without, and somebody enter the open porch.

Barnet went to the door — it was his manservant in search of him.

"I have been trying for some time to find you, sir," he said. "This letter has come by the post, and it is marked immediate. And there's this one from Mr. Downe, who called just now wanting to see you." He searched his pocket for the second.

Barnet took the first letter — it had a black border, and bore the London postmark. It was not in his wife's handwriting, or in that of any person he knew; but conjecture soon ceased as he read the page, wherein he was briefly informed that Mrs. Barnet had died suddenly on the previous day, at the furnished villa she had occupied near London.

Barnet looked vaguely round the empty hall, at the blank walls, out of the doorway. Drawing a long palpitating breath, and with eyes downcast, he turned and climbed the stairs slowly, like a man who doubted their stability. The fact of his wife having, as it were, died once already, and lived on again, had entirely dislodged the possibility of her actual death from his conjecture. He went to the landing, leant over the balusters, and after a reverie, of whose duration he had but the faintest notion, turned to the window and stretched his gaze to the cottage further down the road, which was visible from his landing, and from which Lucy still walked to the solicitor's house by a cross path. The faint words that came from his moving lips were simply, "At last!"

Then, almost involuntarily, Barnet fell down on his knees and murmured some incoherent words of thanksgiving. Surely his virtue in restoring his wife to life had been rewarded! But, as if the impulse struck uneasily on his conscience, he quickly rose, brushed the dust from his trousers, and set himself to think of his next movements. He could not start for London for some hours; and as he had no preparations to make that could not be made in half-an-hour, he mechanically descended and resumed his occupation of turning over the wall-papers. They had all got brighter for him, those papers. It was all changed — who would sit in the rooms that they were to line? He went on to muse upon Lucy's conduct in so frequently coming to the house with the children; her occasional blush in speaking to him; her evident interest in him. What woman can in the long run avoid being interested in a man whom she knows to be devoted to her? If human solicitation could ever effect anything, there should be no going to India for Lucy now. All the papers previously chosen seemed wrong in their shades, and he began from the beginning to choose again.

While entering on the task he heard a forced "Ahem!" from without the porch, evidently uttered to attract his attention, and footsteps again advancing to the door. His man, whom he had quite forgotten in his mental turmoil, was still waiting there.

"I beg your pardon, sir," the man said from round the doorway; "but here's the note from Mr. Downe that you didn't take. He called just after you went out, and as he couldn't wait, he wrote this on your study-table."

He handed in the letter — no black-bordered one now, but a practical-looking note in the well-known writing of the solicitor.

"Dear Barnet" — it ran — "Perhaps you will be prepared for the information I am about to give-that Lucy Savile and myself are going to he married this morning. I have hitherto said nothing as to my intention to any of my friends, for reasons which I am sure you will fully appreciate. The crisis has been brought about by her expressing her intention to join her brother in India. I then discovered that I could not do without her.

"It is to be quite a private wedding; but it is my particular wish that you come down here quietly at ten, and go to church with us; it will add greatly to the pleasure I shall experience in the ceremony, and, I believe, to Lucy's also. I have called on you very early to make the request, in the belief that I should find you at home; but you are beforehand with me in your early rising.   "Yours sincerely,
                    C. DOWNE."

"Need I wait, sir?" said the servant after a dead silence.

"That will do, William. No answer," said Barnet calmly.

When the man had gone Barnet re-read the letter. Turning eventually to the wall-papers, which he had been at such pains to select, he deliberately tore them into halves and quarters, and threw them into the empty fireplace. Then he went out of the house, locked the door, and stood in the front awhile. Instead of returning into the town, he went down the harbour-road and thoughtfully lingered about by the sea, near the spot where the body of Downe's late wife had been found and brought ashore.

Barnet was a man with a rich capacity for misery, and there is no doubt that he exercised it to its fullest extent now. The events that had, as it were, dashed themselves together into one half-hour of this day showed that curious refinement of cruelty in their arrangement which often proceeds from the bosom of the whimsical god at other times known as blind Circumstance. That his few minutes of hope, between the reading of the first and second letters, had carried him to extraordinary heights of rapture was proved by the immensity of his suffering now. The sun blazing into his face would have shown a close watcher that a horizontal line, which had never been seen before, but which was never to be gone thereafter, was somehow gradually forming itself in the smooth of his forehead. His eyes, of a light hazel, had a curious look which can only be described by the word bruised; the sorrow that looked from them being largely mixed with the surprise of a man taken unawares.

The secondary particulars of his present position, too, were odd enough, though for some time they appeared to engage little of his attention. Not a soul in the town knew, as yet, of his wife's death; and he almost owed Downe the kindness of not publishing it till the day was over: the conjuncture, taken with that which had accompanied the death of Mrs. Downe, being so singular as to be quite sufficient to darken the pleasure of the impressionable solicitor to a cruel extent, if made known to him. But as Barnet could not set out on his journey to London, where his wife lay, for some hours (there being at this date no railway within a distance of many miles), no great reason existed why he should leave the town.

Impulse in all its forms characterised Barnet, and when he heard the distant clock strike the hour of ten his feet began to carry him up the harbour-road with the manner of a man who must do something to bring himself to life. He passed Lucy Savile's old house, his own new one, and came in view of the church. Now he gave a perceptible start, and his mechanical condition went away. Before the church gate were a couple of carriages, and Barnet then could perceive that the marriage between Downe and Lucy was at that moment being solemnized within. A feeling of sudden proud self-confidence, an indocile wish to walk unmoved in spite of grim environments, plainly possessed him, and when he reached the wicket-gate he turned in without apparent effort. Pacing up the paved foot-way he entered the church and stood for awhile in the nave passage. A group of people was standing round the vestry door; Barnet advanced through these and stepped into the vestry.

There they were, busily signing their names. Seeing Downe about to look round, Barnet averted his somewhat disturbed face for a second or two; when he turned again front to front he was calm and quite smiling: it was a creditable triumph over himself, and deserved to be remembered in his native town. He greeted Downe heartily, offering his congratulations.

It seemed as if Barnet expected a half-guilty look upon Lucy's face; but no, save the natural flush and flurry engendered by the service just performed, there was nothing whatever in her bearing which showed a disturbed mind: her grey-brown eyes carried in them now as at other times the well-known expression of common-sensed rectitude which never went so far as to touch on hardness. She shook hands with him, and Downe said warmly, "I wish you could have come sooner: I called on purpose to ask you. You'll drive back with us now?"

"No, no," said Barnet; "I am not at all prepared; but I thought I would look in upon you for a moment, even though I had not time to go home and dress. I'll stand back and see you pass out, and observe the effect of the spectacle upon myself as one of the public."

Then Lucy and her husband laughed, and Barnet laughed and retired; and the quiet little party went gliding down the nave and towards the porch, Lucy's new silk dress sweeping with a smart rustle round the base-mouldings of the ancient font, and Downe's little daughters following in a state of round-eyed interest in their position, and that of Lucy, their teacher and friend.

So Downe was comforted after his Emily's death, which had taken place twelve months, two weeks, and three days before that time.

When the two flys had driven off and the spectators had vanished, Barnet followed to the door, and went out into the sun. He took no more trouble to preserve a spruce exterior; his step was unequal, hesitating, almost convulsive; and the slight changes of colour which went on in his face seemed refracted from some inward flame. In the churchyard he became pale as a summer cloud, and finding it not easy to proceed he sat down on one of the tombstones and supported his head with his hand.

Hard by was a sexton filling up a grave which he had not found time to finish on the previous evening. Observing Barnet, he went up to him, and recognising him said, "Shall I help you home, sir?"

"Oh, no, thank you," said Barnet, rousing himself and standing up. The sexton returned to his grave, followed by Barnet, who, after watching him awhile, stepped into the grave, now nearly filled, and helped to tread in the earth.

The sexton apparently thought his conduct a little singular, but he made no observation, and when the grave was full,

Barnet suddenly stopped, looked far away, and with a decided step proceeded to the gate and vanished. The sexton rested on his shovel, and looked after him for a few moments, and then began banking up the mound.

In those short minutes of treading in the dead man Barnet had formed a design, but what it was the inhabitants of that town did not for some long time imagine. He went home, wrote several letters of business, called on his lawyer, an old man of the same place who had been the legal adviser of Barnet's father before him, and during the evening overhauled a large quantity of letters and other documents in his possession. By eleven o'clock the heap of papers in and before Barnet's grate had reached formidable dimensions, and he began to burn them. This, owing to their quantity, it was not so easy to do as he had expected, and he sat long into the night to complete the task.

The next morning Barnet departed for London, leaving a note for Downe to inform him of Mrs. Barnet's sudden death, and that he was gone to bury her; but when a thrice-sufficient time for that purpose had elapsed, he was not seen again in his accustomed walks, or in his new house, or in his old one. He was gone for good, nobody knew whither. It was soon discovered that he had empowered his lawyer to dispose of all his property, real and personal, in the borough, and pay in the proceeds to the account of an unknown person at one of the large London banks. The person was by some supposed to be himself under an assumed name; but few, if any, had certain knowledge of that fact.

The elegant new residence was sold with the rest of his possessions; and its purchaser was no other than Downe, now a thriving man in the borough, and one whose growing family and new wife required more roomy accommodation than was afforded by the little house up the narrow side street. Barnet's old habitation was bought by the trustees of the Congregational Baptist body in that town, who pulled down the time-honoured dwelling and built a new chapel on its site. By the time the last hour of that, to Barnet, eventful year had chimed, every vestige of him had disappeared from the precincts of his native place; and the name became extinct in the borough of Port-Bredy, after having been a living force therein for more than two hundred years.

IX

Twenty-one years and six months do not pass without setting a mark even upon durable stone and triple brass: upon humanity such a period works nothing less than transformation. In Barnet's old birthplace vivacious young children with bones like india-rubber had grown up to be stable men and women, men and women had dried in the skin, stiffened, withered, and sunk into decrepitude; while selections from every class had been consigned to the outlying cemetery. Of inorganic differences the greatest was that a railway had invaded the town, tying it on to a main line at a junction a dozen miles off. Barnet's house on the harbour-road, once so insistently new, had acquired a respectable mellowness, with ivy, Virginia creepers, lichens, damp patches, and even constitutional infirmities of its own like its elder fellows. Its architecture, once so very improved and modern, had already become stale in style, without having reached the dignity of being old-fashioned. Trees about the harbour-road had increased in circumference or disappeared under the saw; while the church had had such a tremendous practical joke played upon it by some facetious restorer or other as to be scarce recognizable

228

by its dearest old friends.

During this long interval George Barnet had never once been seen or heard of in the town of his fathers.

It was the evening of a market-day, and some half-dozen middle-aged farmers and dairymen were lounging round the bar of the Black-Bull Hotel, occasionally dropping a remark to each other, and less frequently to the two barmaids who stood within the pewter-topped counter in a perfunctory attitude of attention, these latter sighing and making a private observation to one another at odd intervals, on more interesting experiences than the present.

"Days get shorter," said one of the dairymen, as he looked towards the street, and noticed that the lamplighter was passing by.

The farmers merely acknowledged by their countenances the propriety of this remark, and finding that nobody else spoke, one of the barmaids said "yes," in a tone of painful duty.

"Come fair-day we shall have to light up before we start for home-along."

"That's true," his neighbour conceded, with a gaze of blankness.

"And after that we shan't see much further difference, all's winter."

The rest were not unwilling to go even so far as this.

The barmaid sighed again, and raised one of her hands from the counter on which they rested to scratch the smallest surface of her face with the smallest of her fingers. She looked towards the door, and presently remarked, "I think I hear the 'bus coming in from station."

The eyes of the dairymen and farmers turned to the glass door dividing the hall from the porch, and in a minute or two the omnibus drew up outside. Then there was a lumbering down of luggage, and then a man came into the hall, followed by a porter with a portmanteau on his poll, which he deposited on a bench.

The stranger was an elderly person, with curly ashen-white hair, a deeply-creviced outer corner to each eyelid, and a countenance baked by innumerable suns to the colour of terra-cotta, its hue and that of his hair contrasting like heat and cold respectively. He walked meditatively and gently, like one who was fearful of disturbing his own mental equilibrium. But whatever lay at the bottom of his breast, had evidently made him so accustomed to its situation there that it caused him little practical inconvenience.

He paused in silence while, with his dubious eyes fixed on the barmaids, he seemed to consider himself. In a moment or two he addressed them, and asked to be accommodated for the night. As he waited he looked curiously round the hall, but said nothing. As soon as invited he disappeared up the staircase, preceded by a chambermaid and candle, and followed by a lad with his trunk. Not a soul had recognised him.

A quarter of an hour later, when the farmers and dairymen had driven off to their homesteads in the country, he came downstairs, took a biscuit and one glass of wine, and walked out into the town, where the radiance from the shop-windows had grown so in volume of late years as to flood with cheerfulness every standing cart, barrow, stall, and idler that occupied the wayside, whether shabby or genteel. His chief interest at present seemed to lie in the names painted over the shop-fronts and on doorways, as far as they were visible; these now differed to an ominous extent from what they had been one-and-twenty years before.

The traveller passed on till he came to the bookseller's, where he looked in through the glass door. A fresh-faced young man was standing behind the counter, otherwise the shop was empty. The grey-haired observer entered, asked for some periodical by way of paying for admission, and with his elbow on the counter began to turn over the pages he had bought, though that he read nothing was obvious.

At length he said, "Is old Mr. Watkins still alive?" in a voice which had a curious youthful cadence in it even now.

"My father is dead, sir," said the young man.

"Ah, I am sorry to hear it," said the stranger. "But it is so many years since I last visited this town that I could hardly expect it should be otherwise." After a short silence he continued, "And is the firm of Barnet, Browse, and Company still in existence? they used to be large flax-merchants and twine-spinners here?"

"The firm is still going on, sir, but they have dropped the name of Barnet. I believe that was a sort of fancy name — at least, I never knew of any living Barnet. 'Tis now Browse and Co."

"And does Andrew Jones still keep on as architect?"

"He's dead, sir."

"And the vicar of St. Mary's — Mr. Melrose?"

"He's been dead a great many years."

"Dear me!" He paused yet longer, and cleared his voice. "Is Mr. Downe, the solicitor, still in practice?"

"No, sir, he's dead. He died about seven years ago."

Here it was a longer silence still; and an attentive observer would have noticed that the paper in the stranger's hand increased its imperceptible tremor to a visible shake. That grey-haired gentleman noticed it himself and rested the paper on the counter. "Is *Mrs.* Downe still alive?" he asked, closing his lips firmly as soon as the words were out of his mouth, and dropping his eyes.

"Yes, sir, she's alive and well. She's living at the old place."

"In East Street?"

"Oh, no; at Château Ringdale. I believe it has been in the family for some generations."

"She lives with her children, perhaps?"

"No; she has no children of her own. There were some Miss Downes; I think they were Mr. Downe's daughters by a former wife; but they are married and living in other parts of the town. Mrs.

Downe lives alone."

"Quite alone?"

"Yes, sir; quite alone."

The newly-arrived gentleman went back to the hotel and dined; after which he made some change in his dress, shaved back his beard to the fashion that had prevailed twenty years earlier, when he was young and interesting, and once more emerging, bent his steps in the direction of the harbour-road. Just before getting to the point where the pavement ceased and the houses isolated themselves, he overtook a shambling, stooping, unshaven man, who at first sight appeared like a professional tramp, his shoulders having a perceptible greasiness as they passed under the gas-light. Each pedestrian momentarily turned and regarded the other, and the tramp-like gentleman started back.

"Good — why — is that Mr. Barnet? 'Tis Mr. Barnet, surely!"

"Yes; and you are Charlson?"

"Yes — ah — you notice my appearance. The Fates have rather ill-used me. By the by, that fifty pounds. I never paid it, did I? . . . But I was not ungrateful!" Here the stooping man laid one hand emphatically on the palm of the other. "I gave you a chance, Mr. George Barnet, which many men would have thought full value received — the chance to marry your Lucy. As far as the world was concerned, your wife was a *drowned woman,* hey?"

"Heaven forbid all that, Charlson!"

"Well, well, 'twas a wrong way of showing gratitude, I suppose. And now a drop of something to drink for old acquaintance sake! And Mr. Barnet, she's again free — there's a chance now if you care for it — ha, ha!" And the speaker pushed his tongue into his hollow cheek and slanted his eye in the old fashion.

"I know all," said Barnet, quickly; and slipping a small present into the hands of the needy, saddening man, he stepped ahead and was soon in the outskirts of the town.

He reached the harbour-road, and paused before the entrance to a well-known house. It was so highly bosomed in trees and shrubs planted since the erection of the building that one would scarcely have recognised the spot as that which had been a mere neglected slope till chosen as a site for a dwelling. He opened the swing-gate, closed it noiselessly, and gently moved into the semicircular drive, which remained exactly as it had been marked out by Barnet on the morning when Lucy

Savile ran to thank him for procuring her the post of governess to Downe's children. But the growth of trees and bushes which revealed itself at every step was beyond all expectation; sun-proof and moon-proof bowers vaulted the walks, and the walls of the house were uniformly bearded with creeping plants as high as the first-floor windows.

After lingering for a few minutes in the dusk of the bending boughs, the visitor rang the door-bell, and on the servant appearing, he announced himself as "an old friend of Mrs. Downe's."

The hall was lighted, but not brightly, the gas being turned low, as if visitors were rare. There was a stagnation in the dwelling: it seemed to be waiting. Could it really be waiting for him? The partitions which had been probed by Barnet's walking-stick when the mortar was green, were now quite brown with the antiquity of their varnish, and the ornamental woodwork of the staircase, which had glistened with a pale yellow newness when first erected, was now of a rich wine-colour. During the servant's absence the following colloquy could be dimly heard through the nearly closed door of the drawing-room.

"He didn't give his name?"

"He only said 'an old friend,' ma'am."

"What kind of gentleman is he?"

"A staidish gentleman, with grey hair."

The voice of the second speaker seemed to affect the listener greatly. After a pause, the lady said, "Very well, I will see him."

And the stranger was shown in face to face with the Lucy who had once been Lucy Savile. The round cheek of that formerly young lady had, of course, alarmingly flattened its curve in her modern representative; a pervasive greyness overspread her once dark brown hair, like morning rime on heather. The parting down the middle was wide and jagged; once it had been a thin white line, a narrow crevice between two high banks of shade. But there was still enough left to form a handsome knob behind, and some curls beneath inwrought with a few hairs like silver wires were very becoming. In her eyes the only modification was that their originally mild rectitude of expression had become a little more stringent than heretofore. Yet she was still girlish — a girl who had been gratuitously weighted by destiny with a burden of five-and-forty years instead of her proper twenty.

"Lucy, don't you know me?" he said, when the servant had closed the door.

"I knew you the instant I saw you!" she returned cheerfully. "I don't know why, but I always thought you would come back to your old town again."

She gave him her hand, and then they sat down. "They said you were dead," continued Lucy, "but I never thought so. We should have heard of it for certain if you had been."

"It is a very long time since we met."

"Yes; what you must have seen, Mr. Barnet, in all these roving years, in comparison with what I have seen in this quiet place!" Her face grew more serious. "You know my husband has been dead a long time? I am a lonely old woman now, considering what I have been; though Mr. Downe's daughters — all married — manage to keep me pretty cheerful."

"And I am a lonely old man, and have been any time these twenty years."

"But where have you kept yourself? And why did you go off so mysteriously?"

"Well, Lucy, I have kept myself a little in America, and a little in Australia, a little in India, a little at the Cape, and so on; I have not stayed in any place for a long time, as it seems to me, and yet more than twenty years have flown. But when people get to my age two years go like one! — Your second question, why did I go away so mysteriously, is surely not necessary. You guessed why, didn't you?"

"No, I never once guessed," she said simply; "nor did Charles, nor did anybody, as far as I know."

"Well, indeed! Now think it over again, and then look at me, and say if you can't guess?"

She looked him in the face with an inquiring smile. "Surely not because of me?" she said, pausing at the commencement of surprise.

Barnet nodded, and smiled again; but his smile was sadder than hers.

"Because I married Charles?" she asked.

"Yes; solely because you married him on the day I was free to ask you to marry me. My wife died four-and-twenty hours before you went to church with Downe. The fixing of my journey at that particular moment was because of her funeral; but once away, I knew I should have no inducement to come back, and took my steps accordingly."

Her face assumed an aspect of gentle reflection, and she looked up and down his form with great interest in her eyes. "I never thought of it!" she said. "I knew, of course, that you had once implied some warmth of feeling towards me, but I concluded that it passed off. And I have always been under the impression that your wife was alive at the time of my marriage. Was it not stupid of me! — But you will have some tea or something? I have never dined late, you know, since my husband's death. I have got into the way of making a regular meal of tea. You will have some tea with me, will you not?"

The travelled man assented quite readily, and tea was brought in. They sat and chatted over the tray, regardless of the flying hour. "Well, well!" said Barnet, presently, as for the first time he leisurely surveyed the room; "how like it all is, and yet how different! Just where your piano stands was a board on a couple of trestles, bearing the patterns of wall-papers, when I was last here. I was choosing them — standing in this way, as it might be. Then my servant came in at the door, and handed me a note, so. It was from Downe, and announced that you were just going to be married to him. I chose no more wall-papers — tore up all those I had selected, and left the house. I never entered it again till now."

"Ah, at last I understand it all," she murmured.

They had both risen and gone to the fireplace. The mantel came almost on a level with her shoulder, which gently rested against it, and Barnet laid his hand upon the shelf close beside her shoulder. "Lucy," he said, "better late than never. Will you marry me now?"

She started back, and the surprise which was so obvious in her wrought even greater surprise in him that it should be so. It was difficult to believe that she had been quite blind to the situation, and yet all reason and common sense went to prove that she was not acting.

"You take me quite unawares by such a question!" she said, with a forced laugh of uneasiness. It was the first time she had shown any embarrassment at all. "Why," she added, "I couldn't marry you for the world."

"Not after all this! Why not?"

"It is — I would — I really think I may say it — I would upon the whole rather marry you, Mr. Barnet, than any other man I have ever met, if I ever dreamed of marriage again. But I don't dream of it — it is quite out of my thoughts; I have not the least intention of marrying again."

"But — on my account — couldn't you alter your plans a little? Come!"

"Dear Mr. Barnet," she said with a little flutter, "I would on your account if on anybody's in existence. But you don't know in the least what it is you are asking — such an impracticable thing — I won't say ridiculous, of course, because I see that you are really in earnest, and earnestness is never ridiculous to my mind."

"Well, yes," said Barnet, more slowly, dropping her hand, which he had taken at the moment of pleading, "I am in earnest. The resolve, two months ago, at the Cape, to come back once more was, it is true, rather sudden, and as I see now, not well considered. But I am in earnest in asking."

"And I in declining. With all good feeling and all kindness, let me say that I am quite opposed to the idea of marrying a second time."

"Well, no harm has been done," he answered, with the same subdued and tender humorousness that he had shown on such occasions in early life. "If you really won't accept me, I must put up with it, I suppose." His eye fell on the clock as he spoke. "Had you any notion that it was so late?" he asked. "How absorbed I have been!"

She accompanied him to the hall, helped him to put on his overcoat, and let him out of the house herself.

242

"Good night," said Barnet, on the door-step, as the lamp shone in his face. "You are not offended with me?"

"Certainly not. Nor you with me?"

"I'll consider whether I am or not," he pleasantly replied. "Good night."

She watched him safely through the gate; and when his footsteps had died away upon the road, closed the door softly and returned to the room. Here the modest widow long pondered his speeches, with eyes dropped to an unusually low level. Barnet's urbanity under the blow of her refusal greatly impressed her. After having his long period of probation rendered useless by her decision, he had shown no anger, and had philosophically taken her words, as if he deserved no better ones. It was very gentlemanly of him, certainly; it was more than gentlemanly; it was heroic and grand. The more she meditated, the more she questioned the virtue of her conduct in checking him so peremptorily; and went to her bedroom in a mood of dissatisfaction. On looking in the glass, she was reminded that there was not so much remaining of her former beauty as to make his frank declaration an impulsive natural homage to her cheeks and eyes; it must undoubtedly have arisen from an old staunch feeling of his, deserving tenderest consideration. She recalled to her mind with much pleasure that he had told her he was staying at the Black-Bull Hotel; so that if, after waiting a day or two, he should not, in his modesty, call again, she might then send him a nice little note. To alter her views for the present was far from her intention; but she would allow herself to be induced to reconsider the case, as any generous woman ought to do.

The morrow came and passed, and Mr. Barnet did not drop in. At every knock, light youthful hues flew across her cheek; and she was abstracted in the presence of her other visitors. In the evening she walked about the house, not knowing what to do with herself; the conditions of existence seemed totally different from those which ruled only four-and-twenty short hours ago. What had been at first a tantalising elusive sentiment was getting acclimatised within her as a definite hope, and her person was so informed by that emotion that she might almost have stood as its emblematical representative by the time the clock struck ten. In short, an interest in Barnet precisely resembling that of her early youth led her present heart to belie her yesterday's words to him, and she longed to see him again.

The next day she walked out early, thinking she might meet him in the street. The growing beauty of her romance absorbed her and she went from the street to the fields, and from the fields to the shore without any consciousness of distance, till reminded by her weariness that she could go no further. He had nowhere appeared. In the evening she took a step which under the circumstances seemed justifiable; she wrote a note to him at the hotel, inviting him to tea with her at six precisely, and signing her note "Lucy."

In a quarter of an hour the messenger came back. Mr. Barnet had left the hotel early in the morning of the day before, but he had stated that he would probably return in the course of the week.

The note was sent back to be given to him immediately on his arrival.

There was no sign from the inn that this desired event had occurred, either on the next day or the day following. On both nights she had been restless, and had scarcely slept half-an-hour.

On the Saturday, putting off all diffidence, Lucy went herself to the Black-Bull, and questioned the staff closely.

Mr. Barnet had cursorily remarked when

leaving that he might return on the Thursday or Friday, but they were directed not to reserve a room for him unless he should write.

He had left no address.

Lucy sorrowfully took back her note, went home, and resolved to wait.

She did wait — years and years — but Barnet never reappeared.

April 1880.

Interlopers at the Knap

I

The north road from Casterbridge is tedious and lonely, especially in winter time. Along a part of its course it connects with Long-Ash Lane, a monotonous track without a village or hamlet for many miles, and with very seldom a turning. Unapprised wayfarers who are too old, or too young, or in other respects too weak for the distance to be traversed, but who, nevertheless, have to walk it, say, as they look wistfully ahead, "Once at the top of that hill, and I must surely see the end of Long-Ash Lane!" But they reach the hill-top, and Long-Ash Lane stretches in front as mercilessly as before.

Some few years ago a certain farmer was riding through this lane in the gloom of a winter evening. The farmer's friend, a dairyman, was riding beside him. A few paces in the rear rode the farmer's man.

All three were well horsed on strong, round-barrelled cobs; and to be well horsed was to be in better spirits about Long-Ash Lane than poor pedestrians could attain to during its passage.

But the farmer did not talk much to his friend as he rode along. The enterprise which had brought him there filled his mind; for in truth it was important. Not altogether so important was it, perhaps, when estimated by its value to society at large; but if the true measure of a deed be proportionate to the space it occupies in the heart of him who undertakes it, Farmer Charles Darton's business to-night could hold its own with the business of kings.

He was a large farmer. His turnover, as it is called, was probably thirty thousand pounds a year. He had a great many draught horses, a great many milch cows, and of sheep a multitude. This comfortable position was, however, none of his own making. It had been created by his father, a man of a very different stamp from the present representative of the line.

Darton, the father, had been a one-idea'd character, with a buttoned-up pocket and a chink-like eye brimming with commercial subtlety. In Darton the son, this trade subtlety had become transmuted into emotional, and the harshness had disappeared; he would have been called a sad man but for his constant care not to divide himself from lively friends by piping notes out of harmony with theirs. Contemplative, he allowed his mind to be a quiet meeting-place for memories and hopes. So that, naturally enough, since succeeding to the agricultural calling, and up to his present age of thirty-two, he had neither advanced nor receded as a capitalist — a stationary result which did not agitate one of his unambitious unstrategic nature, since he had all that he desired. The motive of his expedition to-night showed the same absence of anxious regard for number one.

The party rode on in the slow, safe trot proper to night-time and bad roads, Farmer Darton's head jigging rather unromantically up and down against the sky, and his motions being repeated with bolder emphasis by his friend Japheth Johns; while those of the latter were travestied in jerks still less softened by art in the person of the lad who attended them. A pair of whitish objects hung one on each side of the latter, bumping against him at each step, and still further spoiling the grace of his seat. On close inspection they might have been perceived to be open rush baskets — one containing a turkey, and the other some bottles of wine.

"D'ye feel ye can meet your fate like a man, neighbour Darton?" asked Johns, breaking a silence which had lasted while five-and-twenty hedgerow trees had glided by.

Mr. Darton with a half laugh murmured, "Ay — call it my fate! Hanging and wiving go by destiny." And then they were silent again.

The darkness thickened rapidly, at intervals shutting down on the land in a perceptible flap like the wave of a wing. The customary close of day was accelerated by a simultaneous blurring of the air. With the fall of night had come a mist just damp enough to incommode, but not sufficient to saturate them. Countrymen as they were — born, as may be said, with only an open door between them and the four seasons — they regarded the mist but as an added obscuration, and ignored its humid quality.

They were travelling in a direction that was enlivened by no modern current of traffic, the place of Darton's pilgrimage being an old-fashioned village — one of the Hintocks (several villages of that name, with a distinctive prefix or affix, lying thereabout) — where the people make the best cider and cider-wine in all Wessex, and where the dunghills smell of pomace instead of stable refuse as elsewhere. The lane was sometimes so narrow that the brambles of the hedge, which hung forward like anglers' rods over a stream, scratched their hats and hooked their whiskers as they passed. Yet this neglected lane had been a highway to Queen Elizabeth's subjects and the cavalcades of the past. Its day was over now, and its history as a national artery done for ever.

"Why I have decided to marry her," resumed Darton (in a measured musical voice of confidence which revealed a good deal of his composition) as he glanced round to see that the lad was not too near, "is not only that I like her, but that I can do no better, even from a fairly practical point of view. That I might ha' looked higher is possibly true, though it is really all nonsense. I have had experience enough in looking above me. 'No more superior women for me,' said I — you know when. Sally is a comely, independent, simple character, with no make-up about her, who'll think me as much a superior to her as I used to think — you know who I mean — was to me."

"Ay," said Johns. "However, I shouldn't call Sally Hall simple. Primary, because no Sally is; secondary, because if some could be this one wouldn't. 'Tis a wrong denomination to apply to a woman, Charles, and affects me, as your best man, like cold water. 'Tis like recommending a stage play by saying there's neither murder, villainy, nor harm of any sort in it, when that's what you've paid your half-crown to see."

"Well; may your opinion do you good. Mine's a different one." And turning the conversation from the philosophical to the practical, Darton expressed a hope that the said Sally had received what he'd sent on by the carrier that day.

Johns wanted to know what that was.

"It is a dress," said Darton. "Not exactly a wedding dress, though she may use it as one if she likes. It is rather serviceable than showy — suitable for the winter weather."

"Good," said Johns. "Serviceable is a wise word in a bridegroom. I commend 'ee, Charles."

"For," said Darton, "why should a woman dress up like a rope-dancer because she's going to do the most solemn deed of her life except dying?"

"Faith, why? But she will because she will, I suppose," said Dairyman Johns.

"H'm," said Darton.

The lane they followed had been nearly straight for several miles, but they now left it for a smaller one which after winding uncertainly for some distance forked into two. By night country roads are apt to reveal ungainly qualities which pass without observation during day; and though Darton had travelled this way before, he had not done so frequently, Sally having been wooed at the house of a relative near his own. He never remembered seeing at this spot a pair of alternative ways looking so equally probable as these two did now. Johns rode on a few steps.

"Don't be out of heart, sonny," he cried. "Here's a handpost. Ezra — come and climm this post, and tell us the way."

The lad dismounted, and jumped into the hedge where the post stood under a tree.

"Unstrap the baskets, or you'll smash up that wine!" cried Darton, as the young man began spasmodically to climb the post, baskets and all.

"Was there ever less head in a brainless world?" said Johns. "Here, simple Ezzy, I'll do it." He leapt off, and with much puffing climbed the post, striking a match when he reached the top, and moving the light along the arm, the lad standing and gazing at the spectacle.

"I have faced tantilisation these twenty years with a temper as mild as milk!" said Japheth; "but such things as this don't come short of devilry!" And flinging the match away, he slipped down to the ground.

"What's the matter?" asked Darton.

"Not a letter, sacred or heathen — not so much as would tell us the way to the town of Smokeyhole — ever I should sin to say it! Either the moss and mildew have eat away the words, or we have arrived in a land where the natyves have lost the art o' writing, and should ha' brought our compass like Christopher Columbus."

"Let us take the straightest road," said Darton placidly, "I sha'n't be sorry to get there — 'tis a tiresome ride. I would have driven if I had known."

"Nor I neither, sir," said Ezra. "These straps plough my shoulder like a zull. If 'tis much further to your lady's home, Maister Darton, I shall ask to be let carry half of these good things in my innerds — hee, hee!"

"Don't you be such a reforming radical,

Ezra," said Johns sternly. "Here, I'll take the turkey."

This being done, they went forward by the right-hand lane, which ascended a hill, the left winding away under a plantation. The pit-a-pat of their horses' hoofs lessened up the slope; and the ironical directing-post stood in solitude as before, holding out its blank arms to the raw breeze, which brought a snore from the wood as if Skrymir the Giant were sleeping there.

II

Three miles to the left of the travellers, along the road they had not followed, rose an old house with mullioned windows of Ham-hill stone, and chimneys of lavish solidity. It stood at the top of a slope beside King's-Hintock village-street, only a mile or two from King's-Hintock Court, yet quite shut away from that mansion and its precincts. Immediately in front of it grew a large syca-more-tree, whose bared roots formed a convenient staircase from the road below to the front door of the dwelling. Its situation gave the house what little distinctive name it possessed, namely, "The Knap." Some forty yards off a brook dribbled past, which, for its size, made a great deal of noise. At the back was a dairy barton, accessible for vehicles and live-stock by a side "drong." Thus much only of the character of the homestead could be divined out of doors at this shady evening-time.

But within there was plenty of light to see by, as plenty was construed at Hintock. Beside a Tudor fireplace, whose moulded four-centred arch was nearly hidden by a figured blue-cloth blower, were seated two women — mother and daughter — Mrs Hall, and Sarah, or Sally; for this was a part of the world where the latter modification had not as yet been effaced as a vulgarity by the march of intellect. The owner of the name was the young woman by whose means Mr. Darton proposed to put an end to his bachelor condition on the approaching day.

The mother's bereavement had been so long ago as not to leave much mark of its occurrence upon her now, either in face or clothes. She had resumed the mob-cap of her early married life, enlivening its whiteness by a few rose-du-Barry ribbons. Sally required no such aids to pinkness. Roseate good-nature lit up her gaze; her features showed curves of decision and judgment; and she might have been regarded without much mistake as a warm-hearted, quick-spirited, handsome girl.

She did most of the talking, her mother listening with a half absent air, as she picked up fragments of red-hot wood ember with the tongs, and piled them upon the brands. But the number of speeches that passed was very small in proportion to the meanings exchanged. Long experience together often enabled them to see the course of thought in each other's minds without a word being spoken. Behind them, in the centre of the room, the table was spread for supper, certain whiffs of air laden with fat vapours, which ever and anon entered from the kitchen, denoting its preparation there.

"The new gown he was going to send you stays about on the way like himself," Sally's mother was saying.

"Yes, not finished, I dare say," cried Sally independently. "Lord, I shouldn't be amazed if it didn't come at all! Young men make such kind promises when they are near you, and forget 'em when they go away. But he doesn't intend it as a wed-ding-gown — he gives it to me merely as a gown to wear when I like — a travelling dress is what it would be called by some. Come rathe or come late it don't much matter, as I have a dress of my own to fall back upon. But what time is it?"

She went to the family clock and opened the glass, for the hour was not otherwise discernible by night, and indeed at all times was rather a thing to be investigated than beheld, so much more wall than window was there in the apartment. "It is nearly eight," said she.

"Eight o'clock, and neither dress nor man," said Mrs. Hall.

"Mother, if you think to tantalise me by talking like that, you are much mistaken. Let him be as late as he will — or stay away altogether — I don't care," said Sally. But a tender minute quaver in the negation showed that there was something forced in that statement.

Mrs. Hall perceived it, and drily observed that she was not so sure about Sally not caring. "But perhaps you don't care so much as I do, after all," she said. "For I see what you don't, that it is a good and flourishing match for you; a very honourable offer in Mr. Darton. And I think I see a kind husband in him. So pray God 'twill go smooth, and wind up well."

Sally would not listen to misgivings. Of

course it would go smoothly, she asserted. "How you are up and down, mother!" she went on. "At this moment, whatever hinders him, we are not so anxious to see him as he is to be here, and his thought runs on before him, and settles down upon us like the star in the east. Hark!" she exclaimed, with a breath of relief, her eyes sparkling. "I heard something. Yes — here they are!"

The next moment her mother's slower ear also distinguished the familiar reverberation occasioned by footsteps clambering up the roots of the sycamore.

"Yes, it sounds like them at last," she said. "Well, it is not so very late after all, considering the distance."

The footfall ceased, and they arose, expecting a knock. They began to think it might have been, after all, some neighbouring villager under Bacchic influence, giving the centre of the road a wide berth, when their doubts were dispelled by the newcomer's entry into the passage. The door of the room was gently opened, and there appeared, not the pair of travellers with whom we have already made acquaintance, but a pale-faced man in the garb of extreme poverty — almost in rags.

"Oh, it's a tramp — gracious me!" said Sally, starting back.

His cheeks and eye-orbits were deep concaves — rather, it might be, from natural weakness of constitution than irregular living, though there were indications that he had led no careful life. He gazed at the two women fixedly for a moment; then with an abashed, humiliated demeanour, dropped his glance to the floor, and sank into a chair without uttering a word.

Sally was in advance of her mother, who had remained standing by the fire. She now tried to discern the visitor across the candles.

"Why — mother," said Sally faintly, turning back to Mrs. Hall. "It is Phil, from Australia!"

Mrs. Hall started, and grew pale, and a fit of coughing seized the man with the ragged clothes. "To come home like this!" she said. "Oh, Philip — are you ill?"

"No, no, mother," replied he, impatiently, as soon as he could speak.

"But for God's sake how do you come here — and just now too?"

"Well — I am here," said the man. "How it is I hardly know. I've come home, mother, because I was driven to it. Things were against me out there, and went from bad to worse."

"Then why didn't you let us know? —

260

you've not writ a line for the last two or three years."

The son admitted sadly that he had not. He said that he had hoped and thought he might fetch up again, and be able to send good news. Then he had been obliged to abandon that hope, and had finally come home from sheer necessity — previously to making a new start. "Yes, things are very bad with me," he repeated, perceiving their commiserating glances at his clothes.

They brought him nearer the fire, took his hat from his thin hand, which was so small and smooth as to show that his attempts to fetch up again had not been in a manual direction. His mother resumed her inquiries, and dubiously asked if he had chosen to come that particular night for any special reason.

For no reason, he told her. His arrival had been quite at random. Then Philip Hall looked round the room, and saw for the first time that the table was laid somewhat luxuriously, and for a larger number than themselves; and that an air of festivity pervaded their dress. He asked quickly what was going on.

"Sally is going to be married in a day or two," replied the mother; and she explained how Mr. Darton, Sally's intended husband, was coming there that night with the groomsman, Mr. Johns, and other details. "We thought it must be their step when we heard you," said Mrs. Hall.

The needy wanderer looked again on the floor. "I see — I see," he murmured. "Why, indeed, should I have come to-night! Such folk as I are not wanted here at these times, naturally. And I have no business here — spoiling other people's happiness."

"Phil," said his mother, with a tear in her eye, but with a thinness of lip and severity of manner which were presumably not more than past events justified, "since you speak like that to me, I'll speak honestly to you. For these three years you have taken no thought for us. You left home with a good supply of money, and strength and education, and you ought to have made good use of it all. But you come back like a beggar; and that you come in a very awkward time for us cannot be denied. Your return to-night may do us much harm. But mind — you are welcome to this home as long as it is mine. I don't wish to turn you adrift. We will make the best of a bad job; and I hope you are not seriously ill?"

"Oh, no. I have only this infernal cough."

She looked at him anxiously. "I think you had better go to bed at once," she said.

"Well — I shall be out of the way there," said the son, wearily. "Having ruined myself, don't let me ruin you by being seen in these togs, for Heaven's sake. Who do you say Sally is going to be married to — a Farmer Darton?"

"Yes — a gentleman-farmer — quite a wealthy man. Far better in station than she could have expected. It is a good thing, altogether."

"Well done, little Sal!" said her brother, brightening and looking up at her with a smile. "I ought to have written; but perhaps I have thought of you all the more. But let me get out of sight. I would rather go and jump into the river than be seen here. But have you anything I can drink? I am confoundedly thirsty with my long tramp."

"Yes, yes; we will bring something up stairs to you," said Sally, with grief in her face.

"Ay, that will do nicely. But, Sally and mother —" He stopped, and they waited. "Mother, I have not told you all," he resumed slowly, still looking on the floor between his knees. "Sad as what you see of me is, there's worse behind."

His mother gazed upon him in grieved suspense, and Sally went and leant upon the bureau, listening for every sound, and sighing. Suddenly she turned round, saying, "Let them come, I don't care! Philip, tell the worst, and take your time."

"Well then," said the unhappy Phil, "I am not the only one in this mess. Would to Heaven I were! But —"

"O, Phil!"

"I have a wife as destitute as I."

"A wife?" said his mother.

"Unhappily."

"A wife! Yes, that is the way with sons!"

"And besides —" said he.

"Besides! O Philip, surely —"

"I have two little children."

"Wife and children!" whispered Mrs. Hall, sinking down confounded.

"Poor little things!" said Sally, involuntarily.

His mother turned again to him. "I suppose these helpless beings are left in Australia?"

"No. They are in England."

"Well, I can only hope you've left them in a respectable place."

"I have not left them at all. They are here — within a few yards of us. In short, they are in the stable."

"Where?"

"In the stable. I did not like to bring them indoors till I had seen you, mother, and broken the bad news a bit to you. They were very tired, and are resting out there on some straw."

Mrs. Hall's fortitude visibly broke down. She had been brought up not without refinement, and was even more moved by such a collapse of genteel aims as this than a substantial dairyman's widow would in ordinary have been moved. "Well, it must be borne," she said, in a low voice, with her hands tightly joined. "A starving son, a starving wife, starving children. Let it be. But why is this come to us now, to-day, to-night! Could no other misfortune happen to helpless women than this, which will quite upset my poor girl's chance of a happy life? Why have you done us this wrong, Philip? What respectable man will come here, and marry open-eyed into a family of vagabonds!"

"Nonsense, mother!" said Sally, vehemently, while her face flushed. "Charley isn't the man to desert me! But if he should be, and won't marry me because Phil's come, let him go and marry elsewhere. I won't be ashamed of my own flesh and blood for any man in England — not I!" And then Sally turned away and burst into tears.

"Wait till you are twenty years older and you will tell a different tale," replied her mother.

The son stood up. "Mother," he said bitterly, "as I have come, so I will go. All I ask of you is that you will allow me and mine to lie in your stable to-night. I give you my word that we'll be gone by break of day, and trouble you no further."

Mrs. Hall, the mother, changed at that. "Oh, no," she answered, hastily, "never shall it be said that I sent any of my own family from my door. Bring 'em in, Philip, or take me out to them."

"We will put 'em all into the large bedroom," said Sally, brightening, "and make up a large fire. Let's go and help them in, and call Rebekah." (Rebekah was the woman who assisted at the dairy and housework; she lived in a cottage hard by with her husband who attended to the cows.)

Sally went to fetch a lantern from the back kitchen, but her brother said, "You won't want a light. I lit the lantern that was hanging there."

"What must we call your wife?" asked Mrs. Hall.

"Helena," said Philip.

With shawls over their heads they proceeded towards the back door.

"One minute before you go," interrupted Philip. "I — I haven't confessed all."

"Then Heaven help us!" said Mrs. Hall, pushing to the door and clasping her hands in calm despair.

"We passed through Evershead as we came," he continued, "and I just looked in at the 'Sow-and-Acorn' to see if old Mike still kept on there as usual. The carrier had come in from Sherton Abbas at that moment, and guessing that I was bound for this place — for I think he knew me — he asked me to bring on a dressmaker's parcel for Sally that was marked 'immediate.' My wife had walked on with the children. 'Twas a flimsy parcel, and the paper was torn, and I found on looking at it that it was a thick warm gown. I didn't wish you to see poor Helena in a shabby state. I was ashamed that you should — 'twas not what she was born to. I untied the parcel in the road, took it on to her where she was waiting in the Lower Barn, and told her I had managed to get it for her, and that she was to ask no question. She, poor thing, must have supposed I obtained it on trust, through having reached a place where I was known, for she put it on gladly enough. She has it on now. Sally has other gowns, I dare say."

Sally looked at her mother, speechless.

"You have others, I dare say," repeated Phil, with a sick man's impatience. "I thought to myself, 'Better Sally cry than Helena freeze.' Well, is the dress of great consequence? 'Twas nothing very ornamental, as far as I could see."

"No — no; not of consequence," returned Sally, sadly, adding in a gentle voice, "You will not mind if I lend her another instead of that one, will you?"

Philip's agitation at the confession had brought on another attack of the cough, which seemed to shake him to pieces. He was so obviously unfit to sit in a chair that they helped him up stairs at once; and having hastily given him a cordial and kindled the bedroom fire, they descended to fetch their unhappy new relations.

III

It was with strange feelings that the girl and her mother, lately so cheerful, passed out of the back door into the open air of the barton, laden with hay scents and the herby breath of cows. A fine sleet had begun to fall, and they trotted across the yard quickly. The stable door was open; a light shone from it — from the lantern which always hung there, and which Philip had lighted, as he said. Softly nearing the door, Mrs. Hall pronounced the name "Helena?"

There was no answer for the moment. Looking in she was taken by surprise. Two people appeared before her. For one, instead of the drabbish woman she had expected, Mrs. Hall saw a pale, dark-eyed, lady-like creature, whose personality ruled her attire rather than was ruled by it. She was in a new and handsome gown, Sally's own, and an old bonnet. She was standing up, agitated; her hand was held by her companion — none else than Sally's affianced, Farmer Charles Darton, upon whose fine figure the pale stranger's eyes were fixed, as his were fixed upon her. His other hand held the rein of his horse, which was standing saddled as if just led in.

At sight of Mrs. Hall they both turned, looking at her in a way neither quite conscious nor unconscious, and without seeming to recollect that words were necessary as a solution to the scene. In another moment Sally entered also, when

Mr. Darton dropped his companion's hand, led the horse aside, and came to greet his betrothed and Mrs. Hall.

"Ah!" he said, smiling — with something like forced composure — "this is a round-about way of arriving you will say, my dear Mrs. Hall. But we lost our way, which made us late. I saw a light here, and led in my horse at once — my friend Johns and my man have gone onward to the little inn with theirs, not to crowd you too much. No sooner had I entered than I saw that this lady had taken temporary shelter here — and found I was intruding."

"She is my daughter-in-law," said Mrs. Hall, calmly. "My son, too, is in the house, but he has gone to bed unwell."

Sally had stood staring wonderingly at the scene until this moment, hardly recognising Darton's shake of the hand. The spell that bound her was broken by her perceiving the two little children seated on a heap of hay. She suddenly went forward, spoke to them, and took one on her arm and the other in her hand.

"And two children?" said Mr. Darton, showing thus that he had not been there long enough as yet to understand the situation.

"My grandchildren," said Mrs. Hall,

with as much affected ease as before.

Philip Hall's wife, in spite of this interruption to her first rencounter, seemed scarcely so much affected by it as to feel any one's presence in addition to Mr. Darton's. However, arousing herself by a quick reflection, she threw a sudden critical glance of her sad eyes upon Mrs. Hall; and, apparently finding her satisfactory, advanced to her in a meek initiative. Then Sally and the stranger spoke some friendly words to each other, and Sally went on with the children into the house. Mrs. Hall and Helena followed, and Mr. Darton followed these, looking at Helena's dress and outline, and listening to her voice like a man in a dream.

By the time the others reached the house Sally had already gone up stairs with the tired children. She rapped against the wall for Rebekah to come in and help to attend to them, Rebekah's house being a little "spit-and-daub" cabin leaning against the substantial stonework of Mrs. Hall's taller erection. When she came a bed was made up for the little ones, and some supper given to them. On descending the stairs after seeing this done, Sally went to the sitting-room. Young Mrs. Hall entered it just in advance of her, having in the interim retired with her mother-in-law to take off her bonnet, and otherwise make herself presentable. Hence it was evident that no further communication could have passed between her and Mr. Darton since their brief interview in the stable.

Mr. Japheth Johns now opportunely arrived, and broke up the restraint of the company, after a few orthodox meteorological commentaries had passed between him and Mrs. Hall by way of introduction. They at once sat down to supper, the present of wine and turkey not being produced for consumption to-night, lest the premature display of those gifts should seem to throw doubt on Mrs. Hall's capacities as a provider.

"Drink hearty, Mr. Johns — drink hearty," said that matron, magnanimously. "Such as it is there's plenty of. But perhaps cider-wine is not to your taste? — though there's body in it."

"Quite the contrairy, ma'am — quite the contrairy," said the dairyman. "For though I inherit the malt-liquor principle from my father, I am a cider-drinker on my mother's side. She came from these parts, you know. And there's this to be said for't — 'tis a more peaceful liquor, and don't lie about a man like your hotter drinks. With care, one may live on it a twelvemonth without knocking down a neighbour, or getting a black eye from an old acquaintance."

The general conversation thus begun was continued briskly, though it was in the main restricted to Mrs. Hall and Japheth, who in truth required but little help from anybody. There being slight call upon Sally's tongue she had ample leisure to do what her heart most desired, namely, watch her intended husband and her sister-in-law with a view of elucidating the strange momentary scene in which her mother and herself had surprised them in the stable. If that scene meant anything, it meant, at least, that they had met before. That there had been no time for explanations Sally could see, for their manner was still one of suppressed amazement at each other's presence there. Darton's eyes, too, fell continually on the gown worn by Helena, as if this were an added riddle to his perplexity; though to Sally it was the one feature in the case which was no mystery. He seemed to feel that fate had impishly changed his *vis-à-vis* in the lover's jig he was about to foot; that while the gown had been expected to inclose a Sally, a Helena's face looked out from the bodice;

that some long lost hand met his own from the sleeves.

Sally could see that whatever Helena might know of Darton, she knew nothing of how the dress entered into his embarrassment. And at moments the young girl would have persuaded herself that Darton's looks at her sister-in-law were entirely the fruit of the clothes query. But surely at other times a more extensive range of speculation and sentiment was expressed by her lover's eye than that which the changed dress would account for.

Sally's independence made her one of the least jealous of women. But there was something in the relations of these two visitors which ought to be explained.

Japheth Johns continued to converse in his well known style, interspersing his talk with some private reflections on the position of Darton and Sally, which, though the sparkle in his eye showed them to be highly entertaining to himself, were apparently not quite communicable to the company. At last he withdrew for the night, going off to the roadside inn half-a-mile ahead, whither Darton promised to follow him in a few minutes.

Half an hour passed, and then Mr. Darton also rose to leave, Sally and her sister-in-law simultaneously wishing him good-night as they retired up stairs to their rooms. But on his arriving at the front door with Mrs. Hall a sharp shower of rain began to come down, when the widow suggested that he should return to the fireside till the storm ceased.

Darton accepted her proposal, but insisted that, as it was getting late, and she was obviously tired, she should not sit up on his account, since he could let himself out of the house, and would quite enjoy smoking a pipe by the hearth alone. Mrs. Hall assented; and Darton was left by himself. He spread his knees to the brands, lit up his tobacco as he had said, and sat gazing into the fire and at the notches of the chimney crook which hung above.

An occasional drop of rain rolled down the chimney with a hiss, and still he smoked on; but not like a man whose mind was at rest. In the long run, however, despite his meditations, early hours afield and a long ride in the open air produced their natural result. He began to doze.

How long he remained in this half unconscious state he did not know. He suddenly opened his eyes. The back-brand had burnt itself in two, and ceased to flame; the light which he had placed on the mantelpiece had nearly gone out. But in spite of these deficiencies there was a light in the apartment, and it came from elsewhere. Turning his head, he saw Philip Hall's wife standing at the entrance of the room with a bed candle in one hand, a small brass tea-kettle in the other, and *his* gown, as it certainly seemed, still upon her.

"Helena!" said Darton, starting up.

Her countenance expressed dismay, and her first words were an apology. "I — did not know you were here, Mr. Darton," she said, while a blush flashed to her cheek. "I thought every one had retired — I was coming to make a little water boil; my husband seems to be worse. But perhaps the kitchen fire can be lighted up again."

"Don't go on my account. By all means put it on here as you intended," said Darton. "Allow me to help you." He went forward to take the kettle from her hand, but she did not allow him, and placed it on the fire herself.

They stood some way apart, one on each side of the fireplace, waiting till the water should boil, the candle on the mantel between them, and Helena with her eyes on the kettle. Darton was the first to break the silence. "Shall I call Sally?" he said.

"Oh, no," she quickly returned. "We

have given trouble enough already. We have no right here. But we are the sport of fate, and were obliged to come."

"No right here!" said he in surprise.

"None. I can't explain it now," answered Helena. "This kettle is very slow."

There was another pause; the proverbial dilatoriness of watched pots was never more clearly exemplified.

Helena's face was of that sort which seems to ask for assistance without the owner's knowledge — the very antipodes of Sally's, which was self-reliance expressed. Darton's eyes travelled from the kettle to Helena's face, then back to the kettle, then to the face for rather a longer time. "So I am not to know anything of the mystery that has distracted me all the evening?" he said. "How is it that a woman, who refused me because (as I supposed) my position was not good enough for her taste, is found to be the wife of a man who certainly seems to be worse off than I?"

"He had the prior claim," said she.

"What! you knew him at that time?"

"Yes, yes! And he went to Australia, and sent for me, and I joined him out there!"

"Ah — that was the mystery!"

"Please say no more," she implored. "Whatever my errors I have paid for them during the last five years."

The heart of Darton was subject to sudden overflowings. He was kind to a fault. "I am sorry from my soul," he said, involuntarily approaching her. Helena withdrew a step or two, at which he became conscious of his movement, and quickly took his former place. Here he stood without speaking, and the little kettle began to sing.

"Well, you might have been my wife if you had chosen," he said at last. "But that's all past and gone. However, if you are in any trouble or poverty I shall be glad to be of service, and as your relation by marriage I shall have a right to be. Does your uncle know of your distress?"

"My uncle is dead. He left me without a farthing. And now we have two children to maintain."

"What, left you nothing? How could he be so cruel as that?"

"I disgraced myself in his eyes."

"Now," said Darton earnestly, "let me take care of the children, at least while you are so unsettled. *You* belong to another, so I cannot take care of you."

"Yes you can," said a voice; and suddenly a third figure stood beside them. It was Sally. "You can, since you seem to wish to," she repeated. "She no longer belongs to another. . . . My poor brother is dead!"

Her face was red, her eyes sparkled, and all the woman came to the front. "I have heard it!" she went on to him passionately. "You can protect her now as well as the children!" She turned then to her agitated sister-in-law. "I heard something," said Sally (in a gentle murmur, differing much from her previous passionate words), "and I went into his room. It must have been the moment you left. He went off so quickly, and weakly, and it was so unexpected, that I couldn't leave even to call you."

Darton was just able to gather from the confused discourse which followed that, during his sleep by the fire, Sally's brother whom he had never seen had become worse; and that during Helena's absence for water the end had unexpectedly come. The two young women hastened up stairs, and he was again left alone.

After standing there a short time he went to the front door and looked out; till, softly closing it behind him, he advanced and stood under the large sycamore tree. The stars were flickering coldly, and the dampness which had just descended upon the earth in rain now sent up a chill from it.

Darton was in a strange position, and he felt it. The unexpected appearance, in deep poverty, of Helena — a young lady, daughter of a deceased naval officer, who had been brought up by her uncle, a solicitor, and had refused Darton in marriage years ago — the passionate, almost angry demeanour of Sally at discovering them, the abrupt announcement that Helena was a widow; all this coming together was a conjuncture difficult to cope with in a moment, and made him question whether he ought to leave the house or offer assistance. But for Sally's manner he would unhesitatingly have done the latter.

He was still standing under the tree when the door in front of him opened, and Mrs. Hall came out. She went round to the garden-gate at the side without seeing him. Darton followed her intending to speak. Pausing outside, as if in thought, she proceeded to a spot where the sun came earliest in spring-time, and where the north wind never blew; it was where the row of beehives stood under the wall. Discerning her object, he waited till she had accomplished it.

It was the universal custom thereabout to wake the bees by tapping at their hives whenever a death occurred in the household, under the belief that if this were not done the bees themselves would pine away and perish during the ensuing year. As soon as an interior buzzing responded to her tap at the first hive Mrs. Hall went on to the second, and thus passed down the row. As soon as she came back he met her.

"What can I do in this trouble, Mrs. Hall?" he said.

"Oh — nothing, thank you, nothing," she said in a tearful voice, now just perceiving him. "We have called Rebekah and her husband, and they will do everything necessary." She told him in a few words the particulars of her son's arrival, broken in health — indeed, at death's very door, though they did not suspect it — and suggested, as the result of a conversation between her and her daughter, that the wedding should be postponed.

"Yes, of course," said Darton. "I think now to go straight to the inn and tell Johns what has happened." It was not till after he had shaken hands with her that he turned hesitatingly and added, "Will you tell the mother of his children that, as they are now left fatherless, I shall be glad to take the eldest of them, if it would be any convenience to her and to you?"

Mrs. Hall promised that her son's widow should be told of the offer, and they parted. He retired down the rooty slope and disappeared in the direction of the inn, where he informed Johns of the circumstances. Meanwhile Mrs. Hall had entered the house. Sally was down stairs in the sitting-room alone, and her mother explained to her that Darton had readily assented to the postponement.

"No doubt he has," said Sally, with sad emphasis. "It is not put off for a week, or a month, or a year. I shall never marry him, and she will."

IV

Time passed, and the household on the Knap became again serene under the composing influences of daily routine. A desultory, very desultory, correspondence, dragged on between Sally Hall and Darton, who, not quite knowing how to take her petulant words on the night of her brother's death, had continued passive thus long. Helena and her children remained at the dairy-house, almost of necessity, and Darton therefore deemed it advisable to stay away.

One day, seven months later on, when Mr. Darton was as usual at his farm, twenty miles from King's-Hintock, a note reached him from Helena. She thanked him for his kind offer about her children, which her mother-in-law had duly communicated, and stated that she would be glad to accept it as regarded the eldest, the boy. Helena, had, in truth, good need to do so, for her uncle had left her penniless, and all application to some relatives in the north had failed. There was, besides, as she said, no good school near Hintock to which she could send the child.

On a fine summer day the boy came. He was accompanied half-way by Sally and his mother — to the "White Horse," the fine old Elizabethan inn at Chalk Newton,* where he was handed over to Darton's bailiff in a shining spring-cart, who met them there.

He was entered as a day-scholar at a popular school at Casterbridge, three or four miles from Darton's, having first been taught by Darton to ride a forest-pony, on which he cantered to and from the aforesaid fount of knowledge, and (as Darton

*It is now pulled down, and its site occupied by a modern one in red brick (1912).

hoped) brought away a promising headful of the same at each diurnal expedition. The thoughtful taciturnity into which Darton had latterly fallen was quite dissipated by the presence of this boy.

When the Christmas holidays came it was arranged that he should spend them with his mother. The journey was, for some reason or other, performed in two stages, as at his coming, except that Darton in person took the place of the bailiff, and that the boy and himself rode on horseback.

Reaching the renowned "White Horse," Darton inquired if Miss and young Mrs. Hall were there to meet little Philip (as they had agreed to be). He was answered by the appearance of Helena alone at the door.

"At the last moment Sally would not come," she faltered.

That meeting practically settled the point towards which these long-severed persons were converging. But nothing was broached about it for some time yet. Sally Hall had, in fact, imparted the first decisive motion to events by refusing to accompany Helena. She soon gave them a second move by writing the following note:

[Private]
"DEAR CHARLES,

"Living here so long and intimately with Helena, I have naturally learnt her history, especially that of it which refers to you. I am sure she would accept you as a husband at the proper time, and I think you ought to give her the opportunity. You inquire in an old note if I am sorry that I showed temper (which it *wasn't*) that night when I heard you talking to her. No, Charles, I am not sorry at all for what I said then.

> "Yours sincerely,
> "SALLY HALL."

Thus set in train the transfer of Darton's heart back to its original quarters proceeded by mere lapse of time. In the following July Darton went to his friend Japheth to ask him at last to fulfil the bridal office which had been in abeyance since the previous January twelvemonths.

"With all my heart, man o' constancy!" said Dairyman Johns, warmly. "I've lost most of my genteel fair complexion haymaking this hot weather, 'tis true, but I'll do your business as well as them that look better. There be scents and good hair-oil in the world yet, thank God, and they'll take off the roughest o' my edge. I'll compliment her. 'Better late than never, Sally Hall,' I'll say."

"It is not Sally," said Darton, hurriedly. "It is young Mrs. Hall."

Japheth's face, as soon as he really comprehended, became a picture of reproachful dismay. "Not Sally?" he said. "Why not Sally? I can't believe it! Young Mrs. Hall! Well, well — where's your wisdom!"

Darton shortly explained particulars; but Johns would not be reconciled. "She was a woman worth having if ever woman was," he cried. "And now to let her go!"

"But I suppose I can marry where I like," said Darton.

"H'm," replied the dairyman, lifting his eyebrows expressively. "This don't become you, Charles — it really do not. If I had done such a thing you would have sworn I was a curst no'thern fool to be drawn off the scent by such a red-herring doll-oll-oll."

Farmer Darton responded in such sharp terms to this laconic opinion that the two friends finally parted in a way they had never parted before. Johns was to be no

286

groomsman to Darton after all. He had flatly declined. Darton went off sorry, and even unhappy, particularly as Japheth was about to leave that side of the county, so that the words which had divided them were not likely to be explained away or softened down.

A short time after the interview Darton was united to Helena at a simple matter-of-fact wedding; and she and her little girl joined the boy who had already grown to look on Darton's house as home.

For some months the farmer experienced an unprecedented happiness and satisfaction. There had been a flaw in his life, and it was as neatly mended as was humanly possible. But after a season the stream of events followed less clearly, and there were shades in his reveries. Helena was a fragile woman, of little staying power, physically or morally, and since the time that he had originally known her — eight or ten years before — she had been severely tried. She had loved herself out, in short, and was now occasionally given to moping. Sometimes she spoke regretfully of the gentilities of her early life, and instead of comparing her present state with her condition as the wife of the unlucky Hall, she mused rather on what it had been before she took the first fatal step of clan-destinely marrying him. She did not care to please such people as those with whom she was thrown as a thriving farmer's wife. She allowed the pretty trifles of agricultural domesticity to glide by her as sorry details, and had it not been for the children Darton's house would have seemed but little brighter than it had been before.

This led to occasional unpleasantness, until Darton sometimes declared to himself that such endeavours as his to rectify early deviations of the heart by harking back to the old point mostly failed of success. "Perhaps Johns was right," he would say. "I should have gone on with Sally. Better go with the tide and make the best of its course than stem it at the risk of a capsize." But he kept these unmelodious thoughts to himself, and was outwardly considerate and kind.

This somewhat barren tract of his life had extended to less than a year and a half when his ponderings were cut short by the loss of the woman they concerned. When she was in her grave he thought better of her than when she had been alive; the farm was a worse place without her than with her, after all. No woman short of divine could have gone through such an experience as hers with her first husband without becoming a little soured. Her stagnant sympathies, her sometimes unreasonable manner, had covered a heart frank and well-meaning, and originally hopeful and warm. She left him a tiny red infant in white wrappings. To make life as easy as possible to this touching object became at once his care.

As this child learnt to walk and talk Darton learnt to see feasibility in a scheme which pleased him. Revolving the experiment which he had hitherto made upon life, he fancied he had gained wisdom from his mistakes and caution from his miscarriages.

What the scheme was needs no penetration to discover. Once more he had opportunity to recast and rectify his ill-wrought situations by returning to Sally Hall, who still lived quietly on under her mother's roof at Hintock. Helena had been a woman to lend pathos and refinement to a home; Sally was the woman to brighten it. She would not, as Helena did, despise the rural simplicities of a farmer's fireside. Moreover, she had a preeminent qualification for Darton's household; no other woman could make so desirable a mother to her brother's two children and Darton's one as

Sally — while Darton, now that Helena had gone, was a more promising husband for Sally than he had ever been when liable to reminders from an uncured sentimental wound.

Darton was not a man to act rapidly, and the working out of his reparative designs might have been delayed for some time. But there came a winter evening precisely like the one which had darkened over that former ride to Hintock, and he asked himself why he should postpone longer, when the very landscape called for a repetition of that attempt.

He told his man to saddle the mare, booted and spurred himself with a younger horseman's nicety, kissed the two youngest children, and rode off. To make the journey a complete parallel to the first, he would fain have had his old acquaintance Japheth Johns with him. But Johns, alas, was missing. His removal to the other side of the county had left unrepaired the breach which had arisen between him and Darton; and though Darton had forgiven him a hundred times, as Johns had probably forgiven Darton, the effort of reunion in present circumstances was one not likely to be made.

He screwed himself up to as cheerful a

pitch as he could without his former crony, and became content with his own thoughts as he rode, instead of the words of a companion. The sun went down; the boughs appeared scratched in like an etching against the sky; old crooked men with faggots at their backs said "Good-night, sir," and Darton replied "Good-night" right heartily.

By the time he reached the forking roads it was getting as dark as it had been on the occasion when Johns climbed the directing-post. Darton made no mistake this time. "Nor shall I be able to mistake, thank Heaven, when I arrive," he murmured. It gave him peculiar satisfaction to think that the proposed marriage, like his first, was of the nature of setting in order things long awry, and not a momentary freak of fancy.

Nothing hindered the smoothness of his journey, which seemed not half its former length. Though dark, it was only between five and six o'clock when the bulky chimneys of Mrs. Hall's residence appeared in view behind the sycamore tree. On second thoughts he retreated and put up at the ale-house as in former time; and when he had plumed himself before the inn mirror, called for something to drink, and smoothed out the incipient wrinkles of care, he walked on to the Knap with a quick step.

V

That evening Sally was making "pinners" for the milkers, who were now increased by two, for her mother and herself no longer joined in milking the cows themselves. But upon the whole there was little change in the household economy, and not much in its appearance, beyond such minor particulars as that the crack over the window, which had been a hundred years coming, was a trifle wider; that the beams were a shade blacker; that the influence of modernism had supplanted the open chimney corner by a grate; that Rebekah, who had worn a cap when she had plenty of hair, had left it off now she had scarce any, because it was reported that caps were not fashionable; and that Sally's face had naturally assumed a more womanly and experienced cast.

Mrs. Hall was actually lifting coals with the tongs, as she had used to do.

"Five years ago this very night, if I am not mistaken —" she said laying on an ember.

"Not this very night — though 'twas one

night this week," said the correct Sally.

"Well, 'tis near enough. Five years ago Mr. Darton came to marry you, and my poor boy Phil came home to die." She sighed. "Ah, Sally," she presently said, "if you had managed well Mr. Darton would have had you, Helena, or none."

"Don't be sentimental about that mother," begged Sally. "I didn't care to manage well in such a case. Though I liked him, I wasn't so anxious. I would never have married the man in the midst of such a hitch as that was," she added with decision; "and I don't think I would if he were to ask me now."

"I am not sure about that, unless you have another in your eye."

"I wouldn't; and I'll tell you why. I could hardly marry him for love at this time o' day. And as we've quite enough to live on if we give up the dairy to-morrow, I should have no need to marry for any meaner reason . . . I am quite happy enough as I am, and there's an end of it."

Now it was not long after this dialogue that there came a mild rap at the door, and in a moment there entered Rebekah, looking as though a ghost had arrived. The fact was that that accomplished skimmer and churner (now a resident in the house) had overheard the desultory observations between mother and daughter, and on opening the door to Mr. Darton thought the coincidence must have a grisly meaning in it. Mrs. Hall welcomed the farmer with warm surprise, as did Sally, and for a moment they rather wanted words.

"Can you push up the chimney-crook for me, Mr. Darton? the notches hitch," said the matron. He did it, and the homely little act bridged over the awkward consciousness that he had been a stranger for four years.

Mrs. Hall soon saw what he had come for, and left the principals together while she went to prepare him a late tea, smiling at Sally's recent hasty assertions of indifference, when she saw how civil Sally was. When tea was ready she joined them. She fancied that Darton did not look so confident as when he had arrived; but Sally was quite light-hearted, and the meal passed pleasantly.

About seven he took his leave of them. Mrs. Hall went as far as the door to light him down the slope. On the doorstep he said frankly:

"I came to ask your daughter to marry me; chose the night and everything, with an eye to a favourable answer. But she won't."

"Then she's a very ungrateful girl," emphatically said Mrs. Hall.

Darton paused to shape his sentence, and asked, "I — I suppose there's nobody else more favoured?"

"I can't say that there is, or that there isn't," answered Mrs. Hall. "She's private in some things. I'm on your side, however, Mr. Darton, and I'll talk to her."

"Thank 'ee, thank 'ee!" said the farmer in a gayer accent; and with this assurance the not very satisfactory visit came to an end. Darton descended the roots of the sycamore, the light was withdrawn, and the door closed. At the bottom of the slope he nearly ran against a man about to ascend.

"Can a jack-o'-lent believe his few senses on such a dark night or can't he?" exclaimed one whose utterance Darton recognised in a moment, despite its unexpectedness. "I dare not swear he can, though I fain would." The speaker was Johns.

Darton said he was glad of this opportunity, bad as it was, of putting an end to the silence of years, and asked the dairyman what he was travelling that way for.

Japheth showed the old jovial confidence in a moment. "I'm going to see your — relations — as they always seem to me," he said — "Mrs. Hall and Sally. Well, Charles, the fact is I find the natural barbarousness of man is much increased by a bachelor life, and, as your leavings were always good enough for me, I'm trying civilisation here." He nodded towards the house.

"Not with Sally — to marry her?" said Darton, feeling something like a rill of ice water between his shoulders.

"Yes, by the help of Providence and my personal charms. And I think I shall get her. I am this road every week — my present dairy is only four miles off, you know, and I see her through the window. 'Tis rather odd that I was going to speak practical to-night to her for the first time. You've just called?"

"Yes, for a short while. But she didn't say a word about you."

"A good sign, a good sign. Now that decides me. I'll swing the mallet and get her answer this very night as I planned."

A few more remarks and Darton, wishing his friend joy of Sally in a slightly hollow tone of jocularity, bade him good-bye. Johns promised to write particulars, and ascended, and was lost in the shade of the house and tree. A rectangle of light appeared when Johns was admitted, and all was dark again.

"Happy Japheth!" said Darton. "This, then, is the explanation!"

He determined to return home that night. In a quarter of an hour he passed out of the village, and the next day went about his swede-lifting and storing as if nothing had occurred.

He waited and waited to hear from Johns whether the wedding-day was fixed: but no letter came. He learnt not a single particular till, meeting Johns one day at a horse auction, Darton exclaimed genially — rather more genially than he felt — "When is the joyful day to be?"

To his great surprise a reciprocity of gladness was not conspicuous in Johns. "Not at all," he said, in a very subdued tone. " 'Tis a bad job; she won't have me."

Darton held his breath till he said with treacherous solicitude, "Try again — 'tis coyness."

"Oh, no," said Johns, decisively. "There's been none of that. We talked it over dozens of times in the most fair and square way. She tells me plainly, I don't suit her. 'Twould be simply annoying her to ask her again. Ah, Charles, you threw a prize away when you let her slip five years ago."

"I did — I did," said Darton.

He returned from that auction with a

new set of feelings in play. He had certainly made a surprising mistake in thinking Johns his successful rival. It really seemed as if he might hope for Sally after all.

This time, being rather pressed by business, Darton had recourse to pen and ink, and wrote her as manly and straightforward a proposal as any woman could wish to receive. The reply came promptly: —

"DEAR MR. DARTON,

"I am as sensible as any woman can be of the goodness that leads you to make me this offer a second time. Better women than I would be proud of the honour, for when I read your nice long speeches on mangold-wurzel, and such like topics, at the Casterbridge Farmers' Club, I do feel it an honour, I assure you. But my answer is just the same as before. I will not try to explain what, in truth, I cannot explain — my reasons; I will simply say that I must decline to be married to you. With good wishes as in former times, I am,

"Your faithful friend,
"SALLY HALL."

Darton dropped the letter hopelessly. Beyond the negative, there was just a possibility of sarcasm in it — "nice long speeches on mangold-wurzel" had a suspicious sound. However, sarcasm or none, there was the answer, and he had to be content.

He proceeded to seek relief in a business which at this time engrossed much of his attention — that of clearing up a curious mistake just current in the county, that he had been nearly ruined by the recent failure of a local bank. A farmer named Darton had lost heavily, and the similarity of name had probably led to the error. Belief in it was so persistent that it demanded several days of letter-writing to set matters straight, and persuade the world that he was as solvent as ever he had been in his life. He had hardly concluded this worrying task when, to his delight, another letter arrived in the handwriting of Sally.

Darton tore it open; it was very short.

"DEAR MR. DARTON,

"We have been so alarmed these last few days by the report that you were ruined by the stoppage of —'s Bank, that now it is contradicted, I hasten, by my mother's wish, to say how truly glad we are to find there is no foundation for the report. After your kindness to my poor brother's children, I can do no less than write at such a moment. We had a letter from each of them a few days ago.

"Your faithful friend,
"SALLY HALL."

"Mercenary little woman!" said Darton to himself with a smile. "Then that was the secret of her refusal this time — she thought I was ruined."

Now, such was Darton, that as hours went on he could not help feeling too generously towards Sally to condemn her in this. What did he want in a wife, he asked himself. Love and integrity. What next? Worldly wisdom. And was there really more than worldly wisdom in her refusal to go aboard a sinking ship? She now knew it was otherwise. "Begad," he said, "I'll try her again."

The fact was he had so set his heart upon Sally, and Sally alone, that nothing was to be allowed to baulk him; and his reasoning was purely formal.

Anniversaries having been unpropitious he waited on till a bright day late in May — a day when all animate nature was fancying, in its trusting, foolish way, that it was going to bask under blue sky for evermore. As he rode through Long-Ash Lane it was scarce recognisable as the track of his two winter journeys. No mistake could be made now, even with his eyes shut. The cuckoo's note was at its best between April tentativeness and Midsummer decrepitude, and the reptiles in the sun behaved as winningly as kittens on a hearth. Though afternoon, and about the same time as on the last occasion, it was broad day and sunshine when he entered Hintock, and the details of the Knap dairy-house were visible far up the road. He saw Sally in the garden, and was set vibrating. He had first intended to go on to the inn; but "No," he said; "I'll tie my horse to the garden gate. If all goes well it can soon be taken round: if not, I mount and ride away."

The tall shade of the horseman darkened the room in which Mrs. Hall sat, and made her start, for he had ridden by a side path to the top of the slope, where riders seldom came. In a few seconds he was in the garden with Sally.

Five — ay, three minutes — did the business at the back of that row of bees. Though spring had come, and heavenly blue consecrated the scene, Darton succeeded not. *"No,"* said Sally firmly. "I will never, never marry you, Mr. Darton. I would have done it once; but now I never can."

"But" — implored Mr. Darton. And with a burst of real eloquence he went on to declare all sorts of things that he would do for her. He would drive her to see her mother every week — take her to London — settle so much money upon her — Heavens knows what he did not promise, suggest, and tempt her with. But it availed nothing. She interposed with a stout negative, which closed the course of his argument like an iron gate across a highway. Darton paused.

"Then," said he, simply, "you hadn't heard of my supposed failure when you declined last time?"

"I had not," she said. "That you believed me capable of refusing you for such a reason does not help your cause."

"And 'tis not because of any soreness from my slighting you years ago?"

"No. That soreness is long past."

"Ah — then you despise me, Sally!"

"No," she slowly answered. "I don't altogether despise you. I don't think you quite such a hero as I once did — that's all. The truth is, I am happy enough as I am; and I

302

don't mean to marry at all. Now, may I ask a favour, sir?" She spoke with an ineffable charm which, whenever he thought of it, made him curse his loss of her as long as he lived.

"To any extent."

"Please do not put this question to me any more. Friends as long as you like, but lovers and married never."

"I never will," said Darton. "Not if I live a hundred years."

And he never did. That he had worn out his welcome in her heart was only too plain.

When his step-children had grown up, and were placed out in life, all communication between Darton and the Hall family ceased. It was only by chance that, years after, he learnt that Sally, notwithstanding the solicitations her attractions drew upon her, had refused several offers of marriage, and steadily adhered to her purpose of leading a single life.

May 1884.

The Distracted Preacher

I.   How His Cold Was Cured

Something delayed the arrival of the Wesleyan minister, and a young man came temporarily in his stead. It was on the thirteenth of January, 183–, that Mr. Stockdale, the young man in question, made his humble entry into the village, unknown, and almost unseen. But when those of the inhabitants who styled themselves of his connection became acquainted with him, they were rather pleased with the substitute than otherwise, though he had scarcely as yet acquired ballast of character sufficient to steady the consciences of the hundred-and-forty Methodists of pure blood who, at this time, lived in Nether-Moynton, and to give in addition supplementary support to the mixed race which went to church in the morning and chapel in the evening, or when there was a tea — as many as a hundred and ten people more, all told, and including the parish clerk in the winter-time, when it was too dark for the vicar to observe who passed up the street at seven o'clock — which, to be just to him, he was never anxious to do.

It was owing to this overlapping of creeds that the celebrated population puzzle arose among the denser gentry of the district around Nether-Moynton: how could it be that a parish containing fifteen score of strong, full-grown Episcopalians, and nearly thirteen score of well-matured Dissenters, numbered barely two-and-twenty score adults in all?

The young man being personally interesting, those with whom he came in contact were content to waive for a while the graver question of his sufficiency. It is said that at this time of his life his eyes were affectionate, though without a ray of levity; that his hair was curly, and his figure tall; that he was, in short, a very lovable youth, who won upon his female hearers as soon as they saw and heard him, and caused them to say, "Why didn't we know of this before he came, that we might have gi'ed him a warmer welcome!"

The fact was that, knowing him to be only provisionally selected, and expecting nothing remarkable in his person or doctrine, they and the rest of his flock in Nether-Moynton had felt almost as indifferent about his advent as if they had been the soundest church-going parishioners in the country, and he their true and appointed parson. Thus when Stockdale set foot in the place nobody had secured a lodging for him, and though his journey had given him a bad cold in the head, he was forced to attend to that business himself. On enquiry he learnt that the only possible accommodation in the village would be found at the house of one Mrs. Lizzy Newberry, at the upper end of the street.

It was a youth who gave this information, and Stockdale asked him who Mrs. Newberry might be.

The boy said that she was a widow-woman, who had got no husband, because he was dead. Mr. Newberry, he added, had been a well-to-do man enough, as the saying was, and a farmer; but he had gone off in a decline. As regarded Mrs. Newberry's serious side, Stockdale gathered that she was one of the trimmers who went to church and chapel both.

"I'll go there," said Stockdale, feeling that, in the absence of purely sectarian lodgings, he could do no better.

"She's a little particular, and won't hae

gover'ment folks, or curates, or the pa'son's friends, or such like," said the lad dubiously.

"Ah, that may be a promising sign: I'll call. Or, no; just you go up and ask first if she can find room for me. I have to see one or two persons on another matter. You will find me down at the carrier's."

In a quarter of an hour the lad came back, and said that Mrs. Newberry would have no objection to accommodate him, whereupon Stockdale called at the house. It stood within a garden-hedge, and seemed to be roomy and comfortable. He saw an elderly woman, with whom he made arrangements to come the same night, since there was no inn in the place, and he wished to house himself as soon as possible; the village being a local centre from which he was to radiate at once to the different small chapels in the neighbour-hood. He forthwith sent his luggage to Mrs. Newberry's from the carrier's, where he had taken shelter, and in the evening walked up to his temporary home.

As he now lived there, Stockdale felt it unnecessary to knock at the door; and entering quietly he had the pleasure of hearing footsteps scudding away like mice into the back quarters. He advanced to the parlour, as the front room was called, though its stone floor was scarcely disguised by the carpet, which only overlaid the trodden areas, leaving sandy deserts under the furniture. But the room looked snug and cheerful. The fire-light shone out brightly, trembling on the bulging mouldings of the table-legs, playing with brass knobs and handles, and lurking in great strength on the under surface of the chimney-piece. A deep arm-chair, covered with horsehair, and studded with a countless throng of brass nails, was pulled up on one side of the fireplace. The tea-things were on the table, the teapot cover was open, and a little hand-bell had been laid at that precise point towards which a person seated in the great chair might be expected instinctively to stretch his hand.

Stockdale sat down, not objecting to his experience of the room thus far, and began his residence by tinkling the bell. A little girl crept in at the summons, and made tea for him. Her name, she said, was Marther Sarer, and she lived out there, nodding towards the road and village generally. Before Stockdale had got far with his meal, a tap sounded on the door behind him, and on his telling the enquirer to come in, a rustle of garments caused him to turn his head. He saw before him a fine and extremely well-made young woman, with dark hair, a wide, sensible, beautiful forehead, eyes that warmed him before he knew it, and a mouth that was in itself a picture to all appreciative souls.

"Can I get you anything else for tea?" she said, coming forward a step or two, an expression of liveliness on her features, and her hand waving the door by its edge.

"Nothing, thank you," said Stockdale, thinking less of what he replied than of what might be her relation to the household.

"You are quite sure?" said the young woman, apparently aware that he had not considered his answer.

He conscientiously examined the tea-things, and found them all there. "Quite sure, Miss Newberry," he said.

"It is Mrs. Newberry," she said. "Lizzy Newberry. I used to be Lizzy Simpkins."

"Oh, I beg your pardon, Mrs. Newberry." And before he had occasion to say more, she left the room.

Stockdale remained in some doubt till Martha Sarah came to clear the table. "Whose house is this, my little woman?" said he.

"Mrs. Lizzy Newberry's, sir."

"Then Mrs. Newberry is not the old lady I saw this afternoon?"

"No. That's Mrs. Newberry's mother. It was Mrs. Newberry who comed in to you just by now, because she wanted to see if you was good-looking."

Later in the evening, when Stockdale was about to begin supper, she came again. "I have come myself, Mr. Stockdale," she said. The minister stood up in acknowledgment of the honour. "I am afraid little Marther might not make you understand. What will you have for supper? — there's cold rabbit, and there's a ham uncut."

Stockdale said he could get on nicely with those viands, and supper was laid. He had no more than cut a slice when tap-tap came to the door again. The minister had already learnt that this particular rhythm in taps denoted the fingers of his enkindling landlady, and the doomed young fellow buried his first mouthful under a look of receptive blandness.

"We have a chicken in the house, Mr. Stockdale — I quite forgot to mention it just now. Perhaps you would like Marther Sarer to bring it up?"

Stockdale had advanced far enough in the art of being a young man to say that he did not want the chicken, unless she brought it up herself; but when it was uttered he blushed at the daring gallantry of the speech, perhaps a shade too strong for a serious man and a minister. In three minutes the chicken appeared, but to his great surprise, only in the hands of Martha Sarah. Stockdale was disappointed, which perhaps it was intended that he should be.

He finished supper, and was not in the least anticipating Mrs. Newberry again that night, when she tapped and entered as before. Stockdale's gratified look told that she had lost nothing by not appearing when expected. It happened that the cold in the head from which the young man suffered had increased with the approach of night, and before she had spoken he was seized with a violent fit of sneezing which he could not anyhow repress.

Mrs. Newberry looked full of pity. "Your cold is very bad to-night, Mr. Stockdale."

Stockdale replied that it was rather troublesome.

"And I've a good mind" — she added archly, looking at the cheerless glass of water on the table, which the abstemious minister was going to drink.

"Yes, Mrs. Newberry?"

"I've a good mind that you should have

something more likely to cure it than that cold stuff."

"Well," said Stockdale, looking down at the glass, "as there is no inn here, and nothing better to be got in the village, of course it will do."

To this she replied, "There is something better, not far off, though not in the house. I really think you must try it, or you may be ill. Yes, Mr. Stockdale, you shall." She held up her finger, seeing that he was about to speak. "Don't ask what it is; wait, and you shall see."

Lizzy went away, and Stockdale waited in a pleasant mood. Presently she returned with her bonnet and cloak on, saying, "I am so sorry, but you must help me to get it. Mother has gone to bed. Will you wrap yourself up, and come this way, and please bring that cup with you."

Stockdale, a lonely young fellow, who had for weeks felt a great craving for some-body on whom to throw away superfluous interest, and even tenderness, was not sorry to join her; and followed his guide through the back door, across the garden, to the bottom, where the boundary was a wall. This wall was low, and beyond it Stockdale discerned in the night shades several grey headstones, and the outlines of the church roof and tower.

"It is easy to get up this way," she said, stepping upon a bank which abutted on the wall; then putting her foot on the top of the stonework, and descending by a spring inside, where the ground was much higher, as is the manner of graveyards to be. Stockdale did the same, and followed her in the dusk across the irregular ground till they came to the tower door, which, when they had entered, she softly closed behind them.

"You can keep a secret?" she said in a musical voice.

"Like an iron chest!" said he, fervently.

Then from under her cloak she produced a small lighted lantern, which the minister had not noticed that she carried at all. The light showed them to be close to the singing gallery stairs, under which lay a heap of lumber of all sorts, but consisting mostly of decayed framework, pews, panels, and pieces of flooring, that from time to time had been removed from their original fixings in the body of the edifice and replaced by new.

"Perhaps you will drag some of those boards aside?" she said, holding the lantern over her head to light him better. "Or will you take the lantern while I move them?"

"I can manage it," said the young man, and acting as she ordered, he uncovered, to his surprise, a row of little barrels bound with wood hoops, each barrel being about as large as the nave of a heavy waggon-wheel. When they were laid open Lizzy fixed her eyes on him, as if she wondered what he would say.

"You know what they are?" she asked, finding that he did not speak.

"Yes, barrels," said Stockdale, simply. He was an inland man, the son of highly respectable parents, and brought up with a single eye to the ministry, and the sight suggested nothing beyond the fact that such articles were there.

"You are quite right, they are barrels," she said, in an emphatic tone of candour that was not without a touch of irony.

Stockdale looked at her with an eye of sudden misgiving. "Not smugglers' liquor?" he said.

"Yes," said she. "They are tubs of spirit that have accidentally floated over in the dark from France."

In Nether-Moynton and its vicinity at this date people always smiled at the sort of sin called in the outside world illicit trading; and these little kegs of gin and brandy were as well known to the inhabitants as turnips. So that Stockdale's innocent ignorance, and his look of alarm when he guessed the sinister mystery, seemed to strike Lizzy first as ludicrous, and then as very awkward for the good impression that she wished to produce upon him.

"Smuggling is carried on here by some of the people," she said in a gentle, apologetic voice. "It has been their practice for generations, and they think it no harm. Now, will you roll out one of the tubs?"

"What to do with it?" said the minister.

"To draw a little from it to cure your cold," she answered. "It is so 'nation strong that it drives away that sort of thing in a jiffy. Oh, it is all right about our taking it. I may have what I like; the owner of the tubs says so. I ought to have had some in the house, and then I shouldn't ha' been put to this trouble; but I drink none myself, and so I often forget to keep it indoors."

"You are allowed to help yourself, I suppose, that you may not inform where their hiding-place is?"

"Well, no; not that particularly; but I may take any if I want it. So help yourself."

"I will, to oblige you, since you have a right to it," murmured the minister; and though he was not quite satisfied with his part in the performance, he rolled one of the "tubs" out from the corner into the middle of the tower floor. "How do you wish me to get it out — with a gimlet, I suppose?"

"No, I'll show you," said his interesting companion; and she held up with her other hand a shoemaker's awl and a hammer. "You must never do these things with a gimlet, because the wood-dust gets in; and when the buyers pour out the brandy that would tell them that the tub had been broached. An awl makes no dust, and the hole nearly closes up again. Now tap one of the hoops forward."

Stockdale took the hammer and did so.

"Now make the hole in the part that was covered by the hoop."

He made the hole as directed. "It won't run out," he said.

"O yes it will," said she. "Take the tub between your knees, and squeeze the heads; and I'll hold the cup."

Stockdale obeyed; and the pressure taking effect upon the tub, which seemed to be thin, the spirit spirted out in a stream. When the cup was full he ceased pressing, and the flow immediately stopped. "Now we must fill up the keg with water," said Lizzy, "or it will chuck like forty hens when it is handled, and show that 'tis not full."

"But they tell you you may take it?"

"Yes, the *smugglers;* but the *buyers* must not know that the smugglers have been kind to me at their expense."

"I see," said Stockdale, doubtfully. "I much question the honesty of this proceeding."

By her direction he held the tub with the hole upwards, and while he went through the process of alternately pressing and ceasing to press, she produced a bottle of water, from which she took mouthfuls, conveying each to the keg by putting her pretty lips to the hole, where it was sucked in at each recovery of the cask from pressure. When it was again full he plugged the hole, knocked the hoop down to its place, and buried the tub in the lumber as before.

"Aren't the smugglers afraid that you will tell?" he asked as they recrossed the churchyard.

"O no. They are not afraid of that. I couldn't do such a thing."

"They have put you into a very awkward corner," said Stockdale emphatically. "You must, of course, as an honest person, sometimes feel that it is your duty to inform — really you must."

"Well, I have never particularly felt it as a duty; and, besides, my first husband —" She stopped, and there was some confusion in her voice. Stockdale was so honest and unsophisticated that he did not at once discern why she paused; but at last he did perceive that the words were a slip, and that no woman would have uttered "first husband" by accident unless she had thought pretty frequently of a second. He felt for her confusion, and allowed her time to recover and proceed. "My husband," she said, in a self-corrected tone, "used to know of their doings, and so did my father, and kept the secret. I cannot inform, in fact, against anybody."

"I see the hardness of it," he continued, like a man who looked far into the moral of things. "And it is very cruel that you should be tossed and tantalized between your memories and your conscience. I do hope, Mrs. Newberry, that you will soon see your way out of this unpleasant position."

"Well, I don't just now," she murmured.

By this time they had passed over the wall and entered the house; where she brought him a glass and hot water, and left him to his own reflections. He looked after her vanishing form, asking himself whether he, as a respectable man, and a minister, and a shining light, even though as yet only of the halfpenny-candle sort, were quite justified in doing this thing. A sneeze settled the question; and he found that when the fiery liquor was lowered by the addition of twice or thrice the quantity of water, it was one of the prettiest cures for a cold in the head that he had ever known, particularly at this chilly time of the year.

Stockdale sat in the deep chair about twenty minutes sipping and meditating, till he at length took warmer views of things, and longed for the morrow, when he would see Mrs. Newberry again. He then felt that, though chronologically at a short distance, it would in an emotional sense be very long before tomorrow came, and walked restlessly round the room. His eye was attracted by a framed and glazed sampler in which a running ornament of fir-trees and peacocks surrounded the following pretty bit of sentiment: —

"Rose-leaves smell when roses thrive
Here's my work while I'm alive;
Rose-leaves smell when shrunk and shed,
Here's my work when I am dead.
Lizzy Simpkins. Fear God.
   Honour the King. Aged 11 years."

" 'Tis hers," he said to himself. "Heavens, how I like that name!"

Before he had done thinking that no other name from Abigail to Zenobia would have suited his young landlady so well, tap-tap came again upon the door; and the minister started as her face appeared yet another time, looking so disinterested that the most ingenious would have refrained from asserting that she had come to affect his feelings by her seductive eyes.

"Would you like a fire in your room, Mr. Stockdale, on account of your cold?"

The minister, being still a little pricked in the conscience for countenancing her in watering the spirits, saw here a way to self-chastisement. "No, I thank you," he said firmly, "it is not necessary. I have never been used to one in my life, and it would be giving way to luxury too far."

"Then I won't insist," she said, and disconcerted him by vanishing instantly. Wondering if she was vexed by his refusal, he wished that he had chosen to have a fire, even though it should have scorched him out of bed and endangered his self-discipline for a dozen days. However, he consoled himself with what was in truth a rare consolation for a budding lover, that he was under the same roof with Lizzy; her guest, in fact, to take a poetical view of the term lodger; and that he would certainly see her on the morrow.

The morrow came, and Stockdale rose early, his cold quite gone. He had never in his life so longed for the breakfast hour as he did that day, and punctually at eight o'clock, after a short walk to reconnoitre the premises, he re-entered the door of his dwelling. Breakfast passed, and Martha Sarah attended, but nobody came voluntarily as on the night before to enquire if there were other wants which he had not mentioned, and which she would attempt to gratify. He was disappointed, and went out, hoping to see her at dinner. Dinner-time came; he sat down to the meal, finished it, lingered on for a whole hour, although two new teachers were at that moment waiting at the chapel door to speak to him by appointment. It was useless to wait longer, and he slowly went his way down the lane, cheered by the thought that, after all, he would see her in the evening, and perhaps engage again in the delightful tub-broaching in the neighbouring church tower, which proceeding he resolved to render more moral by steadfastly insisting that no water should be introduced to fill up, though the tub should cluck like all the hens in Christendom. But nothing could disguise the fact that it was a queer business; and his countenance fell when he thought how much more his mind was interested in that matter than in his serious duties.

However, compunction vanished with the decline of day. Night came, and his tea and supper; but no Lizzy Newberry, and no sweet temptations. At last the minister could bear it no longer, and said to his quaint little attendant, "Where is Mrs. Newberry to-day?" judiciously handing a penny as he spoke.

"She's busy," said Martha.

"Anything serious happened?" he asked, handing another penny, and revealing yet additional pennies in the background.

"O no — nothing at all," said she, with breathless confidence. "Nothing ever happens to her. She's only biding upstairs in bed because 'tis her way sometimes."

Being a young man of some honour, he would not question further, and assuming that Lizzy must have a bad headache, or other slight ailment, in spite of what the girl had said, he went to bed dissatisfied, not even setting eyes on old Mrs. Simpkins. "I said last night that I should see her to-morrow," he reflected; "but that was not to be!"

Next day he had better fortune, or worse, meeting her at the foot of the stairs in the morning, and being favoured by a visit or two from her during the day — once for the purpose of making kindly enquiries about his comfort, as on the first evening, and at another time to place a bunch of winter violets on his table, with a promise to renew them when they drooped. On these occasions there was something in her smile which showed how conscious she was of the effect she produced, though it must be said that it was rather a humorous than a designing consciousness, and savoured more of pride than of vanity.

As for Stockdale, he clearly perceived that he possessed unlimited capacity for backsliding, and wished that tutelary saints were not denied to Dissenters. He set a watch upon his tongue and eyes for the space of one hour and a half; after which he found it was useless to struggle further, and gave himself up to the situation. "The other minister will be here in a month," he said to himself when sitting over the fire. "Then I shall be off, and she will distract my mind no more! . . . And then, shall I go on living by myself for ever? No; when my two years of probation are finished, I shall have a furnished house to live in, with a varnished door and a brass knocker; and I'll march straight back to her, and ask her flat, as soon as the last plate is on the dresser."

Thus a titillating fortnight was passed by young Stockdale, during which time things proceeded much as such matters have done ever since the beginning of history: he saw the object of attachment several times one day, did not see her at all the next, met her when he least expected to do so, missed her when hints and signs as to where she should be at a given hour almost amounted to an appointment. This mild coquetry was perhaps fair enough under the circumstances of their being so closely lodged, and Stockdale put up with it as philosophically as he was able. Being in her own house she could, after vexing him or disappointing him of her presence, easily win him back by suddenly surrounding him with those little attentions which her position as his landlady put it in her power to bestow. When he had waited indoors half the day to see her, and on finding that she would not be seen had gone off in a huff to the dreariest and dampest walk he could discover, she would restore equilibrium in the evening with "Mr. Stockdale, I

have fancied you must feel draught o'
nights from your bedroom window, and so
I have been putting up thicker curtains this
afternoon while you were out;" or "I noticed that you sneezed twice again this
morning, Mr. Stockdale. Depend upon it
that cold is hanging about you yet; I am
sure it is — I have thought of it continually; and you must let me make a posset for
you."

Sometimes in coming home he found his
sitting-room rearranged, chairs placed
where the table had stood, and the table
ornamented with the few fresh flowers and
leaves that could be obtained at this
season, so as to add a novelty to the room.
At times she would be standing on a chair
outside the house, trying to nail up a
branch of the monthly rose which the
winter wind had blown down; and of
course he stepped forward to assist her,
when their hands got mixed in passing the
shreds and nails.

Thus they became friends again after a
disagreement. She would utter on these
occasions some pretty and deprecatory remark on the necessity of her troubling him
anew; and he would straightway say that he
would do a hundred times as much for her
if she should so require.

II. How He Saw Two Other Men

Matters being in this advancing state, Stockdale was rather surprised one cloudy evening, while sitting in his room, at hearing her speak in low tones of expostulation to some one at the door. It was nearly dark, but the shutters were not yet closed, nor the candles lighted; and Stockdale was tempted to stretch his head towards the window. He saw outside the door a young man in clothes of a whitish colour, and upon reflection judged their wearer to be the well-built and rather handsome miller who lived below. The miller's voice was alternately low and firm, and sometimes it reached the level of positive entreaty; but what the words were Stockdale could in no way hear.

Before the colloquy had ended, the minister's attention was attracted by a second incident. Opposite Lizzy's home grew a clump of laurels, forming a thick and permanent shade. One of the laurel boughs now quivered against the light background of sky, and in a moment the head of a man peered out, and remained still. He seemed to be also much interested in the conversation at the door, and was plainly lingering there to watch and listen. Had Stockdale stood in any other relation to Lizzy than that of a lover, he might have gone out and investigated the meaning of this; but, being as yet but an unprivileged ally, he did nothing more than stand up and show himself against the firelight, whereupon the listener disappeared, and Lizzy and the miller spoke in lower tones.

Stockdale was made so uneasy by the circumstance, that as soon as the miller was gone, he said, "Mrs. Newberry, are you aware that you were watched just now, and your conversation heard?"

"When?" she said.

"When you were talking to that miller. A man was looking from the laurel-tree as jealously as if he could have eaten you."

She showed more concern than the trifling event seemed to demand, and he added, "Perhaps you were talking of things you did not wish to be overheard?"

"I was talking only on business," she said.

"Lizzy, be frank," said the young man. "If it was only on business, why should anybody wish to listen to you?"

She look curiously at him. "What else do you think it could be, then?"

"Well — the only talk between a young woman and man that is likely to amuse an evesdropper."

"Ah, yes," she said, smiling in spite of her preoccupation. "Well, my cousin Owlett has spoken to me about matrimony, every now and then, that's true; but he was not speaking of it then. I wish he had been speaking of it, with all my heart. It would have been much less serious for me."

"Oh, Mrs. Newberry!"

"It would. Not that I should ha' chimed in with him, of course. I wish it for other reasons. I am glad, Mr. Stockdale, that you have told me of that listener. It is a timely warning, and I must see my cousin again."

"But don't go away till I have spoken," said the minister. "I'll out with it at once, and make no more ado. Let it be Yes or No between us. Lizzy; please do!" And he held out his hand, in which she freely allowed her own to rest, but without speaking.

"You mean Yes by that?" he asked, after waiting awhile.

"You may be my sweetheart, if you will."

"Why not say at once you will wait for me until I have a house and can come back to marry you?"

"Because I am thinking — thinking of something else," she said with embarrassment. "It all comes upon me at once, and I must settle one thing at a time."

"At any rate, dear Lizzy, you can assure

me that the miller shall not be allowed to speak to you except on business? You have never directly encouraged him?"

She parried the question by saying, "You see, he and his party have been in the habit of leaving things on my premises sometimes, and as I have not denied him, it makes him rather forward."

"Things — what things?"

"Tubs — they are called Things here."

"But why don't you deny him, my dear Lizzy?"

"I cannot well."

"You are too timid. It is unfair of him to impose so upon you, and get your good name into danger by his smuggling tricks. Promise me that the next time he wants to leave his tubs here you will let me roll them into the street?"

She shook her head. "I would not venture to offend the neighbours so much as that," said she, "or do anything that would be so likely to put poor Owlett into the hands of the Customs-men."

Stockdale sighed, and said that he thought hers a mistaken generosity when it extended to assisting those who cheated the king of his dues. "At any rate, you will let me make him keep his distance as your lover, and tell him flatly that you are not for him?"

"Please not, at present," she said. "I don't wish to offend my old neighbours. It is not only Mr. Owlett who is concerned."

"This is too bad," said Stockdale impatiently.

"On my honour, I won't encourage him as my lover," Lizzy answered earnestly. "A reasonable man will be satisfied with that."

"Well, so I am," said Stockdale, his countenance clearing.

III.   The Mysterious Great-coat

Stockdale now began to notice more particularly a feature in the life of his fair landlady, which he had casually observed, but scarcely ever thought of before. It was that she was markedly irregular in her hours of rising. For a week or two she would be tolerably punctual, reaching the ground-floor within a few minutes of half-past seven. Then suddenly she would not be visible till twelve at noon, perhaps for three or four days in succession; and twice he had certain proof that she did not leave her room till half-past three in the afternoon. The second time that this extreme lateness came under his notice was on a day when he had particularly wished to consult with her about his future movements; and he concluded, as he always had done, that she had a cold, headache, or other ailment, unless she had kept herself invisible to avoid meeting and talking to him, which he could hardly believe. The former supposition was disproved, however, by her innocently saying, some days later, when they were speaking on a question of health, that she had never had a moment's heaviness, headache, or illness of any kind since the previous January twelvemonth.

"I am glad to hear it," said he. "I thought quite otherwise."

"What, do I look sickly?" she asked, turning up her face to show the impossibility of his gazing on it and holding such a belief for a moment.

"Not at all; I merely thought so from your being sometimes obliged to keep your room through the best part of the day."

"Oh, as for that — it means nothing," she murmured, with a look which some might have called cold, and which was the worst look that he liked to see upon her. "It is pure sleepiness, Mr. Stockdale."

"Never!"

"It is, I tell you. When I stay in my room till half-past three in the afternoon, you may always be sure that I slept soundly till three, or I shouldn't have stayed there."

"It is dreadful," said Stockdale, thinking of the disastrous effects of such indulgence upon the household of a minister, should it become a habit of everyday occurrence. "But then," she said, divining his good and prescient thoughts, "it only happens when I stay awake all night. I don't go to sleep till five or six in the morning sometimes."

"Ah, that's another matter," said Stockdale. "Sleeplessness to such an alarming extent is real illness. Have you spoken to a doctor?"

"O no — there is no need for doing that — it is all natural to me." And she went away without further remark.

Stockdale might have waited a long time to know the real cause of her sleeplessness, had it not happened that one dark night he was sitting in his bedroom jotting down notes for a sermon, which occupied him perfunctorily for a considerable time after the other members of the household had retired. He did not get to bed till one o'clock. Before he had fallen asleep he heard a knocking at the front door, first rather timidly performed, and then louder. Nobody answered it, and the person knocked again. As the house still remained undisturbed, Stockdale got out of bed, went to his window, which overlooked the

333

door, and opening it, asked who was there.

A young woman's voice replied that Susan Wallis was there, and that she had come to ask if Mrs. Newberry could give her some mustard to make a plaster with, as her father was taken very ill on the chest.

The minister, having neither bell nor servant, was compelled to act in person. "I will call Mrs. Newberry," he said. Partly dressing himself, he went along the passage and tapped at Lizzy's door. She did not answer, and, thinking of her erratic habits in the matter of sleep, he thumped the door persistently, when he discovered, by its moving ajar under his knocking, that it had only been gently pushed to. As there was now a sufficient entry for the voice, he knocked no longer, but said in firm tones, "Mrs. Newberry, you are wanted."

The room was quite silent; not a breathing, not a rustle, came from any part of it. Stockdale now sent a positive shout through the open space of the door: "Mrs. Newberry!" — still no answer, or movement of any kind within. Then he heard sounds from the opposite room, that of Lizzy's mother, as if she had been aroused by his uproar though Lizzy had not, and was dressing herself hastily. Stockdale softly closed the younger woman's door and went on to the other, which was opened by Mrs. Simpkins before he could reach it. She was in her ordinary clothes, and had a light in her hand.

"What's the person calling about?" she said in alarm.

Stockdale told the girl's errand, adding seriously, "I cannot wake Mrs. Newberry."

"It is no matter," said her mother. "I can let the girl have what she wants as well as my daughter." And she came out of the room and went downstairs.

Stockdale retired towards his own apartment, saying, however, to Mrs. Simpkins from the landing, as if on second thoughts, "I suppose there is nothing the matter with Mrs. Newberry, that I could not wake her?"

"O no," said the old lady hastily. "Nothing at all."

Still the minister was not satisfied. "Will you go in and see?" he said. "I should be much more at ease."

Mrs. Simpkins returned up the staircase, went to her daughter's room, and came out again almost instantly. "There is nothing at all the matter with Lizzy," she said; and descended again to attend to the applicant, who, having seen the light, had remained quiet during this interval.

Stockdale went into his room and lay down as before. He heard Lizzy's mother open the front door, admit the girl, and then the murmured discourse of both as they went to the store-cupboard for the medicament required. The girl departed, the door was fastened, Mrs. Simpkins came upstairs, and the house was again in silence. Still the minister did not fall asleep. He could not get rid of a singular suspicion, which was all the more harassing, in being, if true, the most unaccountable thing within his experience. That Lizzy Newberry was in her bedroom when he made such a clamour at the door he could not possibly convince himself, notwithstanding that he had heard her come upstairs at the usual time, go into her chamber, and shut herself up in the usual way. Yet all reason was so much against her being elsewhere, that he was constrained to go back again to the unlikely theory of a heavy sleep, though he had heard neither breath nor movement during a shouting and knocking loud enough to rouse the Seven Sleepers.

Before coming to any positive conclusion he fell asleep himself, and did not awake till day. He saw nothing of Mrs. Newberry in the morning, before he went out to meet the rising sun, as he liked to do when the weather was fine; but as this was by no means unusual, he took no notice of it. At breakfast-time he knew that she was not far off by hearing her in the kitchen, and though he saw nothing of her person, that back apartment being rigorously closed against his eyes, she seemed to be talking, ordering, and bustling about among the pots and skimmers in so ordinary a manner, that there was no reason for his wasting more time in fruitless surmise.

The minister suffered from these distractions, and his extemporised sermons were not improved thereby. Already he often said Romans for Corinthians in the pulpit, and gave out hymns in strange cramped metres, that hitherto had always been skipped, because the congregation could not raise a tune to fit them. He fully resolved that as soon as his few weeks of stay approached their end he would cut the matter short, and commit himself by proposing a definite engagement, repenting at leisure if necessary.

With this end in view, he suggested to her on the evening after her mysterious sleep that they should take a walk together just before dark, the latter part of the proposition being introduced that they might return home unseen. She consented to go; and away they went over a stile, to a shrouded foot-path suited for the occasion. But, in spite of attempts on both sides, they were unable to infuse much spirit into the ramble. She looked rather paler than usual, and sometimes turned her head away.

"Lizzy," said Stockdale reproachfully, when they had walked in silence a long distance.

"Yes," said she.

"You yawned — much my company is to you!" He put it in that way, but he was really wondering whether her yawn could possibly have more to do with physical weariness from the night before than mental weariness of that present moment. Lizzy apologised, and owned that she was rather tired, which gave him an opening for a direct question on the point; but his modesty would not allow him to put it to her; and he uncomfortably resolved to wait.

The month of February passed with alternations of mud and frost, rain and sleet, east winds and north-westerly gales. The hollow places in the ploughed fields showed themselves as pools of water, which had settled there from the higher levels, and had not yet found time to soak away. The birds began to get lively, and a single thrush came just before sunset each evening, and sang hopefully on the large elm tree which stood nearest to Mrs. Newberry's house. Cold blasts and brittle earth had given place to an oozing dampness more unpleasant in itself than frost; but it suggested coming spring, and its unpleasantness was of a bearable kind.

Stockdale had been going to bring about a practical understanding with Lizzy at least half-a-dozen times; but, what with the mystery of her apparent absence on the night of the neighbour's call, and her curious way of lying in bed at unaccountable times, he felt a check within him whenever he wanted to speak out. Thus they still lived on as indefinitely affianced lovers, each of whom hardly acknowledged the other's claim to the name of chosen one. Stockdale persuaded himself that his hesitation was owing to the postponement of the ordained minister's arrival, and the consequent delay in his own departure, which did away with all necessity for haste in his courtship; but perhaps it was only that his discretion was re-asserting itself, and telling him that he had better get clearer ideas of Lizzy before arranging for the grand contract of his life with her. She, on her part, always seemed ready to be urged further on that question than he had hitherto attempted to go; but she was none the less independent, and to a degree which would have kept from flagging the passion of a far more mutable man.

On the evening of the 1st of March he went casually into his bedroom about dusk, and noticed lying on a chair a great-coat, hat, and breeches. Having no recollection of leaving any clothes of his own in that spot, he went and examined them as well as he could in the twilight, and found that they did not belong to him. He paused for a moment to consider how they might have got there. He was the only man living in the house; and yet these were not his garments, unless he had made a mistake. No, they were not his. He called up Martha Sarah.

"How did these things come in my room?" he said, flinging the objectionable articles to the floor.

Martha said that Mrs. Newberry had given them to her to brush, and that she had brought them up there thinking they must be Mr. Stockdale's, as there was no other gentleman a-lodging there.

"Of course you did," said Stockdale. "Now take them down to your mis'ess, and say they are some clothes I have found here and know nothing about."

As the door was left open he heard the conversation downstairs. "How stupid!" said Mrs. Newberry, in a tone of confusion. "Why, Marther Sarer, I did not tell you to take 'em to Mr. Stockdale's room."

"I thought they must be his as they was so muddy," said Martha, humbly.

"You should have left 'em on the clothes-horse," said the young mistress, severely; and she came upstairs with the garments on her arm, quickly passed Stockdale's room, and threw them forcibly into a closet at the end of a passage. With this the incident ended, and the house was silent again.

There would have been nothing remarkable in finding such clothes in a widow's house had they been clean; or moth-eaten, or creased, or mouldy from long lying by; but that they should be splashed with recent mud bothered Stockdale a good deal. When a young pastor is in the aspen stage of attachment, and open to agitation at the merest trifles, a really substantial incongruity of this complexion is a disturbing thing. However, nothing further occurred at that time; but he became watchful, and given to conjecture, and was unable to forget the circumstance.

One morning, on looking from his window, he saw Mrs. Newberry herself brushing the tails of a long drab great-coat, which, if he mistook not, was the very same garment as the one that had adorned the chair of his room. It was densely splashed up to the hollow of the back with neighbouring Nether-Moynton mud, to judge by its colour, the spots being distinctly visible to him in the sunlight. The previous day or two having been wet, the inference was irresistible that the wearer had quite recently been walking some considerable distance about the lanes and fields. Stockdale opened the window and looked out, and Mrs. Newberry turned her head. Her face became slowly red; she never had looked prettier, or more incomprehensible. He waved his hand affectionately, and said good-morning; she answered with embarrassment, having ceased her occupation on the instant that she saw him, and rolled up the coat half-cleaned.

Stockdale shut the window. Some simple explanation of her proceeding was doubtless within the bounds of possibility; but he himself could not think of one; and he wished that she had placed the matter beyond conjecture by voluntarily saying something about it there and then.

But, though Lizzy had not offered an explanation at the moment, the subject was brought forward by her at the next time of their meeting. She was chatting to him concerning some other event, and remarked that it happened about the time when she was dusting some old clothes that had belonged to her poor husband.

"You keep them clean out of respect to his memory?" said Stockdale, tentatively.

"I air and dust them sometimes," she said, with the most charming innocence in the world.

"Do dead men come out of their graves and walk in mud?" murmured the minister, in a cold sweat at the deception that she was practising.

"What did you say?" asked Lizzy.

"Nothing, nothing," said he, mournfully. "Mere words — a phrase that will do for my sermon next Sunday." It was too plain that Lizzy was unaware that he had seen fresh pedestrian splashes upon the skirts of the tell-tale overcoat, and that she imagined him to believe it had come direct from some chest or drawer.

The aspect of the case was now considerably darker. Stockdale was so much depressed by it that he did not challenge her explanation, or threaten to go off as a missionary to benighted islanders, or reproach her in any way whatever. He simply parted from her when she had done talking, and lived on in perplexity, till by degrees his natural manner became sad and constrained.

IV.   At the Time of the New Moon

The following Thursday was changeable, damp, and gloomy; and the night threatened to be windy and unpleasant. Stockdale had gone away to Knollsea in the morning, to be present at some commemoration service there, and on his return he was met by the attractive Lizzy in the passage. Whether influenced by the tide of cheerfulness which had attended him that day, or by the drive through the open air, or whether from a natural disposition to let bygones alone, he allowed himself to be fascinated into forgetfulness of the great-coat incident, and upon the whole passed a pleasant evening; not so much in her society as within sound of her voice, as she sat talking in the back parlour to her mother, till the latter went to bed. Shortly after this Mrs. Newberry retired, and then Stockdale prepared to go upstairs himself. But before he left the room he remained standing by the dying embers awhile, thinking long of one thing and another; and was only aroused by the flickering of his candle in the socket as it suddenly declined and went out. Knowing that there were a tinder-box, matches, and another candle in his bedroom, he felt his way upstairs without a light. On reaching his chamber he laid his hand on every possible ledge and corner for the tinder-box, but for a long time in vain. Discovering it at length, Stockdale produced a spark, and was kindling the brimstone, when he fancied that he heard a movement in the passage. He blew harder at the lint, the match flared up, and looking by aid of the blue light through the door, which had been standing open all this time, he was surprised to see a male figure vanishing round the top of the staircase with the evident intention of escaping unobserved. The personage wore the clothes which Lizzy had been brushing, and something in the outline and gait suggested to the minister that the wearer was Lizzy herself.

But he was not sure of this; and, greatly excited, Stockdale determined to investigate the mystery, and to adopt his own way for doing it. He blew out the match without lighting the candle, went into the passage, and proceeded on tiptoe towards Lizzy's room. A faint grey square of light in the direction of the chamber-window as he approached told him that the door was open, and at once suggested that the occupant was gone. He turned and brought down his fist upon the handrail of the staircase: "It was she; in her late husband's coat and hat!"

Somewhat relieved to find that there was no intruder in the case, yet none the less surprised, the minister crept down the stairs, softly put on his boots, overcoat, and hat, and tried the front door. It was fastened as usual: he went to the back door, found this unlocked, and emerged into the garden. The night was mild and moonless, and rain had lately been falling, though for the present it had ceased. There was a sudden dropping from the trees and bushes every now and then, as each passing wind shook their boughs. Among these sounds Stockdale heard the faint fall of feet upon the road outside, and he guessed from the step that it was Lizzy's. He followed the sound, and, helped by the circumstance of the wind blowing from the direction in which the pedestrian moved, he got nearly close to her, and kept there, without risk of being overheard. While he thus followed her up the street or lane, as it might indifferently be called, there being more hedge than houses on either side, a figure came forward to her from one of the cottage doors. Lizzy stopped; the minister stepped upon the grass and stopped also.

"Is that Mrs. Newberry?" said the man who had come out, whose voice Stockdale recognised as that of one of the most devout members of his congregation.

"It is," said Lizzy.

"I be quite ready — I've been here this quarter-hour."

"Ah John," said she, "I have bad news; there is danger to-night for our venture."

"And d'ye tell o't! I dreamed there might be."

"Yes," she said hurriedly; "and you must go at once round to where the chaps are waiting, and tell them they will not be wanted till to-morrow night at the same time. I go to burn the lugger off."

"I will," he said; and instantly went off through a gate, Lizzy continuing her way.

On she tripped at a quickening pace till the lane turned into the turnpike road, which she crossed, and got into the track for Ringsworth. Here she ascended the hill without the least hesitation, passed the lonely hamlet of Holworth, and went down the vale on the other side. Stockdale had never taken any extensive walks in this direction, but he was aware that if she persisted in her course much longer she would draw near to the coast, which was here between two and three miles distant from Nether-Moynton; and as it had been about a quarter-past eleven o'clock when they set out, her intention seemed to be to reach the shore about midnight.

Lizzy soon ascended a small mound, which Stockdale at the same time adroitly skirted on the left; and a dull monotonous roar burst upon his ear. The hillock was about fifty yards from the top of the cliffs, and by day it apparently commanded a full view of the bay. There was light enough in the sky to show her disguised figure against it when she reached the top, where she paused, and afterwards sat down. Stockdale, not wishing on any account to alarm her at this moment, yet desirous of being near her, sank upon his hands and knees, crept a little higher up, and there stayed still.

The wind was chilly, the ground damp, and his position one in which he did not care to remain long. However, before he had decided to leave it, the young man heard voices behind him. What they signified he did not know; but, fearing that Lizzy was in danger, he was about to run forward and warn her that she might be seen, when she crept to the shelter of a little bush which maintained a precarious existence in that exposed spot; and her form was absorbed in its dark and stunted outline as if she had become part of it. She had evidently heard the men as well as he. They passed near him, talking in loud and careless tones, which could be heard above the uninterrupted washings of the sea, and which suggested that they were not engaged in any business at their own risk. This proved to be the fact: some of their words floated across to him, and caused him to forget at once the coldness of his situation.

"What's the vessel?"

"A lugger, about fifty tons."

"From Cherbourg, I suppose?"

"Yes, 'a b'lieve."

"But it don't all belong to Owlett?"

"Oh no. He's only got a share. There's another or two in it — a farmer and such like, but the names I don't know."

The voices died away, and the heads and shoulders of the men diminished towards the cliff, and dropped out of sight.

"My darling has been tempted to buy a share by that unbeliever Owlett," groaned the minister, his honest affection for Lizzy having quickened to its intensest point during these moments of risk to her person and name. "That's why she's here," he said to himself. "Oh, it will be the ruin of her!"

His perturbation was interrupted by the sudden bursting out of a bright and increasing light from the spot where Lizzy was in hiding. A few seconds later, and before it had reached the height of a blaze, he heard her rush past him down the hollow like a stone from a sling, in the direction of home. The light now flared high and wide, and showed its position clearly. She had kindled a bough of furze and stuck it into the bush under which she had been crouching; the wind fanned the flame, which crackled fiercely, and threatened to consume the bush as well as the bough. Stockdale paused just long enough to notice thus much, and then followed rapidly the route taken by the young woman. His intention was to overtake her, and reveal himself as a friend; but run as he would he could see nothing of her. Thus he flew across the open country about Holworth, twisting his legs and ankles in unexpected fissures and descents, till, on coming to the gate between the downs and the road, he was forced to pause to get breath. There was no audible movement either in front or behind him, and he now concluded that she had not outrun him, but that, hearing him at her heels, and believing him one of the excise party, she had hidden herself somewhere on the way, and let him pass by.

He went on at a more leisurely pace towards the village. On reaching the house he found his surmise to be correct, for the gate was on the latch, and the door unfastened, just as he had left them. Stockdale closed the door behind him, and waited silently in the passage. In about ten minutes he heard the same light footstep that he had heard in going out; it paused at the gate, which opened and shut softly, and then the door-latch was lifted, and Lizzy came in.

Stockdale went forward and said at once, "Lizzy, don't be frightened. I have been waiting up for you."

She started, though she had recognised the voice. "It is Mr. Stockdale, isn't it?" she said.

"Yes," he answered, becoming angry now that she was safe indoors, and not alarmed. "And a nice game I've found you out in to-night. You are in man's clothes, and I am ashamed of you."

Lizzy could hardly find a voice to answer this unexpected reproach.

"I am only partly in man's clothes," she faltered, shrinking back to the wall. "It is only his great-coat and hat and breeches that I've got on, which is no harm, as he was my own husband; and I do it only because a cloak blows about so, and you can't use your arms. I have got my own dress under just the same — it is only tucked in! Will you go away upstairs and let me pass? I didn't want you to see me at such a time as this."

"But I have a right to see you. How do you think there can be anything between us now?" Lizzy was silent. "You are a smuggler," he continued sadly.

"I have only a share in the run," she said.

"That makes no difference. Whatever did you engage in such a trade as that for, and keep it such a secret from me all this time?"

"I don't do it always. I only do it in winter-time when 'tis new moon."

"Well, I suppose that's because it can't be done anywhen else. . . . You have regularly upset me, Lizzy."

"I am sorry for that," Lizzy meekly replied.

"Well now," said he more tenderly, "no harm is done as yet. Won't you for the sake of me give up this blamable and dangerous practice altogether?"

"I must do my best to save this run," said she, getting rather husky in the throat. "I don't want to give you up — you know that; but I don't want to lose my venture. I don't know what to do now! Why I have kept it so secret from you is that I was afraid you would be angry if you knew."

"I should think so. I suppose if I had married you without finding this out you'd have gone on with it just the same?"

"I don't know. I did not think so far ahead. I only went to-night to burn the folks off, because we found that the preventive-men knew where the tubs were to be landed."

"It is a pretty mess to be in altogether, is this," said the distracted young minister. "Well, what will you do now?"

Lizzy slowly murmured the particulars of their plan, the chief of which were that they meant to try their luck at some other point of the shore the next night; that three landing places were always agreed upon before the run was attempted, with the understanding that, if the vessel was "burnt off" from the first point, which was Ringsworth, as it had been by her to-night, the crew should attempt to make the second, which was Lulwind Cove, on the second night; and if there, too, danger threatened, they should on the third night try the third place, which was behind a headland further west.

"Suppose the officers hinder them landing there too?" he said, his attention to this interesting programme displacing for a moment his concern at her share in it.

"Then we shan't try anywhere else all this dark — that's what we call the time be-tween moon and moon — and perhaps they'll string the tubs to a stray-line, and sink 'em a little-ways from shore, and take the bearings; and then when they have a chance they'll go to creep for 'em."

"What's that?"

"Oh, they'll go out in a boat and drag a creeper — that's a grapnel — along the bottom till it catch hold of the stray-line."

The minister stood thinking; and there was no sound within doors but the tick of the clock on the stairs, and the quick breathing of Lizzy, partly from her walk and partly from agitation, as she stood close to the wall, not in such complete darkness but that he could discern against its whitewashed surface the great-coat, breeches, and broad hat which covered her.

"Lizzy, all this is very wrong," he said. "Don't you remember the lesson of the tribute-money? 'Render unto Caesar the things that are Caesar's.' Surely you have heard that read times enough in your growing up."

"He's dead," she pouted.

"But the spirit of the text is in force just the same."

"My father did it, and so did my grandfather, and almost everybody in Nether-Moynton lives by it, and life would be so dull if it wasn't for that, that I should not care to live at all."

"I am nothing to live for, of course," he replied bitterly. "You would not think it worth while to give up this wild business and live for me alone?"

"I have never looked at it like that."

"And you won't promise, and wait till I am ready?"

"I cannot give you my word to-night." And, looking thoughtfully down, she gradually moved and moved away, going into the adjoining room, and closing the door between them. She remained there in the dark till he was tired of waiting, and had gone up to his own chamber.

Poor Stockdale was dreadfully depressed all the next day by the discoveries of the night before. Lizzy was unmistakably a fascinating young woman; but as a minister's wife she was hardly to be contemplated. "If I had only stuck to father's little grocery business, instead of going in for the ministry, she would have suited me beautifully!" he said sadly, until he remembered that in that case he would never have come from his distant home to Nether-Moynton, and never have known her.

The estrangement between them was not complete, but it was sufficient to keep them out of each other's company. Once during the day he met her in the garden-path, and said, turning a reproachful eye upon her, "Do you promise, Lizzy?" But she did not reply. The evening drew on, and he knew well enough that Lizzy would repeat her excursion at night — her half-offended manner had shown that she had not the slightest intention of altering her plans at present. He did not wish to repeat his own share of the adventure; but, act as he would, his uneasiness on her account increased with the decline of day. Supposing that an accident should befall her, he would never forgive himself for not being there to help, much as he disliked the idea of seeming to countenance such unlawful escapades.

V. How They Went to Lulwind Cove

As he had expected, she left the house at the same hour at night, this time passing his door without stealth, as if she knew very well that he would be watching, and were resolved to brave his displeasure. He was quite ready, opened the door quickly, and reached the back door almost as soon as she.

"Then you will go, Lizzy?" he said as he stood on the step beside her, who now again appeared as a little man with a face altogether unsuited to his clothes.

"I must," she said, repressed by his stern manner.

"Then I shall go too," said he.

"And I am sure you will enjoy it!" she exclaimed, in more buoyant tones. "Everybody does who tries it."

"God forbid that I should," he said. "But I must look after you."

They opened the wicket and went up the road abreast of each other, but at some distance apart, scarcely a word passing between them. The evening was rather less favourable to smuggling enterprise than the last had been, the wind being lower, and the sky somewhat clear towards the north.

"It is rather lighter," said Stockdale.

" 'Tis, unfortunately," said she. "But it is only from those few stars over there. The moon was new to-day at four o'clock, and I expected clouds. I hope we shall be able to do it this dark, for when we have to sink 'em for long it makes the stuff taste bleachy, and folks don't like it so well."

Her course was different from that of the preceding night, branching off to the left over Lord's Barrow as soon as they had got out of the lane and crossed the highway. By the time they reached Shaldon Down, Stockdale, who had been in perplexed thought as to what he should say to her, decided that he would not attempt expostulation now, while she was excited by the adventure, but wait till it was over, and endeavour to keep her from such practices in future. It occurred to him once or twice, as they rambled on, that should they be surprised by the Preventive-guard, his situation would be more awkward than hers, for it would be difficult to prove his true motive in coming to the spot; but the risk was a slight consideration beside his wish to be with her.

They now arrived at a ravine which lay on the outskirts of Shaldon, a village two miles on their way towards the point of the shore they sought. Lizzy broke the silence this time: "I have to wait here to meet the carriers. I don't know if they have come yet. As I told you, we go to Lulwind Cove to-night, and it is two miles further than Ringsworth."

It turned out that the men had already come; for while she spoke two or three dozen heads broke the line of the slope, and a company of them at once descended from the bushes where they had been lying in wait. These carriers were men whom Lizzy and other proprietors regularly employed to bring the tubs from the boat to a hiding-place inland. They were all young fellows of Nether-Moynton, Shaldon, and the neighbourhood, quiet and inoffensive persons, even though some held heavy sticks, who simply engaged to carry the cargo for Lizzy and her cousin Owlett, as they would have engaged in any other labour for which they were fairly well paid.

At a word from her they closed in together. "You had better take it now," she said to them; and handed to each a packet. It contained six shillings, their re-muneration for the night's undertaking, which was paid beforehand without refer-ence to success or failure; but, besides this, they had the privilege of selling as agents when the run was successfully made. As soon as it was done, she said to them, "The place is the old one, Dagger's Grave, near Lulwind Cove"; the men till that moment not having been told whither they were bound, for obvious reasons. "Mr. Owlett will meet you there," added Lizzy. "I shall follow behind, to see that we are not watched."

The carriers went on, and Stockdale and Mrs. Newberry followed at a distance of a stone's-throw. "What do these men do by day?" he said.

"Twelve or fourteen of them are la-bouring men. Some are brickmakers, some carpenters, some shoemakers, some thatchers. They are all known to me very well. Nine of 'em are of your own congre-gation."

"I can't help that," said Stockdale.

"O, I know you can't. I only told you. The others are more church-inclined, be-cause they supply the pa'son with all the spirits he requires, and they don't wish to show unfriendliness to a customer."

"How do you choose 'em?" said Stock-dale.

"We choose 'em for their closeness, and because they are strong and surefooted, and able to carry a heavy load a long way without being tired."

Stockdale sighed as she enumerated each particular, for it proved how far involved in the business a woman must be who was so well acquainted with its conditions and needs. And yet he felt more tenderly towards her at this moment than he had felt all the foregoing day. Perhaps it was that her experienced manner and bold indifference stirred his admiration in spite of himself.

"Take my arm, Lizzy," he murmured.

"I don't want it," she said. "Besides, we may never be to each other again what we once have been."

"That depends upon you," said he, and they went on again as before.

The hired carriers paced along over Shaldon Down with as little hesitation as if it had been day, avoiding the cart-way, and leaving the village of East Shaldon on the left, so as to reach the crest of the hill at a lonely trackless place not far from the ancient earthwork called Round Pound. A quarter-hour more of brisk walking brought them within sound of the sea, to the place called Dagger's Grave, not many hundred yards from Lulwind Cove. Here they paused, and Lizzy and Stockdale came up with them, when they went on together to the verge of the cliff. One of the men now produced an iron bar, which he drove firmly into the soil a yard from the edge, and attached to it a rope that he had uncoiled from his body. They all began to descend, partly stepping, partly sliding down the incline, as the rope slipped through their hands.

"You will not go to the bottom, Lizzy?" said Stockdale anxiously.

"No. I stay here to watch," she said. "Mr. Owlett is down there."

The men remained quite silent when they reached the shore; and the next thing audible to the two at the top was the dip of heavy oars, and the dashing of waves against a boat's bow. In a moment the keel gently touched the shingle, and Stockdale heard the footsteps of the thirty-six carriers running forwards over the pebbles towards the point of landing.

There was a sousing in the water as of a brood of ducks plunging in, showing that the men had not been particular about keeping their legs, or even their waists, dry from the brine; but it was impossible to see what they were doing, and in a few minutes the shingle was trampled again. The iron bar sustaining the rope, on which Stockdale's hand rested, began to swerve a little, and the carriers one by one appeared climbing up the sloping cliff, dripping audibly as they came, and sustaining themselves by the guide-rope. Each man on reaching the top was seen to be carrying a pair of tubs, one on his back and one on his chest, the two being slung together by cords passing round the chine hoops, and resting on the carrier's shoulders. Some of the stronger men carried three by putting an extra one on the top behind, but the customary load was a pair, these being quite weighty enough to give their bearer the sensation of having chest and backbone in contact after a walk of four or five miles.

"Where is Mr. Owlett?" said Lizzy to one of them.

"He will not come up this way," said the carrier. "He's to bide on shore till we be safe off." Then, without waiting for the rest, the foremost men plunged across the down; and, when the last had ascended, Lizzy pulled up the rope, wound it round her arm, wriggled the bar from the sod, and turned to follow the carriers.

"You are very anxious about Owlett's safety," said the minister.

"Was there ever such a man!" said Lizzy. "Why, isn't he my cousin?"

"Yes. Well, it is a bad night's work," said Stockdale heavily. "But I'll carry the bar and rope for you."

"Thank God, the tubs have got so far all right," said she. Stockdale shook his head, and, taking the bar, walked by her side towards the downs; and the moan of the sea was heard no more.

"Is this what you meant the other day when you spoke of having business with Owlett?" the young man asked.

"This is it," she replied. "I never see him on any other matter."

"A partnership of that kind with a young man is very odd."

"It was begun by my father and his, who were brother-laws."

Her companion could not blind himself to the fact that where tastes and pursuits were so akin as Lizzy's and Owlett's, and where risks were shared, as with them, in every undertaking, there would be a peculiar appropriateness in her answering Owlett's standing question on matrimony in the affirmative. This did not soothe Stockdale, its tendency being rather to stimulate in him an effort to make the pair as inappropriate as possible, and win her away from this nocturnal crew to correctness of conduct and a minister's parlour in some far-removed inland county.

They had been walking near enough to the file of carriers for Stockdale to perceive that, when they got into the road to the village, they split up into two companies of unequal size, each of which made off in a direction of its own. One company, the smaller of the two, went towards the church, and by the time that Lizzy and Stockdale reached their own house these men had scaled the churchyard wall, and were proceeding noiselessly over the grass within.

"I see that Mr. Owlett has arranged for one batch to be put in the church again," observed Lizzy. "Do you remember my taking you there the first night you came?"

"Yes, of course," said Stockdale. "No wonder you had permission to broach the tubs — they were his, I suppose?"

"No, they were not — they were mine; I had permission from myself. The day after that they went several miles inland in a waggon-load of manure, and sold very well."

At this moment the group of men who

had made off to the left some time before began leaping one by one from the hedge opposite Lizzy's house, and the first man, who had no tubs upon his shoulders, came forward.

"Mrs. Newberry, isn't it?" he said hastily.

"Yes, Jim," said she. "What's the matter?"

"I find that we can't put any in Badger's Clump to-night, Lizzy," said Owlett. "The place is watched. We must sling the apple-tree in the orchet if there's time. We can't put any more under the church lumber than I have sent on there, and my mixen hev already more in en than is safe."

"Very well," she said. "Be quick about it — that's all. What can I do?"

"Nothing at all, please. Ah, it is the minister — you two that can't do anything had better get indoors and not be zeed."

While Owlett thus conversed, in a tone so full of contraband anxiety and so free from lover's jealousy, the men who followed him had been descending one by one from the hedge; and it unfortunately happened that when the hindmost took his leap, the cord slipped which sustained his tubs: the result was that both the kegs fell into the road, one of them being stove in by the blow.

" 'Od drown it all!" said Owlett, rushing back.

"It is worth a good deal, I suppose?" said Stockdale.

"O no — about two guineas and half to us now," said Lizzy, excitedly. "It isn't that — it is the smell. It is so blazing strong before it has been lowered by water, that it smells dreadfully when spilt in the road like that! I do hope Latimer won't pass by till it is gone off."

Owlett and one or two others picked up the burst tub and began to scrape and trample over the spot, to disperse the liquor as much as possible; and then they all entered the gate of Owlett's orchard, which adjoined Lizzy's garden on the right. Stockdale did not care to follow them, for several on recognising him had looked wonderingly at his presence, though they said nothing. Lizzy left his side and went to the bottom of the garden, looking over the hedge into the orchard, where the men could be dimly seen bustling about, and apparently hiding the tubs. All was done noiselessly, and without a light; and when it was over they dispersed in different directions, those who had taken their cargoes to the church having already gone off to their homes.

Lizzy returned to the garden-gate, over which Stockdale was still abstractedly leaning. "It is all finished: I am going indoors now," she said gently. "I will leave the door ajar for you."

"O no — you needn't," said Stockdale; "I am coming too."

But before either of them had moved, the faint clatter of horses' hoofs broke upon the ear, and it seemed to come from the point where the track across the down joined the hard road.

"They are just too late!" cried Lizzy exultingly.

"Who?" said Stockdale.

"Latimer, the riding-officer, and some assistant of his. We had better go indoors."

They entered the house, and Lizzy bolted the door. "Please don't get a light, Mr. Stockdale," she said.

"Of course I will not," said he.

"I thought you might be on the side of the king," said Lizzy, with faintest sarcasm.

"I am," said Stockdale. "But, Lizzy Newberry, I love you, and you know it perfectly well; and you ought to know, if you do not, what I have suffered in my conscience on your account these last few days."

"I guess very well," she said hurriedly.

"Yet I don't see why. Ah, you are better than I!"

The trotting of the horses seemed to have again died away, and the pair of listeners touched each other's fingers in the cold "Good-night" of those whom something seriously divided. They were on the landing, but before they had taken three steps apart, the tramp of the horsemen suddenly revived, almost close to the house. Lizzy turned to the staircase-window, opened the casement about an inch, and put her face close to the aperture. "Yes, one of 'em is Latimer," she whispered. "He always rides a white horse. One would think it was the last colour for a man in that line."

Stockdale looked, and saw the white shape of the animal as it passed by; but before the riders had gone another ten yards, Latimer reined in his horse, and said something to his companion which neither Stockdale nor Lizzy could hear. Its drift was, however, soon made evident, for the other man stopped also; and sharply turning the horses' heads they cautiously retraced their steps. When they were again opposite Mrs. Newberry's garden, Latimer dismounted, and the man on the dark horse did the same.

Lizzy and Stockdale, intently listening and observing the proceedings, naturally put their heads as close as possible to the slit formed by the slightly opened casement; and thus it occurred that at last their cheeks came positively into contact. They went on listening, as if they did not know of the singular incident which had happened to their faces, and the pressure of each to each rather increased than lessened with the lapse of time.

They could hear the Customs-men sniffing the air like hounds as they paced slowly along. When they reached the spot where the tub had burst, both stopped on the instant.

"Ay, ay, 'tis quite strong here," said the second officer. "Shall we knock at the door?"

"Well, no," said Latimer. "Maybe this is only a trick to put us off the scent. They wouldn't kick up this stink anywhere near their hiding-place. I have known such things before."

"Anyhow, the things, or some of 'em, must have been brought this way," said the other.

"Yes," said Latimer musingly. "Unless 'tis all done to tole us the wrong way. I have a mind that we go home for to-night without saying a word, and come the first thing in the morning with more hands. I know they have storages about here, but we can do nothing by this owl's light. We will look round the parish and see if everybody is in bed, John; and if all is quiet, we will do as I say."

They went on, and the two inside the window could hear them passing leisurely through the whole village, the street of which curved round at the bottom and entered the turnpike-road at another junction. This way the officers followed, and the amble of their horses died quite away.

"What will you do?" said Stockdale, withdrawing from his position.

She knew that he alluded to the coming search by the officers, to divert her attention from their own tender incident by the casement, which he wished to be passed over as a thing rather dreamt of than done. "Oh, nothing," she replied, with as much coolness as she could command under her disappointment at his manner. "We often have such storms as this. You would not be frightened if you knew what fools they are. Fancy riding o' horseback through the place: of course they will hear and see nobody while they make that noise; but they are always afraid to get off, in case some of our fellows should burst out upon 'em, and tie them up to the gate-post, as they have done before now. Good-night, Mr. Stockdale."

She closed the window and went to her room, where a tear fell from her eyes; and that not because of the alertness of the riding officers.

VI. The Great Search at Nether-Moynton

Stockdale was so excited by the events of the evening, and the dilemma that he was placed in between conscience and love, that he did not sleep, or even doze, but remained as broadly awake as at noonday. As soon as the grey light began to touch ever so faintly the whiter objects in his bedroom he arose, dressed himself, and went downstairs into the road.

The village was already astir. Several of the carriers had heard the well-known canter of Latimer's horse while they were undressing in the dark that night, and had already communicated with each other and Owlett on the subject. The only doubt seemed to be about the safety of those tubs which had been left under the church gallery-stairs, and after a short discussion at the corner of the mill, it was agreed that these should be removed before it got lighter, and hidden in the middle of a double hedge bordering the adjoining field. However, before anything could be carried into effect, the footsteps of many men were heard coming down the lane from the highway.

"Damn it, here they be," said Owlett, who, having already drawn the hatch and started his mill for the day, stood stolidly at the mill door covered with flour, as if the interest of his whole soul was bound up in the shaking walls around him.

The two or three with whom he had been talking dispersed to their usual work, and when the Customs-officers, and the formidable body of men they had hired, reached the village cross, between the mill and Mrs. Newberry's house, the village wore the natural aspect of a place beginning its morning labours.

"Now," said Latimer to his associates, who numbered thirteen men in all, "what I know is that the things are somewhere in this here place. We have got the day before us, and 'tis hard if we can't light upon 'em and get 'em to Budmouth Custom-house before night. First we will try the fuel-houses, and then we'll work our way into the chimmers, and then to the ricks and stables, and so creep round. You have nothing but your noses to guide ye, mind, so use 'em to-day if you never did in your lives before."

Then the search began. Owlett, during the early part, watched from his mill-window, Lizzy from the door of her house, with the greatest self-possession. A farmer down below, who also had a share in the run, rode about with one eye on his fields and the other on Latimer and his myrmidons, prepared to put them off the scent if he should be asked a question. Stockdale, who was no smuggler at all, felt more anxiety than the worst of them, and went about his studies with a heavy heart, coming frequently to the door to ask Lizzy some question or other on the consequences to her of the tubs being found.

"The consequences," she said quietly, "are simply that I shall lose 'em. As I have none in the house or garden, they can't touch me personally."

"But you have some in the orchard."

"Mr. Owlett rents that of me, and he lends it to others. So it will be hard to say who put any tubs there if they should be found."

There was never such a tremendous sniffing known as that which took place in Nether-Moynton parish and its vicinity this day. All was done methodically, and mostly on hands and knees. At different hours of the day they had different plans. From day-break to breakfast-time the officers used their sense of smell in a direct and straightforward manner only, pausing nowhere but at such places as the tubs might be supposed to be secreted in at that very moment, pending their removal on the following night. Among the places tested and examined were —

Hollow trees   Chimney-flues
Potato-graves   Rainwater-butts
Fuel-houses   Pigsties
Bedrooms   Culverts
Apple-lofts   Hedgerows
Cupboards   Faggot-ricks
Clock-cases   Haystacks
Coppers and ovens.

After breakfast they recommenced with renewed vigour, taking a new line; that is to say, directing their attention to clothes that might be supposed to have come in contact with the tubs in their removal from the shore; such garments being usually tainted with the spirit, owing to its oozing between the staves. They now sniffed at

> Smock-frocks
> Old shirts and waistcoats
> Coats and hats
> Breeches and leggings
> Women's shawls and gowns
> Smiths' and shoemakers' aprons
> Knee-naps and hedging-gloves
> Tarpaulins
> Market-cloaks
> Scarecrows.

And, as soon as the midday meal was over, they pushed their search into places where the spirits might have been thrown away in alarm: —

> Horse-ponds   Cesspools
> Stable-drains   Sinks in yards
> Cinder-heaps   Road-scrapings, and
> Mixens   Back-door gutters.
> Wet ditches

But still these indefatigable Custom-house men discovered nothing more than the original tell-tale smell in the road opposite Lizzy's house, which even yet had not passed off.

"I'll tell ye what it is, men," said Latimer, about three o'clock in the afternoon; "we must begin over again. Find them tubs I will."

The men, who had been hired for the day, looked at their hands and knees, muddy with creeping on all fours so frequently, and rubbed their noses, as if they had almost had enough of it; for the quantity of bad air which had passed into each one's nostril had rendered it nearly as insensible as a flue. However, after a moment's hesitation they prepared to start anew, except three, whose power of smell had quite succumbed under the excessive wear and tear of the day.

By this time not a male villager was to be seen in the parish. Owlett was not at his mill, the farmers were not in their fields, the parson was not in his garden, the smith had left his forge, and the wheelwright's shop was silent.

"Where the divil are the folk gone?" said Latimer, waking up to the fact of their absence, and looking round. "I'll have 'em up for this! Why don't they come and help us? There's not a man about the place but the Methodist parson; and he's an old woman. I demand assistance in the king's name."

"We must find the jineral public afore we

can demand that," said his lieutenant.

"Well, well, we shall do better without 'em," said Latimer, who changed his moods at a moment's notice. "But there's great cause of suspicion in this silence and this keeping out of sight, and I'll bear it in mind. Now we will go across to Owlett's orchard, and see what we can find there."

Stockdale, who heard this discussion from the garden-gate, over which he had been leaning, was rather alarmed, and thought it a mistake of the villagers to keep so completely out of the way. He himself, like the Preventives, had been wondering for the last half-hour what could have become of them. Some labourers were of necessity engaged in distant fields, but the master-workmen should have been at home; though one and all, after just showing themselves at their shops, had apparently gone off for the day. He went in to Lizzy, who sat at a back window sewing, and said, "Lizzy, where are the men?"

Lizzy laughed. "Where they mostly are when they're run so hard as this." She cast her eyes to heaven. "Up there," she said.

Stockdale looked up. "What — on the top of the church tower?" he asked, seeing the direction of her glance.

"Yes."

"Well, I expect they will soon have to come down," said he, gravely. "I have been listening to the officers, and they are going to search the orchard over again; and then every nook in the church."

Lizzy looked alarmed for the first time. "Will you go and tell our folk?" she said. "They ought to be let know." Seeing his conscience struggling within him like a boiling pot, she added, "No, never mind, I'll go myself."

She went out, descended the garden, and climbed over the churchyard wall at the same time that the preventive-men were ascending the road to the orchard. Stockdale could do no less than follow her. By the time that she reached the tower-entrance he was at her side, and they entered together.

Nether-Moynton church tower was, as in many villages, without a turret, and the only way to the top was by going up to the singers' gallery, and thence ascending by a ladder to a square trap-door in the floor of the bell-loft; above which a permanent ladder was fixed, passing through the bells to a hole in the roof. When Lizzy and Stockdale reached the gallery and looked up, nothing but the trap-door and the five holes for the bell-ropes appeared. The ladder was gone.

"There's no getting up," said Stockdale.

"O yes there is," said she. "There's an eye looking at us at this moment through a knot-hole in that trap-door."

And as she spoke the trap opened, and the dark line of the ladder was seen descending against the white-washed wall. When it touched the bottom Lizzy dragged it to its place, and said, "If you'll go up, I'll follow."

The young man ascended, and presently found himself among consecrated bells for the first time in his life, nonconformity having been in the Stockdale blood for some generations. He eyed them uneasily, and looked round for Lizzy. Owlett stood here, holding the top of the ladder.

"What, be you really one of us?" said the miller.

"It seems so," said Stockdale, sadly.

"He's not," said Lizzy, who overheard. "He's neither for nor against us. He'll do us no harm."

She stepped up beside them, and then they went on to the next stage, which, when they had clambered over the dusty bell-carriages, was of easy ascent, leading towards the hole through which the pale sky appeared, and into the open air. Owlett remained behind for a moment, to pull up the lower ladder.

"Keep down your heads," said a voice, as soon as they set foot on the flat.

Stockdale here beheld all the missing parishioners, lying on their stomachs on the tower-roof, except a few who, elevated on their hands and knees, were peeping through the embrasures of the parapet. Stockdale did the same, and saw the village lying like a map below him, over which moved the figures of the Customs-men, each foreshortened to a crab-like object, the crown of his hat forming a circular disc in the centre of him. Some of the men had turned their heads when the young preacher's figure arose among them.

"What, Mr. Stockdale?" said Matt Grey, in a tone of surprise.

"I'd as lief that it hadn't been," said Jim Clarke. "If the pa'son should see him a trespassing here in his tower, 'twould be none the better for we, seeing how 'a do hate chapel-members. He'd never buy a tub of us again, and he's as good a customer as we have got this side o' Warm'll."

"Where is the pa'son?" said Lizzy.

"In his house to be sure, that he may see nothing of what's going on — where all good folks ought to be, and this young man likewise."

"Well, he has brought some news," said Lizzy. "They are going to search the orchard and church; can we do anything if they should find?"

"Yes," said her cousin Owlett. "That's what we've been talking o', and we have settled our line. Well, be dazed!"

The exclamation was caused by his perceiving that some of the searchers, having got into the orchard, and begun stooping and creeping hither and thither, were pausing in the middle, where a tree smaller than the rest was growing. They drew closer, and bent lower than ever upon the ground.

"O my tubs!" said Lizzy, faintly, as she peered through the parapet at them.

"They have got 'em, 'a b'lieve," said Owlett.

The interest in the movements of the officers was so keen that not a single eye was looking in any other direction; but at that moment a shout from the church beneath them attracted the attention of the smugglers, as it did also of the party in the orchard, who sprang to their feet and went towards the churchyard wall. At the same time those of the Government men who had entered the church unperceived by the smugglers cried aloud, "Here be some of 'em at last."

The smugglers remained in a blank silence, uncertain whether "some of 'em" meant tubs or men; but again peeping cautiously over the edge of the tower they learnt that tubs were the things descried; and soon these fated articles were brought one by one into the middle of the churchyard from their hiding place under the gallery stairs.

"They are going to put 'em on Hinton's vault till they find the rest," said Lizzy hopelessly. The Customs-men had, in fact, begun to pile up the tubs on a large stone slab which was fixed there; and when all were brought out from the tower, two or three of the men were left standing by them, the rest of the party again proceeding to the orchard.

The interest of the smugglers in the next manœuvres of their enemies became painfully intense. Only about thirty tubs had been secreted in the lumber of the tower, but seventy were hidden in the orchard, making up all that they had brought ashore as yet, the remainder of the cargo having been tied to a sinker and dropped overboard for another night's operations. The Preventives, having re-entered the orchard, acted as if they were positive that here lay hidden the rest of the tubs, which they were determined to find before nightfall. They spread themselves out round the field, and advancing on all fours as before, went anew round every apple-tree in the enclosure. The young tree in the middle again led them to pause, and at length the whole company gathered there in a way which signified that a second chain of reasoning had led to the same results as the first.

When they had examined the sod hereabouts for some minutes, one of the men rose, ran to a disused part of the church where tools were kept, and returned with the sexton's pickaxe and shovel, with which they set to work.

"Are they really buried there?" said the minister, for the grass was so green and uninjured that it was difficult to believe it had been disturbed. The smugglers were too interested to reply, and presently they saw, to their chagrin, the officers stand several on each side of the tree; and stooping and applying their hands to the soil, they bodily lifted the tree and the turf around it. The apple-tree now showed itself to be growing in a shallow box, with handles for lifting at each of the four sides. Under the site of the tree a square hole was revealed, and an officer went and looked down.

"It is all up now," said Owlett quietly. "And now all of ye get down before they notice we are here; and be ready for our next move. I had better bide here till dark, or they may take me on suspicion, as 'tis on my ground. I'll be with ye as soon as daylight begins to pink in."

"And I?" said Lizzy.

"You please look to the linch-pins and screws; then go indoors and know nothing at all. The chaps will do the rest."

The ladder was replaced, and all but Owlett descended, the men passing off one by one at the back of the church, and vanishing on their respective errands. Lizzy walked boldly along the street, followed closely by the minister.

"You are going indoors, Mrs. Newberry?" he said.

She knew from the words "Mrs. Newberry" that the division between them had widened yet another degree.

"I am not going home," she said. "I have a little thing to do before I go in. Martha Sarah will get your tea."

"O, I don't mean on that account," said Stockdale. "What *can* you have to do further in this unhallowed affair?"

"Only a little," she said.

"What is that? I'll go with you."

"No. I shall go by myself. Will you please go indoors? I shall be there in less than an hour."

"You are not going to run any danger, Lizzy?" said the young man, his tenderness reasserting itself.

"None whatever — worth mentioning," answered she, and went down towards the Cross.

Stockdale entered the garden-gate, and stood behind it looking on. The Preventive-men were still busy in the orchard, and at last he was tempted to enter, and watch their proceedings. When he came closer he found that the secret cellar, of whose existence he had been totally unaware, was formed by timbers placed across from side to side about a foot under the ground, and grassed over.

The officers looked up at Stockdale's fair and downy countenance, and evidently thinking him above suspicion, went on with their work again. As soon as all the tubs were taken out, they began tearing up the turf, pulling out the timbers, and breaking in the sides, till the cellar was wholly dismantled and shapeless, the apple-tree lying with its roots high to the air. But the hole which had in its time held so much contraband merchandise was never completely filled up, either then or afterwards, a depression in the greensward marking the spot to this day.

VII.   The Walk to Warm'ell Cross; and Afterwards

As the goods had all to be carried to Budmouth that night, the next object of the Custom-House officers was to find horses and carts for the journey, and they went about the village for that purpose. Latimer strode hither and thither with a lump of chalk in his hand, marking broad-arrows so vigorously on every vehicle and set of harness that he came across, that it seemed as if he would chalk broad arrows on the very hedges and roads. Stockdale, who had had enough of the scene, turned indoors thoughtful and depressed. Lizzy was already there, having come in at the back, though she had not yet taken off her bonnet. She looked tired, and her mood was not much brighter than his own. They had but little to say to each other; and the minister went away and attempted to read; but at this he could not succeed, and he shook the little bell for tea.

Lizzy herself brought in the tray, the girl having run off into the village during the afternoon, too full of excitement at the proceedings to remember her state of life. However, almost before the sad lovers had said anything to each other, Martha came in in a steaming state.

"O there's such a stoor, Mrs. Newberry and Mr. Stockdale! The king's officers can't get the carts ready nohow at all! They pulled Thomas Artnell's, and William Rogers's, and Stephen Sprake's carts into the road, and off came the wheels, and down fell the carts; and they found there was no linch-pins in the arms; and then they tried Samuel Shane's waggon, and found that the screws were gone from he, and at last they looked at the dairyman's cart, and he's got none neither! They have gone now to the blacksmith's to get some made, but he's nowhere to be found!"

Stockdale looked at Lizzy, who blushed very slightly, and went out of the room followed by Martha Sarah. But before they had got through the passage there was a rap at the front door, and Stockdale recognised Latimer's voice addressing Mrs. Newberry, who had turned back.

"For God's sake, Mrs. Newberry, have you seen Hardman the blacksmith up this way? If we could get hold of him, we'd e'en a'most drag him by the hair of his head to his anvil, where he ought to be."

"He's an idle man, Mr. Latimer," said Lizzy archly. "What do you want him for?"

"Why there isn't a horse in the place that has got more than three shoes on, and some have only two. The waggon-wheels be without strakes, and there's no linch-pins to the carts. What with that, and the bother about every set of harness being out of order, we shan't be off before night-fall — upon my soul we shan't. 'Tis a rough lot, Mrs. Newberry, that you've got about you here; but they'll play at this game once too often, mark my words they will. There's not a man in the parish that don't deserve to be whipped."

It happened that Hardman was at that moment a little further up the lane, smoking his pipe behind a holly bush. When Latimer had done speaking he went on in this direction, and Hardman, hearing the riding-officer's steps, found curiosity too strong for prudence. He peeped out from the bush at the very moment that Latimer's glance was on it. There was nothing left for him to do but to come forward with unconcern.

"I've been looking for you for the last

hour!" said Latimer, with a glare in his eye.

"Sorry to hear that," said Hardman. "I've been out for a stroll, to look for more hid tubs, to deliver 'em up to Gover'ment."

"O yes, Hardman, we know it," said Latimer, with withering sarcasm. "We know that you'll deliver 'em up to Gover'ment. We know that all the parish is helping us, and have been all day. Now you please walk along with me down to your shop, and kindly let me hire ye in the king's name."

They went down the lane together; and presently there resounded from the smithy the ring of a hammer not very briskly swung. However, the carts and horses were got into some sort of travelling condition, but it was not until after the clock had struck six, when the muddy roads were glistening under the horizontal light of the fading day. The smuggled tubs were soon packed into the vehicles, and Latimer, with three of his assistants, drove slowly out of the village in the direction of the port of Budmouth, some considerable number of miles distant, the other men of the Preventive-guard being left to watch for the remainder of the cargo, which they knew to have been sunk somewhere between

Ringsworth and Lulwind Cove, and to un-earth Owlett, the only person clearly impli-cated by the discovery of the cave.

Women and children stood at the doors as the carts, each chalked with the Govern-ment pitchfork, passed in the increasing twilight; and as they stood they looked at the confiscated property with a melancholy expression that told only too plainly the re-lation which they bore to the trade.

"Well, Lizzy," said Stockdale, when the crackle of the wheels had nearly died away. "This is a fit finish to your adventure. I am truly thankful that you have got off without suspicion, and the loss only of the liquor. Will you sit down and let me talk to you?"

"By-and-by," she said. "But I must go out now."

"Not to that horrid shore again?" he said blankly.

"No, not there. I am only going to see the end of this day's business."

He did not answer to this, and she moved towards the door slowly, as if waiting for him to say something more.

"You don't offer to come with me," she added at last. "I suppose that's because you hate me after all this?"

"Can you say it, Lizzy, when you know I only want to save you from such practices?

Come with you! — of course I will, if it is only to take care of you. But why will you go out again?"

"Because I cannot rest indoors. Something is happening, and I must know what. Now, come." And they went into the dusk together.

When they reached the turnpike-road she turned to the right, and he soon perceived that they were following the direction of the Preventive-men and their load. He had given her his arm, and every now and then she suddenly pulled it back, to signify that he was to halt a moment and listen. They had walked rather quickly along the first quarter of a mile, and on the second or third time of standing still she said, "I hear them ahead — don't you?"

"Yes," he said; "I hear the wheels. But what of that?"

"I only want to know if they get clear away from the neighbourhood."

"Ah," said he, a light breaking upon him. "Something desperate is to be attempted! — and now I remember there was not a man about the village when we left."

"Hark!" she murmured. The noise of the cart-wheels had stopped, and given place to another sort of sound.

" 'Tis a scuffle!" said Stockdale.

392

"There'll be murder. Lizzy, let go my arm; I am going on. On my conscience, I must not stay here and do nothing!"

"There'll be no murder, and not even a broken head," she said. "Our men are thirty to four of them: no harm will be done at all."

"Then there *is* an attack!" exclaimed Stockdale; "and you knew it was to be. Why should you side with men who break the laws like this?"

"Why should you side with men who take from country traders what they have honestly bought wi' their own money in France?" said she firmly.

"They are not honestly bought," said he.

"They are," she contradicted. "I and Mr. Owlett and the others paid thirty shillings for every one of the tubs before they were put on board at Cherbourg, and if a king who is nothing to us sends his people to steal our property, we have a right to steal it back again."

Stockdale did not stop to argue the matter, but went quickly in the direction of the noise, Lizzy keeping at his side. "Don't you interfere, will you, dear Richard?" she said anxiously, as they drew near. "Don't let us go any closer: 'tis at Warm'ell Cross where they are seizing 'em. You can do no good, and you may meet with a hard blow."

"Let us see first what is going on," he said. But before they had got much further the noise of the cart-wheels began again; and Stockdale soon found that they were coming towards him. In another minute the three carts came up, and Stockdale and Lizzy stood in the ditch to let them pass.

Instead of being conducted by four men, as had happened when they went out of the village, the horses and carts were now accompanied by a body of from twenty to thirty, all of whom, as Stockdale perceived to his astonishment, had blackened faces. Among them walked six or eight huge female figures whom, from their wide strides, Stockdale guessed to be men in disguise. As soon as the party discerned Lizzy and her companion four or five fell back, and when the carts had passed, came close to the pair.

"There is no walking up this way for the present," said one of the gaunt women, who wore curls a foot long, dangling down the sides of her face, in the fashion of the time. Stockdale recognised this lady's voice as Owlett's.

"Why not?" said Stockdale. "This is the public highway."

"Now look here, youngster," said Owlett. "Oh, 'tis the Methodist parson! — what, and Mrs. Newberry! Well, you'd better not go up that way, Lizzy. They've all run off, and folks have got their own again."

The miller then hastened on and joined his comrades. Stockdale and Lizzy also turned back. "I wish all this hadn't been forced upon us," she said regretfully. "But if those Coast-men had got off with the tubs, half the people in the parish would have been in want for the next month or two."

Stockdale was not paying much attention to her words, and he said, "I don't think I can go back like this. Those four poor Preventives may be murdered for all I know."

"Murdered!" said Lizzy impatiently. "We don't do murder here."

"Well, I shall go as far as Warm'ell Cross to see," said Stockdale decisively; and, without wishing her safe home or anything else, the minister turned back. Lizzy stood looking at him till his form was absorbed in the shades; and then, with sadness, she went in the direction of Nether-Moynton.

The road was lonely, and after nightfall at this time of the year there was often not a passer for hours. Stockdale pursued his way without hearing a sound beyond that of his own footsteps; and in due time he passed beneath the trees of the plantation which surrounded the Warm'ell Cross-road. Before he had reached the point of intersection he heard voices from the thicket.

"Hoi-hoi-hoi! Help, help!"

The voices were not at all feeble or despairing, but they were unmistakably anxious. Stockdale had no weapon, and before plunging into the pitchy darkness of the plantation he pulled a stake from the hedge, to use in case of need. When he got among the trees he shouted — "What's the matter — where are you?"

"Here," answered the voices; and, pushing through the brambles in that direction, he came near the objects of his search.

"Why don't you come forward?" said Stockdale.

"We be tied to the trees."

"Who are you?"

"Poor Will Latimer the Customs-officer," said one, plaintively.

"Just come and cut these cords, there's a good man. We were afraid nobody would pass by to-night."

Stockdale soon loosened them, upon

which they stretched their limbs and stood at their ease.

"The rascals!" said Latimer, getting now into a rage, though he had seemed quite meek when Stockdale first came up. " 'Tis the same set of fellows. I know they were Moynton chaps to a man."

"But we can't swear to 'em," said another. "Not one of 'em spoke."

"What are you going to do?" said Stockdale.

"I'd fain go back to Moynton, and have at 'em again!" said Latimer.

"So would we!" said his comrades.

"Fight till we die!" said Latimer.

"We will, we will!" said his men.

"But," said Latimer, more frigidly, as they came out of the plantation, "we don't *know* that these chaps with black faces were Moynton men? And proof is a hard thing."

"So it is," said the rest.

"And therefore we won't do nothing at all," said Latimer, with complete dispassionateness. "For my part, I'd sooner be them than we. The clitches of my arms are burning like fire from the cords those two strapping women tied round 'em. My opinion is, now I have had time to think o't, that you may serve your Gover'ment at too high a price. For these two nights and days I have not had an hour's rest; and, please God, here's for home-along."

The other officers agreed heartily to this course; and, thanking Stockdale for his timely assistance, they parted from him at the Cross, taking themselves the western road, and Stockdale going back to Nether-Moynton.

During that walk the minister was lost in reverie of the most painful kind. As soon as he got into the house, and before entering his own rooms, he advanced to the door of the little back parlour in which Lizzy usually sat with her mother. He found her there alone. Stockdale went forward, and, like a man in a dream, looked down upon the table that stood between him and the young woman, who had her bonnet and cloak still on. As he did not speak, she looked up from her chair at him, with misgiving in her eye.

"Where are they gone?" he then said listlessly.

"Who? — I don't know. I have seen nothing of them since. I came straight in here."

"If your men can manage to get off with those tubs, it will be a great profit to you, I suppose?"

"A share will be mine, a share my cousin Owlett's, a share to each of the two farmers, and a share divided amongst the men who helped us."

"And you still think," he went on slowly, "that you will not give this business up?"

Lizzy rose, and put her hand upon his shoulder. "Don't ask that," she whispered. "You don't know what you are asking. I must tell you, though I meant not to do it. What I make by that trade is all I have to keep my mother and myself with."

He was astonished. "I did not dream of such a thing," he said. "I would rather have scraped the roads, had I been you. What is money compared with a clear conscience?"

"My conscience is clear. I know my mother, but the king I have never seen. His dues are nothing to me. But it is a great deal to me that my mother and I should live."

"Marry me, and promise to give it up. I will keep your mother."

"It is good of you," she said, moved a little. "Let me think of it by myself. I would rather not answer now."

She reserved her answer till the next day, and came into his room with a solemn face. "I cannot do what you wished," she said passionately. "It is too much to ask.

399

My whole life ha' been passed in this way." Her words and manner showed that before entering she had been struggling with herself in private, and that the contention had been strong.

Stockdale turned pale, but he spoke quietly. "Then, Lizzy, we must part. I cannot go against my principles in this matter, and I cannot make my profession a mockery. You know how I love you, and what I would do for you; but this one thing I cannot do."

"But why should you belong to that profession?" she burst out. "I have got this large house; why can't you marry me, and live here with us, and not be a Methodist preacher any more? I assure you, Richard, it is no harm, and I wish you could only see it as I do. We only carry it on in winter: in summer it is never done at all. It stirs up one's dull life at this time o' the year, and gives excitement, which I have got so used to now that I should hardly know how to do 'ithout it. At nights, when the wind blows, instead of being dull and stupid, and not noticing whether it do blow or not, your mind is afield, even if you are not afield yourself; and you are wondering how the chaps are getting on; and you walk up and down the room, and look out o' window, and then you go out yourself, and know your way about as well by night as by day, and have hair-breadth escapes from old Latimer and his fellows, who are too stupid ever to really frighten us, and only make us a bit nimble."

"He frightened you a little last night, anyhow; and I would advise you to drop it before it is worse."

She shook her head. "No, I must go on as I have begun. I was born to it. It is in my blood, and I can't be cured. O Richard, you cannot think what a hard thing you have asked, and how sharp you try me when you put me between this and my love for 'ee!"

Stockdale was leaning with his elbow on the mantelpiece, his hands over his eyes. "We ought never to have met, Lizzy," he said. "It was an ill day for us! I little thought there was anything so hopeless and impossible in our engagement as this. Well, it is too late now to regret consequences in this way. I have had the happiness of seeing you and knowing you at least."

"You dissent from Church, and I dissent from State," she said. "And I don't see why we are not well matched."

He smiled sadly, while Lizzy remained

looking down, her eyes beginning to over-flow.

That was an unhappy evening for both of them, and the days that followed were unhappy days. Both she and he went mechanically about their employments, and his depression was marked in the village by more than one of his denomination with whom he came in contact. But Lizzy, who passed her days indoors, was unsuspected of being the cause; for it was generally understood that a quiet engagement to marry existed between her and her cousin Owlett, and had existed for some time.

Thus uncertainly the week passed on; till one morning Stockdale said to her: "I have had a letter, Lizzy. I must call you that till I am gone."

"Gone?" said she blankly.

"Yes," he said. "I am going from this place. I felt it would be better for us both that I should not stay after what has happened. In fact, I couldn't stay here, and look on you from day to day, without becoming weak and faltering in my course. I have just heard of an arrangement by which the other minister can arrive here in about a week; and let me go elsewhere."

That he had all this time continued so firmly fixed in his resolution came upon her as a grievous surprise. "You never loved me," she said bitterly.

"I might say the same," he returned; "but I will not. Grant me one favour. Come and hear my last sermon on the day before I go."

Lizzy, who was a church-goer on Sunday mornings, frequently attended Stockdale's chapel in the evening with the rest of the double-minded; and she promised.

It became known that Stockdale was going to leave, and a good many people outside his own sect were sorry to hear it. The intervening days flew rapidly away, and on the evening of the Sunday which preceded the morning of his departure Lizzy sat in the chapel to hear him for the last time. The little building was full to overflowing, and he took up the subject which all had expected, that of the contraband trade so extensively practised among them. His hearers, in laying his words to their own hearts, did not perceive that they were most particularly directed against Lizzy, till the sermon waxed warm, and Stockdale nearly broke down with emotion. In truth his own earnestness, and her sad eyes looking up at him, were too much for the young man's equanimity. He hardly knew how he ended. He saw Lizzy, as through a mist, turn and go away with the rest of the congregation; and shortly afterwards followed her home.

She invited him to supper, and they sat down alone, her mother having, as was usual with her on Sunday nights, gone to bed early.

"We will part friends, won't we?" said Lizzy, with forced gaiety, and never alluding to the sermon: a reticence which rather disappointed him.

"We will," he said, with a forced smile on his part; and they sat down.

It was the first meal that they had ever shared together in their lives, and probably the last that they would so share. When it was over, and the indifferent conversation could no longer be continued, he arose and took her hand. "Lizzy," he said, "do you say we must part — do you?"

"You do," she said solemnly. "I can say no more."

"Nor I," said he. "If that is your answer, good-bye."

Stockdale bent over her and kissed her, and she involuntarily returned his kiss. "I shall go early," he said hurriedly. "I shall not see you again."

And he did leave early. He fancied, when

404

stepping forth into the grey morning light, to mount the van which was to carry him away, that he saw a face between the parted curtains of Lizzy's window; but the light was faint, and the panes glistened with wet; so he could not be sure. Stockdale mounted the vehicle, and was gone; and on the following Sunday the new minister preached in the chapel of the Moynton Wesleyans.

One day, two years after the parting, Stockdale, now settled in a midland town, came into Nether-Moynton by carrier in the original way. Jogging along in the van that afternoon he had put questions to the driver, and the answers that he received interested the minister deeply. The result of them was that he went without the least hesitation to the door of his former lodging. It was about six o'clock in the evening, and the same time of year as when he had left; now, too, the ground was damp and glistening, the west was bright, and Lizzy's snowdrops were raising their heads in the border under the wall.

Lizzy must have caught sight of him from the window, for by the time that he reached the door she was there holding it open; and then, as if she had not sufficiently considered her act of coming out, she drew herself back, saying with some constraint, "Mr. Stockdale!"

"You knew it was," said Stockdale, taking her hand. "I wrote to say I should call."

"Yes, but you did not say when," she answered.

"I did not. I was not quite sure when my business would lead me to these parts."

"You only came because business brought you near?"

"Well, that is the fact; but I have often thought I should like to come on purpose to see you . . . But what's all this that has happened? I told you how it would be, Lizzy, and you would not listen to me."

"I would not," she said sadly. "But I had been brought up to that life; and it was second nature to me. However, it is all over now. The officers have blood-money for taking a man dead or alive, and the trade is going to nothing. We were hunted down like rats."

"Owlett is quite gone, I hear."

"Yes. He is in America. We had a dreadful struggle that last time, when they tried to take him. It is a perfect miracle that he lived through it; and it is a wonder that I was not killed. I was shot in the hand. It was not by aim; the shot was really meant for my cousin; but I was behind, looking on as usual, and the bullet came to me. It bled terribly, but I got home without fainting; and it healed after a time. You know how he suffered?"

"No," said Stockdale. "I only heard that he just escaped with his life."

"He was shot in the back; but a rib turned the ball. He was badly hurt. We would not let him be took. The men carried him all night across the meads to Kingsbere, and hid him in a barn, dressing his wound as well as they could, till he was so far recovered as to be able to get about. Then he was caught, and tried with the others at the assizes; but they all got off. He had given up his mill for some time; and at last he went to Bristol, and took a passage to America, where he's settled."

"What do you think of smuggling now?" said the minister, gravely.

"I own that we were wrong," said she. "But I have suffered for it. I am very poor now, and my mother has been dead these twelve months. . . . But won't you come in, Mr. Stockdale?"

Stockdale went in; and it is to be supposed that they came to an understanding; for a fortnight later there was a sale of

Lizzy's furniture, and after that a wedding at a chapel in a neighbouring town.

He took her away from her old haunts to the home that he had made for himself in his native county, where she studied her duties as a minister's wife with praiseworthy assiduity. It is said that in after years she wrote an excellent tract called *Render unto Caesar; or, the Repentant Villagers*, in which her own experience was anonymously used as the introductory story. Stockdale got it printed, after making some corrections, and putting in a few powerful sentences of his own; and many hundreds of copies were distributed by the couple in the course of their married life.

April 1879.

NOTE. — The ending of this story with the marriage of Lizzy and the minister was almost *de rigueur* in an English magazine at the time of writing. But at this late date, thirty years after, it may not be amiss to give the ending that would have been preferred by the writer to the convention used above. Moreover it corresponds more closely with the true incidents of which the tale is a vague and flickering shadow. Lizzy

did not, in fact, marry the minister, but —
much to her credit in the author's
opinion — stuck to Jim the smuggler, and
emigrated with him after their marriage, an
expatrial step rather forced upon him by
his adventurous antecedents. They both
died in Wisconsin between 1850 and 1860.
(May 1912.)

We hope you have enjoyed this Large Print Edition. Other Thorndike, Wheeler or Chivers Press Large Print books are available at your library or directly from the publishers.

For more information about current and upcoming titles, please call or write, without obligation, to:

Publisher
Thorndike Press
295 Kennedy Memorial Drive
Waterville, ME   04901
Tel. (800) 223-1244

Or visit our Web site at:
www.gale.com/thorndike
www.gale.com/wheeler

OR

Chivers Large Print
published by BBC Audiobooks Ltd
St James House, The Square
Lower Bristol Road
Bath BA2 3SB
England
Tel. +44(0) 800 136919
email: bbcaudiobooks@bbc.co.uk
www.bbcaudiobooks.co.uk

All our Large Print titles are designed for easy reading, and all our books are made to last.